On the *Plus* Side

Chubby Girl Chronicles

On the

Plus

Side

Tabatha Vargo

For Matthew, thank you for making me feel beautiful everyday for the last eleven years...even when I'm wearing the poodle puff and ugly sleep pants. I love you mostest!

On the *Plus* Side

Chubby Girl Chronicles

One

Devin Michaels

"But, Dev, he hit me first... kind of," Jenny said as she handed me a socket wrench. I was under the car, of course. Under the hood of a vehicle was my second home.

"It's not my fault he didn't protect his balls. You *always* protect your balls. Even I know that, and I'm a chick." She bit her nails as she talked. I could tell by her muffled voice.

"That's debatable. Me and Dad aren't so sure anymore," I chuckled as she kicked my booted foot that stuck out from under the car. "Also, could you please *not* talk about balls with me? I'm pretty sure there's like a rule about little sisters saying the word balls anywhere in the vicinity of their brother. If there isn't, let's just go ahead and put that rule on the books." I released the old oil from the engine.

It splattered up from the oil pan and landed on my grease-covered shirt. I pulled the rag from my back pocket and wiped my hands so that I could get a better grip on the ratchet.

1

"I'm assuming the new rule applies to the word cock, too?" she laughed.

"Yes!" I said a little too loudly. "*That* word is strictly forbidden."

"Don't be a little bitch, Dev," she said as she slipped a new oil filter under the car to me.

"Watch your damn mouth, Jenny. Could you at least attempt to be a lady? Ladies don't kick boys in their balls because they win a game of Halo. I'd be pissed if I was him, too. You need to call him and apologize. Josh has been your best friend too long—don't let a stupid game ruin that."

"First of all, he did *not* win and B, I was raised by two dudes. I'm pretty sure the lady train left the station when I was nine." She popped open a can of soda and sighed. "Whatever, I guess I'll run him over some gummy worms later and say sorry. He's such a baby. It's just balls. He smacked me in the boob once and you didn't hear me bitchin' and moanin'," she said as she left the garage and headed toward the back door of the house.

"You said balls again!" I yelled from under the car.

I couldn't hear her response over the loud smack of the screened door.

I finished up the oil change then worked on a dent that I acquired at the grocery store. Poor Lucy, my sixty-nine Chevy Camaro, didn't stand a chance against the wayward grocery cart.

She was a gift from my dad. When I got her she was just a big heap of junk, wouldn't even crank. My dad isn't one for gifts, but being a mechanic has its perks every now and again. When a

2

customer couldn't pay for the new transmission my dad dropped in his truck, a trade for the cash was offered and I got Lucy. To me, she's worth every minute we put into that man's piece-of-shit truck. Dad might not agree with me on that, but what can I say, I got the better part of that deal.

Lucy's the epitome of beauty. You can't buy the kind of character that an old muscle car has these days and Lucy had character. I'd rather be out there secluded in the garage with her, than any other place in the world. I'd spent hours overhauling my car and I'd spend every dime on the project, if I had a dime.

At my age, I should have a steady woman in my life, but cars are better than women. They're gorgeous, powerful, and they purr when you handle them. They do all that without the mandatory attachment that women require.

"Devin! Are you gonna stay in that garage under that car all day? I need ya to come in for a minute, boy!" Dad yelled from the back door of the house.

"I'm comin'!" I hollered back. "Is this man ever gonna give me a break?" I sighed to myself.

It wouldn't be so bad if I actually made some money working in the shop with Dad. Since I make such a crappy paycheck, the least he could do is give me five minutes to dwell on my less-than-stellar life. Instead, he pushes me harder and harder every day. You'd think he'd appreciate the fact that I haven't ran off and left him high and dry, but oh no...not Harold Michaels, a.k.a., the town drunk.

If my dad could fix a car as fast as he could take out a six
pack of beer, I swear we'd be rich. Even drunk as a skunk the
man knows his way around an engine. That fact kept the people
in our small town from caring that he did business with
Budweiser on his breath. One of the plus sides of living in a
town full of truck owners is the fact that once the good ole boys
found a good mechanic, they stuck with him. Who cares that he
couldn't stand up straight or speak without a slur as long as the
job got done right?

That was the biggest reason our small father-and-son
shop stayed afloat. The other reason, of course, was because I'm
a Whiz at the books. Last year alone, I saved dad three grand in
taxes. I should've stayed in school, and then maybe I could've
gone somewhere else in this world.

Instead, here I was, twenty-two years old, stuck with
Renee, a wannabe girlfriend, who drove me nuts, and a father
who was a slave driver. Let's not forget my fifteen-year-old
sister, Jenny, who should've been a boy. I guess things could've
been worse; I could be all alone in this big bad world.

I pulled myself out from under Lucy and stood there for a
minute before running out of the garage and across the yard to
the house.

The screened door snapped back making a loud slamming
noise when I walked in. Dad was sitting at the kitchen table
sorting through a massive stack of bills. He shook his head in
disgust. For as much business as we made here at our little

4

shop, it never seemed to be enough. We barely kept our heads above water.

The last couple of months had been the worst we'd had in a long while though. A new mechanic shop just opened on the outskirts of town. Even though I knew all the customers would come back once the new place got old, I couldn't help but worry about us until then.

It happened in our line of business. Some new shop with bright paint and fresh tools would pop up and stay open just long enough to make us financially uncomfortable. Another advantage to living in a small town...people don't like change. They always came back to what they knew, and the people in Walterboro knew my dad.

"What's up, Pops?" I said as I tapped the top on a cold Mountain Dew.

"Son, we got ourselves a bit of a problem. It seems we're a little behind on some loans. We gotta come up with some cash, fast."

"OK. Which loans are we talking about and how much?" I pinched my lips together like a disappointed mom.

I knew exactly which loans we were talking about, or should I say which loan. The loan we were talking about was the loan on the house and the garage. Back before I started taking care of the books for dad, he'd gotten so deep in debt with the I.R.S he actually had to take a loan out on anything he had of value. From the look on his face, I could tell the amount was going to chap my ass.

5

"What's the damage and what can we do?" I said impatiently.

"Well, it's along the lines of eight grand and there's nothin' comin' to mind. You got any ideas?"

Eight thousand dollars! I switched out my Mountain Dew for a beer.

"How long do we have?" I sighed.

"The final notice says ninety days. I don't see how we can come up with eight grand by then. I just hope somethin' comes up."

It pissed me off that he kept saying "me" and "us" like I had something to do with it. He was the one who let it get this bad. He was the one that needed to go back to school and learn basic math, not me!

I stared back at Dad for a minute and let the last few sentences he uttered fill my brain and make sense.

"Dad, I'm gonna take a drive and try to figure some stuff out. You want me to grab you anything while I'm out?

"No, don't be gone long, though. Morgan's bringin' over that ford that's been tickin'. I want you to look it over for me," I heard him say as I walked back out the door—the screen door snapped back and made an even louder banging noise.

All the work I put into this stupid shop trying to save it, and all the time I spared in the garage with him, were a waste. I could have a real job somewhere far from here. I could have my own place and take care of myself. I've always been a hard

6

worker and I've always hated the fact that I was stuck here going nowhere fast.

I've been working in Dad's garage ever since I was twelve or so. I used to come home from school, eat a peanut butter and jelly sandwich, and then head straight out back where I'd spend the rest of my night under the hood of something. That was back when mom was still around. She left when Jenny was six.

The year I turned thirteen was the hardest year of my life. Not only was I officially a teenager dealing with all the new hormones and growth spurts, but my mom left me like I was nothing. You'd think she would have at least stuck around to see Jenny grow up. What kind of woman leaves a six-year-old girl behind with two males? Leaving me with dad could almost be excused, but a young girl needs a mom to teach her girly stuff.

My mom was a beauty and apparently, every man in town thought so. I can remember the nights my mom and dad would argue. I always wondered why he would let her run around on him like she did. If I knew as a boy what was going on, then you know everyone in town knew. My dad must've looked like a dumbass.

There were some happy times when they were together, but most days I'd sit back and watch as Dad tried everything to make her happy. The day she left she didn't even say goodbye to me and Jenny. I could hear Dad begging her to stay and telling her how much he loved her.

At one point during the conversation he asked, "What about the kids? You just gonna walk out on the kids?"

I couldn't hear her response, but apparently we didn't matter too much. She gave up on us, and you never get over the pain of losing a mother. It would've been easier if she had died. I wouldn't hate her as much for leaving if it wasn't by choice.

I haven't been the same since she left and I've always blamed her for my fear of attachment. Though I'd never talk about it, deep down she's the reason I have trust issues. She's the reason I refused to bind myself to anyone. The fear of feeling the way I felt the day she left is unbearable. I would never put myself in the position to get hurt like my dad did. I've never even had a serious girlfriend.

Jenny's the reason I stuck around here. I'd die before I walked out on her. She's the only reason I still work at dad's shop—the reason I'd do almost anything to get this money and save our home.

"Shit!" I said as I pounded my hand on the steering wheel.

Eight thousand dollars! Where in the hell was I going to find that kind of money so fast? I could always rob a bank. Bank robbers always get caught, but maybe I could hide the money somewhere for dad and Jenny to find, like in one of those awesome action movies.

After driving around aimlessly for an hour, I ended up in front of Renee's house. I was in need of a good dose of stress relief.

I spotted her sitting on her front porch gossiping on her cell phone. She ended the conversation and smiled as soon as she saw me.

She's a pretty girl—tall and lean, the way I like them. I wouldn't call her beautiful, since most of the attractive things about her are fake—box-dyed blonde hair, false nails, and a rigid smile. It would suck to find out that her blue eyes were contacts.

Physically she's not perfect for me, since I liked natural girls better, but emotionally, she was my exact match. She was aware of my limits, which made things comfortable. No expectations made for an easy ride.

Thanks to her reputation for being a freak in the sheets, some guys called me lucky to have her. I knew differently. Her self-centered nature made her active in bed, but as for being a freak...not so much.

She slammed her slender body against mine and wrapped her arms around my neck. I leaned down and pecked her on the mouth.

"Is that all I get? I swear, Devin, I don't know why I bother with you." Her deep southern twang stabbed into my ear drums. "I guess it's too much to ask for a flirty phone call every now and again? I wish you would've called to let me know you were comin' by. I have a nail appointment then Nicole's coming over for a movie night. Oh! I almost forgot, I talked to Matt the other day...did you know that Cassie's brother went to Afghanistan?" She rambled on and on until finally she realized I wasn't talking and stopped. "Why are you staring at me like that?" she asked.

9

I imagined myself choking her to death and laughing hysterically like one of those crazy scary movie psycho freaks. I almost laughed out loud at the thought. My dad would kick my ass for just thinking a thing like that. I was raised to never put my hands on a female.

"You talk too much. Let's go inside and do this," I said flatly.

There was no need to bullshit her into thinking I was there for any other reason but to get laid.

She leaned in and kissed me, slipping her tongue into my mouth. Before long we were in her small, two-bedroom house falling over things trying to make it to her bedroom. Mindy, her roommate, was nowhere in sight, thankfully.

Afterward, I sat back in her bed surrounded by fluffy pink pillows and lace. She's definitely the girly type, nothing like my little sister Jenny. I'd probably die if I saw anything pink in her room. Renee quietly slept with her legs wrapped around mine. I felt so much better. Sex was what I needed, sex is the main reason I keep her around. Shit, she uses me, why the hell shouldn't I use her? I looked over at the pink alarm clock on the side table. It was getting pretty late. I really needed to get up and head home and I seriously needed to find eight thousand dollars...fast.

With that final thought I quickly and quietly got out of Renee's bed. I slipped on my clothes and slid through the house to the front door. The evening air rushed through my hair as I slammed the door behind me. The entire way home my thoughts were on money. There had to be a way, there was always a way.

Two

Lilly Sheffield

Yesterday, at a charity benefit my mom pretended to be interested in, a miniature man on a massive stage was trying to get everyone to donate to a multitude of charities. I'm usually the biggest donator, mainly because the people who run these things knew me so well—they prey on my conscience and make me feel like a monster for having money. Once they pull out the slide shows of starving children, I'm done for. I leave with at least a hundred grand missing from my bank account.

Anyway, this little man said something that made me really evaluate my world. He asked the group of multi-millionaires what they'd be willing to give up to make a difference in someone else's life. It made me think of the things that I'd *never* give up. Money isn't really a problem, especially for me, but what in my life do I hold dear?

My list is pretty pathetic for a twenty- year-old woman. Really pathetic!

There are few things in my life that you'd have to pry from my cold, dead fingers before they were ever taken from me. The first thing is my Spanx. Which, in my opinion, are the best man-made contraptions ever, better than electricity or chocolate. The creators of these life changing pieces of cloth should be put on a pedestal for all the chubby girls of the world to worship. Spanx, the body shaping devices of the fatty girl world...I bow down to you.

I don't know what they're made of, or who came up with this fantastical idea, but they're a godsend. If it wasn't for my Spanx, every fat roll I own would spill forth like frothy white volcano lava. It keeps the back fat to a minimum, too. Everyone with extra poundage can appreciate that. There's just nothing like walking around feeling like you have an extra pair of double D's strapped to your back.

The second thing I hold dear, is my paid for, but not really nice anymore, ninety-seven black Honda Accord. Yes, I have money to purchase a new car. Yes, I probably should purchase a new car, but my car's been with me through thick and thin. Well, not really the thin, more like the thick and thicker. Referring to anything in my life as *thin* is just wrong in so many ways.

Finally, the third thing that I couldn't live without is ice cream. As far as I was concerned, ice cream could heal broken bones if applied directly to the skin. Think about it. If you

13

considered how many broken hearts ice cream has mended, it wouldn't really seem that outlandish. Not to mention, ice cream is full of calcium.

Calcium + bones = good!

I think doctors everywhere should buy stock in ice cream products. It would save a ton of money in health care.

This kind of logic is what gets me through a pint of cookies and cream without the guilt of knowing two more pounds are coming my way. Hey, whatever gets you through your day, right?

Needless to say, the amount of suckage in my life was mind blowing for a girl with more money than she could count. I should've been happy. I should've been lying on a warm beach somewhere while my newly liposuctioned body was being massaged by my sexy boyfriend who had a really hot name like, Damon. I wasn't. Instead, I went to work. I sat behind a jewelry counter working for money that I didn't need in an attempt to achieve any form of normalcy.

The space between my chin and the heel of my palm started to sweat as I stared out the store window at the people walking by. OK, so today was going to be a bad day. Technically, since my day at work was almost over, it was already a bad day. Not to mention I had a coffee date with my mom that was rapidly approaching. Other than the fact that I'd have a reason to leave work early, I dreaded meeting my mom. Our little coffee dates rarely ended on a good note.

As much as I'd love to put off facing the dragon, it was time to go.

"Shannon! I'm gonna go ahead and leave, OK? I'll keep my cell close in case you need me," I yelled.

I seriously doubted that anything would happen in the next thirty minutes that would require my excellent management skills, especially considering we may have had one or two customers all day.

"Go ahead, honey. See you when I get home!" She called back.

"Remember, call my cell if you need anything and please don't forget to lock the top lock. Mrs. Franklin will have a fit if you forget again," I said as she came from the back of the store.

I watched as Shannon stumbled around with way too many tiny jewelry boxes piled in her arms. She tossed them on the front counter and smiled innocently. A stray lock of bright red hair attacked her eyes and I laughed at the face she made as she blew it out of her vision.

"I got ya' covered, Lil. Have fun with your mom," she teased.

Rolling my eyes, I walked out of the store and made my way toward my car.

When I got my license, my mom tried to convince me to let her buy me an expensive sports car. I think she was more worried about my sixteen-year-old reputation than I was. As if a girl like me would ever be happy with a car that's *too* small. I've had to deal with things that were "too small" my entire life, why the hell would I torture myself more? Did she seriously think I'd want to stuff myself into a skinny girl car every day? Um...no thanks! Feeling like a sardine was never my thing.

All skinny sports cars aside, things mean more when you buy them for yourself anyway. If I let my mom buy me everything she offered I wouldn't have room in my life for anything.

Thankfully, my mom moved past the point of trying to live my life. That was only after years of trying to make her understand that I was nothing like her.

I've always been the kind of person who likes to do things for myself. I want to work for anything that I acquire in my life. For instance, I love my car, and not because it's the greatest car ever, but because I paid for it with my own money. Money I earned back before my life was changed forever, before grandma died and left me millions. It's *my* car. My mom doesn't understand that. She's never worked a day in her life.

I've never hated her for that, she's just playing the cards she was dealt. My grandparents were always wealthy, so she's never known any different. I was raised with money, too, but my dad dumped tons of reality into my life before he ran off to California without me.

Simply put, the money's mine. The huge amount was dropped on me from my grandma's will. I received it on my twentieth birthday, but I'd give it all back for just one more day with her.

She was a lot like my mom, meaning she loved to spend money. The difference was she wanted me to be happy with myself—she never made me feel like a disappointment. Her pride in me was evident, while my mom always looked down on me, made me feel like I was just one step below where I should be.

My mom always was a snob, though she'd never admit it. If you removed her impressive bitch mask, you'd see that she has a seriously diluted sense of self-worth. If she had an honest moment, she'd admit that having money makes her feel superior to everyone else. I think she gets off on it.

I've never felt the need to make my life less abnormal than it's always been by being flashy with cash that I never wanted to begin with.

Normalcy has been in short supply for me. My permanent single status ruled the all-girls private school I grew up in, and I was dubbed Large Lilly, a.k.a. the Virgin Mary. Just call me the president of the twenty-year-old virgins club! The member list includes me and a bunch of unattractive nuns.

When it finally happens for me, it'll be real. I have no desire to be in the kind of relationship my parents had before they divorced. They were miserable and hated each other. It was the perfect example of what *not* to be. I want love...the kind they write books about, but my fear of rejection refuses to make it possible.

A special shout out to all the awesome high school girls who taunted me daily. Thanks for the fabulous fat girl complex.

There's a sense a comedy surrounding my situation. Technically, I could have anything I want. I could buy anything, but the one thing I can't buy is the one thing I crave. It's not like you could run thru the closest drive thru and grab a relationship.

One hot boy toy to go, please!

My inner ranting was cut short by the bell over the door to Mirabelle's, my favorite little cafe. My mom was already seated as she sipped her vanilla espresso. I hated the fact that she chose to sit in a booth instead of a table. I'd pull my fingernails out before I admitted that the booths were too small for me.

Guess who gets to play squeeze the fat girl in the tiny booth today?

"How was work?" Mom asked.

My presence didn't even warrant her to look up from her daily newspaper—the financial pages, no doubt.

"Good," I said. "How was the spa?"

I held my breath as I sucked in my stomach and slid into the seat. The table dug into my mini muffin top.

She ignored my spa question.

"Your father called. He says it's been nearly two weeks since he's heard from you."

"Yeah, I know. I need to call him. I've just have been so busy at work. We got a brand new shipment in for the fall. Me and Shannon have been killing ourselves trying to get it all set up. You should come by, Mom. We have tons of stuff I know you'd love."

She looked up at me like I'd lost my mind. Her newspaper rattled to the table.

"Honey, no offense, but you know I don't shop at those kinds of places. I wish you'd quit that awful job, or at least consider working somewhere more appropriate. Your grandfather's probably turning in his grave at the thought of his angel working countless hours. You weren't bred for that, Lilly." She blew on her espresso, sending the scent of vanilla my way.

"I know, Mom, but I enjoy it there. Mrs. Franklin's talking about making me area manager over all three stores. I hope I get the job."

"If we're being honest with each other, I hope you get fired from that pitiful place," she sniffed.

A mocha latte was placed in front of me. Going to the same café almost every day has its benefits. They always know what I want. I walk in and they get it ready for me.

"Here you go, Lilly. Having a good day?" Joey smirked at me.

He's the only male worker at Mirabelle's and a joker to boot.

"Oh yeah, today's been a *fabulous* day. It's getting better, too," I said, sarcastically.

It was an inside joke between me and the people that work at the café. Since Mirabelle's has always been my meeting place with mom, they've figured out how well our little meeting is going by how many lattes I order. One latte usually means it was a pleasant conversation, quick and to the point. Two lattes means things didn't go so well. Three means I'm probably about three minutes away from pulling my hair out and hanging my mother by a make shift napkin noose.

"Mom!" I said in a hushed tone after Joey leaves the table. "Why would you say that? You hope I get fired? I can't believe you'd wish bad things on me like that. I have to have that job for sanity purposes. I'm *so* sorry that I refuse to live like you, but that's no reason for you to say mean things to me."

I rolled my eyes before nursing my latte and wishing I had told her I couldn't get out of work.

Mom continued on and on about me not needing to work. I tuned her out. It's always about money with her. Normal families argued because the children constantly asked the parents for money. In my case, we argued because I refused to blow it.

There have been a few times when expensive name brand handbags and shoes would mysteriously show up at my door—brand names I can't even pronounce. Normal people don't wear twelve-hundred dollar shoes. Needless to say, Shannon has a pretty impressive closet.

As I continued to tune my mom out, I noticed a cute couple at a corner table. They were gazing lovingly into each other's eyes. Their elbows were rested on the table for balance as they each leaned in to get closer to the other. It was adorable to watch as he smiled at her and softly rubbed her hand. Her cheeks were turning pink as he whispered sweet nothings to her from across the table.

I smiled secretly to myself at the love story that was unfolding in front of me. Their love for each other was evident. It was written in their smiles and seeped out of their eyes. I couldn't look away. I hated myself for being a crazy, romance stalker, but the longing that crashed over me was paralyzing.

"Lilly! What's gotten into you? Are you even listening to me?"

I snapped my attention back to my mom.

"Of course I'm listening. I have a lot on my mind right now."

"Sweetie, you know you can talk to me about anything. Go ahead, exactly what's bothering you?"

The couple in the corner caught my attention once more.

"Mom, did you love dad?"

She straightened her body as if reflecting the awkward question with her chest.

"I loved your father very much. Unfortunately, my love wasn't enough for the both of us. Why do you ask such a strange question?"

"No reason," I said. "Just curious what it felt like."

She looked at me sadly as she proceeded to pat my hand in an attempt to be motherly.

"OK, enough with this nonsense. Let's do something fun. Let's go shopping! We can buy whatever you want, anything that'll make you happy. Just tell me what it is and I'll make sure you get it."

Growing up, anytime some skinny girl at school would laugh at me or we had a school dance that I never had a date to—mom was always the first one to blow it off as no big deal. She'd buy something fun and after a while I'd get over it. It was her way. The only way she knew how to show affection was to buy things. Instead of the sweet words and motherly hugs, I got gifts.

"Money can't buy everything, Mom," I said as I looked back to the cute couple who was now making out in their little corner.

Mom looked at them, too. She knew right away what I meant.

"Are you lonely, Sweetie? Because I'll be the first to tell you that you do *not* need a man to make you happy. Trust me. I had one for twenty years and I was miserable." She laughed at her little joke.

I smiled at her and then gave her a forced laugh.

"Just forget it, Mom. Let's go shopping. I could use a few new shirts and a pair of shoes," I said, hoping she would forget what she had just witnessed.

I hated shopping for clothes. Trying to find something decent to fit me was my idea of Hell. I'd gladly go through Hell if it meant my mom would forget the conversation we just had. The last thing I wanted was my mom trying any stupid match making schemes with a bunch of idiot men who'd rather be celibate than touch me. Of course, it worked.

I listened as she went over all the stores she wanted to visit and the things she wanted to buy. I followed her out of the café barely paying attention.

Today wasn't my day. All the mushy love thoughts and the "no one wants me" whining was starting to get on my nerves. Aunt Flo's definitely knocking at my door, and she brought the bitch triplets P, M, and S with her.

I stood in the first store we went to and daydreamt of a hot bubble bath, candles, and Christina Perri on low volume. All this shopping for expensive crap that would never fit, when all I really wanted was a nice hot bubble bath and a naughty threesome with Ben & Jerry's. So much for that idea!

Three

The Proposition

I haven't worn a tie since my grandfather's funeral when I was fifteen. These bank officials damn well better appreciate that. I'd already spent most of the morning stuck in traffic all the way from Walterboro to downtown Charleston. It's usually a thirty minute trip, if you take the interstate. Today it took me damn near an hour and a half.

I sat in the lobby and silently prayed that these bank boys would give us a shot at an extension. I just needed some extra time...anything that would keep me and my little family in our home. Maybe they could give us two more months on top of the ninety days? What's two more months?

The devil on my shoulder stuffed negative thoughts into my brain. What if they refused? We'd have to start over fresh somehow. That's not really a scary thought for me, except for that fact that poor dad wouldn't know what to do with himself. The shop is all he's ever known.

The minutes felt like hours and I found myself dazing in and out. I picked up a magazine and flipped through it without even looking at the pages. I felt like I was being watched so I looked around the room once more. I noticed a lady sitting across from me, an attractive lady actually. She was older, late forties maybe? Not really my type, but she was still kind of sexy in a cougar dominatrix kind of way.

She was openly staring back at me. Doing nothing to hide the fact that she was checking me out, her eyes moved from my eyes down to my crotch. The way she stared at me didn't match her look. Legs crossed all prim and proper like, she smiled seductively at me. I smiled back. Hey, if she wanted to play, I could play, too. Then her face dropped and her smile was replaced with a sarcastically lifted brow and a pinched mouth.

I shook my head and looked away. I didn't have time for an old tease.

Finally, after what felt like days, the lady behind the desk called me back. I stepped through the door of the bank manager's office.

"Mr. Michaels, I presume?" The man behind the desk asked.

He stood and held out his hand, I shook it. My sweaty palm made a squishing noise when I squeezed it, giving away my nerves.

This has to work. It's our last resort.

"My name is Mr. Schaefer. What can I help you with?"

I took my seat and started to fidget a little. This was the most important thing I've ever done and getting refused just wasn't an option at this point.

"Well, Mr. Schaefer, I won't waste your valuable time so I'm gonna get straight to the point. We owe this bank more money than we got and we only have ninety days to come up with that money. I'm here to ask you for more time, an extra sixty days, maybe?" I said quickly.

He picked up a small stack of papers and tapped them against the desk as he organized them.

"Mr. Michaels, I'm going to be completely honest with you. I've taken a good look at your file and there's just nothing more we can do. I feel horrible about this, I really do, but if the balance isn't paid in the next ninety days, we're going to be forced to foreclose on all of your father's properties, the business included. I'm deeply sorry. If there's anything else I can help you with, you just let me know."

"You're tellin' me there's no other option?" I said loudly.

I knew the people in the waiting room could hear me, but I didn't care. This was my life he was messing with. This was Jenny's life he was messing with. Our home and our work, the way we survived.

"Mr. Schaefer, I appreciate the fact that this is your job and everything, but you gotta find another way!" I yelled. "There's no way that we can come up with that kind of money

26

that fast and I'll be damned if you or any of these little stuck up bastards you got working here are gonna take our home."

"Mr. Michaels, I think it'd best if you left before I have to call security."

"Then I guess you better call security because I'm not leaving until we come to some kind of agreement."

"I understand that you and your *daddy* are having money issues, but it's not really mine or the bank's problem. If we handed out free money or more time to every poor person that walked through the door we'd go out of business, too. Maybe your father should think about the way he runs things," he snapped.

Before I knew it, I was standing over Mr. Schaefer with a sore fist and his blood on my knuckles. That bastard better be glad I didn't keep going. He had the audacity to talk down about me and my dad...in my face, no less. His high-horsed ass needed a big reality check and I'm glad I was the one to give it to him.

Security arrived just as I was backing away toward the door and I knew I was going to jail.

I came here to try and fix things, but because I couldn't control my damn temper, dad was going to have to dip into our measly savings to get me out of jail. I really screwed up this time.

Four hours later, I laid on the little bunk that the jail provided and ran different ideas through my head. I decided against calling dad to bail me out. I could spend a night in jail. I knew they'd let me out in the morning and to be honest I'd rather dad worry about me for the night than to use money we needed to bail my stupid ass out of jail. It was worth being behind these bars. That bastard got what he deserved.

The cell door opened and a police officer stepped into the tiny space.

"OK, Michaels, time to go," he said.

"What do you mean? I just got here."

"Your bail's paid. You're free to go."

I followed the officer out of the cell and down the hall to the front desk of the police station. I collected all my stuff, my empty wallet included, and turned to face my dad.

He was nowhere to be found. I did one more quick check around the police station trying to find him. He definitely wasn't there.

Maybe he went to wait in the truck?

I walked out of the police station and checked the parking lot. Dad's truck was nowhere in sight, which meant that he was so pissed off that he left me here.

I was about to start walking toward home, when I noticed the cougar lady from the bank lobby standing across the parking lot. She was perched against a long, black limo as she motioned for me to come to her with a finger.

Today had officially become the most fucked up day ever, and it didn't look like it was going to get any better. First, I get eye raped by an old broad in the bank. Then, I beat the hell out of the bank manager, which got me a swollen hand and jail time. Then, I get mysteriously bailed out only to find the female eye rapist waiting on me outside the police station.

I made my way over to the limo.

"It's about time. I was beginning to think they took my money and left you there," she said in a husky voice.

"You bailed me out?" I asked, confused.

"Well, how else was I going to talk to you?"

"I'm sorry...do I know you?" I continued to question.

"Don't be ridiculous. Ordinarily, I'd never be caught dead socializing with someone like you."

Fire cut across my chest as my anger started to spike.

"Then what the hell are you doing socializing with *someone like me*?" I said in a mocking tone.

One more stuck up bastard in my face tonight and I was going to snap.

"Let's cut the small talk. I heard you pitching a fit at the bank today. You need money and I have plenty, so let's talk business," she said.

"Look, Lady, I don't know how y'all do things in your world, but in mine selling yourself will get you at least thirty days. Being that I just stepped out of the jailhouse I'd prefer..."

She cut me off with a burst of laughter.

"I *know* you don't think I'm suggesting I pay you for sex, do you?" She laughed out loud one more time. "Don't get me wrong, kid, you're nice to look at, but I'm into men, not boys."

"Then what the hell do you want?" I asked rudely.

"I have a business proposition for you." She pulled open the limo door and climbed in. "Care to join me?" she asked.

"I already said I'm not a..."

"Don't flatter yourself!" She cut me off again. "Trust me...I'm far too much woman for a boy like you. Now, are you getting in the damn limo or not?" she growled.

I stood there debating what to do. Finally, I stepped toward the limo and jumped in shutting the door behind me.

"Where to?" she asked

"Walterboro...off of Clements Road."

"My God you *are* a country bumpkin," she huffed.

I sat there while she called orders to the driver and then pushed a little button causing a barrier to rise between us and him.

"Now, let's get back to business," she said. "I need you to do something for me and since you need money so badly I'm prepared to pay you nicely, as long as you don't screw it up."

"OK, is this something illegal? Because I'm no criminal."

"No, it's not illegal."

"OK, shoot me with it."

She grinned and then slid farther back into her seat.

"I'd like to pay you to date my daughter,'" she smirked as she poured a brown liquid out of a crystal container into a crystal glass. It smelled like liquor, which was fitting since I was almost positive this bitch was drunk.

"You wanna pay me to do what?"

"You heard me."

"You're joking, right?" I snorted.

"No, this is no joking matter and I'd appreciate it if you didn't treat it like one. I'm offering you a serious business proposition," she said aggressively.

I sobered and got rid of my smile. If this lady was serious, I was going to be serious, too. This could very well be the break me and dad were hoping for. Still, being paid to date someone didn't sit well with me. This girl must be some kind of God-awful creature if her mom had to pay a dude to date her.

"What's wrong with her?" I asked.

"Excuse me?"

"No offense, but if you gotta pay someone to date your daughter, there's gotta be something wrong with her."

"There's nothing wrong with my daughter. There's something wrong with all the boys who can't see how wonderful she is."

"So, she's ugly?"

"Absolutely not!" she snapped. "She has a small weight problem, but she's beautiful and that's exactly how you treat her. Take her out, show her a fabulous time, and make her feel like she's the most gorgeous creature you've ever seen."

"Basically you want me to blow smoke up her ass?"

"Stay away from her ass, but yes...whatever you have to do."

"Exactly what do I get out of this and how long do I have to do it?" I asked.

"In return for you dating my daughter, I'll pay your unpaid balance to the bank. If I heard correctly, you have ninety days.

31

When the ninety days are up and as long as my daughter's happy and you've done your job correctly...I'll pay it."

"You can't be serious." I choked. "You're gonna pay me eight thousand dollars to date your kid? How old is she anyway? She not like some high school kid or anything is she?" I asked.

"Is that all you owe? Sounds perfect. Yes, I'll definitely pay you eight thousand dollars and no, my daughter's not a high school student. She'll be twenty-one next month; you're kind of an early birthday present."

This couldn't have happened at a better time. Actually, it was kind of freaky how convenient it was, but at this point I'd be willing to do almost anything. I couldn't refuse if I wanted to. It's not likely that another opportunity like this would fall into my lap.

Eight grand was pocket change for this woman.

"Make it fifteen thousand and we got a deal," I said.

If I'm doing this, I might as well get something out of it, too. Lucy was going to look good with her new paint job.

The car wasn't moving anymore and the silence in the small space was suffocating as she thought it over. I still couldn't believe this was happening. It was wrong to lead some poor, fat girl around making her think that I wanted her, but I knew I could pull it off. We needed this money—I could do this for Jenny.

"Fine," she gave in. "I'll pay you three grand to start. We'll call it a courtesy payment. There are a few rules, though. You screw this up and you will *not* get the other twelve grand in ninety days. Plus, I'll personally make your life a living Hell. I'll make it my mission to make sure that you and your loved ones lose everything...and Mr. Michaels, I'm filthy rich. Don't think for one minute that I can't ruin you."

"What are the rules?" I snapped.

I wasn't too happy with being verbally threatened.

"First of all, don't put your filthy hands on my daughter. I understand that you're probably going to kiss her. You'll be dating her for at least three months and I know that kids do that sort of thing in that time period. You're *not* allowed to do anything more than that. The last thing I want is my daughter getting knocked up by some countrified chop shop boy," she huffed. "Do you understand?"

"Well, golly jeez, Miss, I think I reckon I understand what you're sayin'!" I said sarcastically with my deepest fake southern drawl.

Kissing? Hah! It wouldn't even go that far. I could make this girl feel like a princess without touching her. Playing women is kind of my niche.

"How can I find her?" I asked.

"She works. As much as I hate it, she's the manager at Franklin's Jewelry store downtown on Meeting Street. You can find her there. Also, she spends a lot of free time with friends at a little café called Mirabelle's. Are you familiar with these places?" she asked.

"Yeah," I said, as I opened the limo door to get out.

"And, Mr. Michaels...my daughter better not ever find out about this agreement, do you understand?

"Yeah, I got it!" I snapped.

"Good. I'm glad we understand each other. Her name's Lilly and you better not screw this up. I'll be in touch and you'll get your first installment when I'm sure that you've started the job, so I suggest you get to it." She straightened her top.

"I gotcha covered," I said as I climbed out of the big, black limo that was now parked in front of my house.

It's a little creepy that she knew where I lived without telling her. It's like she had done her homework and dug up information on me. This lady was clever, and clever ladies are dangerous. I'll be watching my back around this one.

"See you soon, kid," she said as I slammed the door in her face.

I watched the limo drive off. The whole scheme was crazy, but I had to do what needed to be done. One thing was for sure, dad would never approve, which meant he and Jenny could never know. I needed to think long and hard about where I'd tell him I got the money from, but that would come later. One thing at a time, and right now, I had a chubby chick to enchant. Doing hurtful things to strangers wasn't my thing, but extreme situations called for extreme measures.

I now had three things that I have to do first thing in the morning. One, I had to make Renee think that I'll be out of town for a while. I'll just make up an uncle in Georgia or something. There's no way she'd keep her trap shut long enough for me to finish the job if she thought another girl was getting something she wasn't. Of course there was money involved so maybe I could just buy her something and shut her up.

Second, I had to clean myself up a bit. If I was going to win some girl over, I really needed a good shave and a haircut. Third, I had to put on my charming face. I had to get rid of "asshole Devin" and bring out the nice boy that I knew I could be.

It could be fun. I'd get to go out a little on someone else's money with a girl that I'd never have to see again in three months. It wasn't really a bad deal.

I stripped down to my boxers and jumped into my bed. Before I could do anything, I needed some sleep. Within minutes, I passed out and slept better than I had in the last two weeks.

Four

Picking a Lilly

After finally convincing Renee that I was going to visit family for a while, I made my way toward Charleston. I drove with the windows down and let the cool wind cut across my face. I could use as much fresh air as humanly possible. The radio was off as I contemplated how to go about pursuing this girl. As crazy as it sounded, I've never really had to pursue a female before.

The rumble of Lucy's engine soothed me. I had to stay focused. I'd be fine as long as I remembered that this wasn't just for me and Dad. I was doing this for Jenny, for our home and our business. No matter what, I couldn't allow my conscience to get the best of me. This was a cut and dry job, and all I had to do was *not* get involved. Being emotionally disconnected was easy for me, so this job should've been a piece of cake.

I got to Franklin's Jewelry store and it took me three tries at parallel parking before I got it right. Digging out some change for the parking meter, I sat and gave myself a "hell yeah" pep talk. I'm sure I looked like a creeper just sitting in my car, but I wanted to plan. I just needed to go in, buy something, and get a good look at her so I'd know what I was dealing with. I should've asked to see a picture so I'd at least know who she was. Hopefully, she was the only fat girl working there.

After putting two dollars in the parking meter, I walked to the store. The entire time I prayed that everyone inside wore name tags.

It'd be more believable if I approached her at the little café, so right now called for just a little harmless flirting as I browsed the jewelry. Getting her to notice me was my number one goal.

The little bell over the door rang out as I walked into the empty store. The only reason I knew the place was even open was because of the big, bright open sign in the front window.

I walked to one of the jewelry counters and started to look at all the expensive rings in the case. I made my way down to the earrings and decided they were more in my price range. In all reality, I didn't have a price range, but I figured this was worth digging out of the savings for the loan payment. Besides, if this worked I'd have all the money we needed plus more.

"Anything in particular you're looking for?" A female voice called from in front of me.

I looked up at the girl on the other side of the counter. She was short and chunky. Long, dark hair cascaded over her shoulders and down her back while a thick set of bangs swooped over her right eye. Her cute, round face boasted clear skin and a juicy set of pouty lips.

Stylishly dressed in a low cut top, I was able to see the rise of her soft cleavage from my height. One of the perks of being a big girl had to be an amazing rack because she sure as hell had a nice set of tits on her.

She reached up and pushed her bangs from her face. The movement pushed a wave feminine scent straight at me. She smelled amazing, like vanilla and cherries. It was really nice, not too over bearing like the horrible perfumes Renee liked to smother herself in.

I took a better look at her as she pushed her hair out of her face and smiled. She had the biggest brown eyes, deep-set bedroom eyes with a sexy tilt that hid the secrets of a sensual woman. Honestly, she was kind of pretty, in a chunky cute girl kind of way, if you're into that.

While I checked out her tits, her name tag popped out at me. She was Lilly, my financial savior.

"Actually, I'm kind of lost when it comes to jewelry," I said, as I nibbled my bottom lip. I was happy to see her eyes dip to my mouth. "I'm not really sure what she likes." I shot her my "I want you" smile and let my eyes noticeably wander over her face.

I relished in the deep blush that invaded her cheeks since it signified that I was doing my job well. I was just getting started and she was already blushing. This was going to be a walk in the park.

"What kind of girl is she? What do you think she'd like?" She nervously bit the inside of her mouth.

"I don't really know. What do *you* like?" I leaned my elbows against the counter to be eye level with her.

"I like lots of things." She quietly giggled as she started to fidget. It was charming. "But she may not like what I like."

"Ah, come on. Play along with me. If you could have anything in here what would it be?" I asked.

I kept hoping she'd show me something that wasn't too expensive. This chick was rich and I didn't want her thinking I was a poor guy when I couldn't afford what she picked out.

"You're serious? You want me to pick out jewelry for someone I don't know?" She flashed me a weird confused look.

"No, I want you to pick out jewelry that you like. I'm positive that if you like it then she will, too. Humor me, please." I tilted my head and gave her my puppy dog eyes.

Her face turned pink again and I felt a rush of primal satisfaction. I've affected woman before, but for some strange reason seeing her reaction gave me a rush.

"OK, well—um—I'm more of a necklace girl," she said as she walked down to another case with necklaces in it.

"I'm not really into expensive jewelry," she continued. "So, that knocks out everything on this side of the case."

A rich girl who didn't like expensive jewelry? Fascinating.

I listened as she continued picking out the perfect necklace for herself.

"I prefer silver over gold, so that knocks out half of the necklaces on this side of the case."

Her fingers moved softly over the different necklaces and for a brief moment I wondered what those hands would feel like against my skin. She had cute fingers...nice nails, too. I appreciated that her medium length, baby pink nails were her own. I hated those God-awful acrylic nails that most girls wore. Short was fine, but some girls went overboard with the length. My boys and I would laugh as we wondered how girls wiped their asses with nails that long.

She swung her hair around once more and again the light scent of vanilla and cherries rushed me.

"What kind of perfume are you wearing?" I blurted out without thinking.

"Um...I'm not wearing any perfume. Why? Does something stink?" Her perfect brow pulled down in question.

"Actually, something smells really good and since I didn't smell it until you came around, I just assumed it was you. You smell sweet...I like it," I said, as I threw out another flirty smile.

Her face lit up darker than before and I swam in my playboy ego for a bit. She didn't stand a chance...poor girl. Her breathing picked up and her large chest pressed against her low top with every breath. It'd been a while since I held a good handful that weren't bags of silicone and Lilly was definitely more than a *real* handful. My mouth watered with the thought of tasting vanilla and cherries. Oh, she'd been a sweet snack if I were allowed to taste.

Maybe this wouldn't be so bad after all. She was untouchable to me, but I was in need of a good tease.

Brown eyes flickered away from me as she put her head down. Her deep breaths cut through our silence until finally she snapped her head up and held out a necklace.

"What about this? Do you think she'd like this?" she asked.

She wasn't making any eye contact at all.

After being with so many aggressive women like Renee, her shyness was kind of a turn on. I liked how sexy she made me feel without even realizing it. I made her uncomfortable in a good way and she couldn't even look me in the face without blushing. It was a boost to my manly pride since her reactions were genuine, and not like the usual overly dramatic reactions of a slutty girl trying to get laid. I liked her response to me. I liked how she made me feel. A soft growl of appreciation slipped from my throat and it earned me a brief flicker of chocolate eyes. I fought the tilt of my mouth.

The necklace she held up was nice. It was a sterling silver rope chain with a little silver heart shaped locket. It was only a hundred and fifty bucks so I could afford it, and she liked it so I'd buy it.

"I think she would," I said. "What do I put in it?"

"Anything you want really. You could put a picture of the two of you in it or maybe have something engraved on the inside. That's completely up to you."

"OK, I'll take it."

I followed her up to the cash register and watched as she neatly put the necklace in a little red box. She did everything so softly, she wasn't in any rush. Her plump fingers brushed gently across the necklace and then lightly over the box. I watched as she rang it up, touching the cash register again with what seemed like the softest touch. I found myself wondering how soft her hands felt. Her touch was relaxing and it blasted me with a quick rush of chills.

I looked up at her when she gave me the total, again noticing how deep her eyes were.

"You have really beautiful eyes," I blurted out.

That wasn't a part of my strategy. It was a stupid moment of unwelcomed honesty. I'd be sure that didn't happen again.

The tips of her cheeks warmed.

"Are you flirting with me?" Genuine confusion laced her expression.

I didn't have to be a mind reader to know she was thinking of how unlikely it was for a man like me to be flirting with a girl like her. Either that or she really had no idea what flirting looked like and really wanted to know for reference purposes.

"Maybe," I smirked and shrugged my shoulders.

Her eyes filled with panic and the part of me I never used with strangers lit up with sorrow for her. She really had no idea how to respond to me and my tiny advances.

"Um...thank you, I guess. For...for the eye comment," she stuttered.

"Don't thank me...it's the truth." I held out the money to her.

She finished the transaction and then put my receipt in the little black bag containing the necklace. I stood there a minute smiling at her and enjoying how nervous I made her, before I thanked her and left the store.

Part one of my mission was complete.

I ended up sitting in the café her mother told me about and drinking way too much cappuccino. I paid close attention to all the people coming in. I heard every order they made...a double shot of this and an extra pump of that. I'd never sleep again if I drank something like that. Shit, I'm probably not going to sleep tonight after all this cappuccino.

"Come on already, Lilly," I whispered into the lid of my coffee cup.

I was about five minutes away from giving up for the day and trying again tomorrow when I noticed her through the window. She walked in and breezed right by me. I was happy she didn't notice me right away. I pretended to focus on the car magazine I had in my hand as I listened closely to her order.

"Hey, Joey, just the usual," she said.

"Hey, girl! How's it going? No mom meeting today?" he laughed.

"That's not funny, punk," she giggled. "No, there's no meeting today. I'm on my lunch break. Go ahead and throw in a turkey sandwich with that."

She sat at a little table in the corner across the café from me. I watched as she pulled out a little book and started to write something. This was it, this was the perfect time to go and join her. I stood up and grabbed my cappuccino. Slowly, I walked over to her table. She was so involved in what she was writing she didn't even hear me approach.

"If it isn't the brown-eyed beauty from the jewelry store," I said.

She looked up at me and her full lips spread into a tiny smile.

"If it isn't the guy who knows nothing about his girlfriend," she said, as she sat her pen down.

"Girlfriend? Who says that locket was for my girlfriend? Maybe it's for my mom or my sister or..."

"OK, are you seriously gonna play the *no girlfriend* game with me?" She lifted a cocky brow.

"I'm sorry...I'm not sure I'm familiar with any game like that."

"I seriously doubt you're single," she said.

"And why is that?"

I slipped into the chair next to her and rested my chin against my fist. This was getting pretty interesting. She was going to attempt to psychoanalyze me. Good luck, sweet girl.

"Guys like you are *never* single."

"Guys like me?" I laughed "And exactly what kind of guy am I?"

"You want me to be honest or you want me to sugar coat it?"

"I've always been a fan of honesty." I bit my bottom lip and smiled inside when her eyes followed my action. She was thinking of what it would be like to kiss me...good. I wanted her to think things like that.

"You're *that* guy—tall, dark, handsome and *totally* untouchable. You're mysterious, which drives the girls wild, and all that confidence you have wrapped around yourself is a turn on, too. You're a challenge and it's like encoded in human DNA to go after a challenge. I'm willing to bet you have a hundred different walls up to keep people out, which of course makes the girls even crazier. They all want to be the first one to know the real you and I bet you love your car...which is probably some really great classic mustang that you've named *Bertha* or some other horrible old lady name." She paused.

Finally, she looked me in the eye and I felt her deep gaze inside my boxers. Holy shit! She was turning me on.

"Am I warm?" She asked with a questioning tilt to her head.

I sat there sifting through everything she had said. She was so close to the truth it freaked me out.

"You're hot," I gave her a direct gaze as I let the different meanings behind my words sink in. "Have you been watching me, naughty girl?" I attempted to shake the seriousness away.

"Are you saying that I was right?" she smiled.

She was so right it wasn't even funny anymore.

"No, I'm just curious where all that came from."

"I just described any man that would have *nothing* to do with me, so now my question to you is...why are you talking to me?" she lifted one eyebrow as if accusing me of something.

This girl was very strange. Obviously she had self-esteem issues, but at the same time she was the most confident, outspoken woman I'd ever met...other than my sister, Jenny.

Her honest eyes flipped my insides and I felt a tiny bit of panic run up my spine. I was slowly losing control of the conversation, which was completely unacceptable. I internally shook myself and went in for the kill.

"You think I'm handsome?" I flirted.

"Don't change the subject," she blushed.

"No, I think it's you who's changing the subject. Then it's settled!" I said as I playfully smacked the table top.

"What's settled?"

"As long as you're not seeing anyone and since you obviously think I'm *handsome*...I'm taking you out."

"What do you mean out? Like a date, out?"

"Yes, like a date out. What do ya say?" I shrugged.

I was praying that I made some kind of impression on this girl, at least enough to get her to agree to go on a date with me. Everything was riding on this girl and making her happy for three months.

Five

Luck of the Rolls

"I don't even know your name and you want me to go out with you?"

This day couldn't have gotten any more bizarre. First, Shannon gets a mystery illness and I have to fill in all day long on a day that was supposed to be my half day. That worked out well though because I got to cancel my coffee date with my mom. Then, when I thought I was going to die from boredom at the store, this tall, sexy somebody comes walking in and actually starts to flirt with me. Which I have to admit, I kind of enjoyed that part.

Then, to top it all off, when I get to Mirabelle's for my lunch break, who else but tall and sexy is sitting, practically waiting on me. Stranger things have happened, but I couldn't help but want to pinch myself to see if I was dreaming.

I stared back at the gorgeous man sitting across from me. He couldn't have been more perfect. It was like someone took all the physical qualities that I found attractive and put them all into this one extremely sexual stranger. It was almost unnatural that this beautiful man even spared me a look, much less talked to me, and yet, he was here and he was asking me out.

Even sitting his tall frame towered over me. He made me feel small and anything that made a girl my size feel small was a damn good thing. His dark, wavy tresses melted down the side of his face and connected with his facial hair. I enjoyed the way his thin mustache and light goatee encircled his seductive mouth and turned it into a target for kissing.

His wandering green gaze held sexual secrets and promised fulfillment as it slid over my face, down my neck, and then very brazenly over my cleavage. He was fearless, confident, and it was such a huge turn on.

I remember at the jewelry store having to look up at him and the way he smiled when he looked down at me. Can you say sexy? Because I sure as hell can! The man had a smile that could bring a girl right to her knees, which would be bad considering I'd have a hell of a time getting back up. He had on a hunter green sweatshirt and relaxed jeans that looked like they were specifically made for him. He was born and bred to be eye candy. No other qualifications necessary with a man like this.

I realized then that he was talking to me and I had no idea what he was saying. Embarrassment seeped in when I was caught gawking at him like a drooling dog, or should I say like a drooling, fat sow? I almost burst out laughing at my own thoughts, but instead, a huge, goofy grin spread across my face. He smiled back at me and got quiet.

"I'm sorry, what did you say?" I could feel my face burning.

He chuckled a little before answering. It was as if he'd heard all my crazy thoughts.

"I said my name is Devin...and you're Lilly?" He leaned over and ran his finger softly across my name tag, which was practically on my left boob.

I felt his touch through my clothing and soon I felt my nipples getting hard inside my bra. They were probably pointing out like daggers saying, "Hey, hot guy! Look at me, look at me!" I put my head down and took a deep breath. My nervousness was becoming annoying. You'd think I'd never talked to a hot guy before in my life. It's not like they're lined out my door waiting to have a conversation with me or anything, but I've spoken with attractive men. Of course, those conversations were nothing like the one we were having. He was verbally screwing my brains out as far as I was concerned.

I had to pull it together and fast. I wasn't some fifteen-year-old virgin...I was a twenty-year-old virgin. The extra age alone should give me more nerve control. Not to mention, with my undying virginal status, it was obvious that I was in need of some male attention. My nipples practically leapt from my body with a single caress of my damn name tag. I was minutes away from stripping naked and screaming, "Oh yeah, baby, finger my name tag!"

I made a mistake by letting my eyes dip to his mouth again and his smile knocked me stupid once more.

"Yes, my name's Lilly. It's nice to meet you, Devin."

"It's nice to meet you, too. Now, are you gonna put me out of my misery and go out with me?"

His voice was so rich and creamy. Yes...creamy. It was becoming obvious to me that I watched entirely too many cooking shows since the only word that even came close to describing his voice was creamy. The word made me imagine him smoothing peanut butter all over me and licking it off. I'd make myself a Lilly peanut butter cup for this man...no questions asked.

He asked again and again his voice shook me. It vibrated through me like the sound waves were attacking my nervous system and all I could think about for a minute was the little colorful penis toys that my friend Erin had purchased at the local sex toy store.

What could one date hurt?

"I will," I said breathlessly.

The words came out before I could stop them. What I really wanted to say was, "why me?" but I thought that might have been unattractive, so instead I just smiled and shook my head yes or no to his questions. I pretty much acted like I belonged on the short bus during our entire conversation.

He asked me how Friday night sounded. After telling him I had to work Friday, we agreed that he would pick me up after work. I heard him say something about dinner and a movie. He was doing something to my senses. I pretty much went deaf, dumb, and blind all at the same time. The man knocked me senseless!

I gave him my number and he wrote his number down on a napkin. I enjoyed the way his thick fingers maneuvered the pen. Then, just as quickly as he came, he was leaving me. I watched him walk out of the café. He slipped my number into his back pocket once he made it to the door. I was sad to see him go, but I enjoyed watching him leave.

I couldn't wait to tell Shannon and I can't believe I am saying this, but I had to get my ass to the nearest fat girl friendly store and buy some new clothes for our date, which just so happened to be my first date ever.

After work, I practically broke down Shannon's bedroom door to tell her the news. I was out of breath and had broken a sweat by the time I made it there. We jumped around like sixteen-year-old girls and then collapsed on her bed while I described how unbelievably hot he was. I explained why I was so confused and didn't understand why *he* would want to take *me* out.

"Lil, you're crazy! Why wouldn't he want to take you out? You're gorgeous!"

"Thanks, but guys like little skinny girls...and hello?" I grabbed at my fat roll and laughed.

"Not all guys like skinny women, babe. Some guys love a thick woman. They like a little junk in the trunk." She popped her butt out in emphasis. "We call them chubby chasers."

I laughed so hard I almost pissed myself. Chubby chasers? Thank God I had an awesome sense of humor about all this. Of course, I always have. Whenever I watched a comedian on TV I always laughed at the fat jokes. Why not? They're funny and since I'm a fat girl I'm allowed to either laugh or be offended. Getting mad would be a waste of my time. If I got offended every time someone said something funny about fat people I'd spend my life pissed off.

Shannon's a plus size girl, too, technically, except she's the kind of plus size that barely registers on the fat-o-meter. She's stuck in between worlds...too skinny to be in the fat girl club, but too fat to be skinny. She was only considered plus size because her jeans had a double digit size. Instead of calling her a big girl we just called her thick. Personally, I laughed in the face of size fourteen!

She has long auburn hair that never seems to be in control and pretty hazel eyes that show her sweetness, which was the only way you'd see it. Her height gave her a slimmer appearance, while her firecracker attitude and the random trickle of freckles across her cheeks matched the red in her hair. I'm sure her sarcastic come backs made high school a breeze for her, but still, her witty smartass nature won me over. I couldn't ask for a better best friend.

I met her three years ago when she first came into Franklin's looking for a job and we've been inseparable since. She's a year younger than me and acted like the unruly little sister that I never had. She was my first real friend and even though I've never said it, I think she knew it.

We finished our uplifting "power to the fat girls" conversation and started getting everything ready for game night. Every Wednesday night a group of our friends came over and we had a few drinks and played board games.

There were six of us all together. Me and Shannon, of course, and then there was Erin, who was tall and bronze with long black hair. We called her our beautiful Indian friend, but she was made to be a plus size model.

There was Anna, who was the shortie of the group—five-foot-one, round, and adorable with shoulder length dark hair and green cat eyes that I'm sure you could see in the dark. Her soon to be veterinary status was perfect for her sweet and giggly personality. A rabid dog would love on Anna. The response she got from animals was freaky, so we all called her the pet detective.

Meg was the skinny blonde in the group. She wasn't your average skinny blonde, though. She was different. We liked to call Meg, "a fat girl stuck in a skinny girl's body." She may look like the cheerleader you'd love to hate, but she had the personality of the sweet round band geek.

Last, but never the least, was Randy. He was the girlie one in the group and the only one who was getting any action in the sex department. Occasionally, he brought along a new boy toy, but most of the time he kept his love life at the gay club down the street, which, by the way, was the best place to have a good time around here.

Once everyone showed up to game night, we got in an all-out Phase 10 war followed by a very long game of perverted Scrabble. Shannon, of course, blabbed about my date with a hot stranger, which had Randy fanning himself.

"Oh, honey, there ain't nothing like some hot stranger sex! Let me tell you!"

We all laughed even though I doubted any of us, with the exception of Randy, knew anything about stranger sex.

It felt like a whole other day when I finally laid my head on my pillow at one in the morning. I didn't dream that night and as soon as I closed my eyes to go to sleep the alarm clock went off at seven.

I stopped off at Mirabelle's for a coffee before I unlocked and opened the store for the day. Shannon and I watched TV in between customers and soon it was time to close for lunch. I was sitting at the corner table. It was now my favorite table in Mirabelle's thanks to the inspiring love birds from a few weeks before.

When I didn't have pockets in my pants, my bra became my phone holder. So, when my cell phone rang it vibrated my boob and caused me to jerk. I touched my screen and accepted the call from the number I didn't know.

"Hello!" I answered happily

"Is this Lilly?"

"That's me!"

"Hey, this is Devin. Can you talk for a few or are you busy?"

Six

Dirty Work

Today was a slow day. After I finished with the new water pump on an old Ford Dad left for me, I gave Lucy a bath. I grabbed a quick shower and soon it was noon and I had absolutely nothing to do. After I stuffed a ham sandwich and a coke down my throat, I decided to call Renee. I could use a little afternoon delight.

I was about to call her and make up a lie about coming home early, when I noticed the napkin with Lilly's number lying across my dresser.

Why not?

It only rang twice before she picked up.

"Hello!" She sang into the phone.

"Is this Lilly?"

"That's me!"

"Hey, this is Devin. Can you talk for a few or are you busy?"

The other line got quiet for a minute and I thought maybe she had hung up on me.

"Yeah, I can talk...what's up?"

"I know I just got your number yesterday and we have a date tomorrow night, but I couldn't stop thinking about you." I smiled to myself.

It was more like I was completely bored and there was nothing better to do than sit on the phone handing out fake flattery. Work was work. I might as well have some fun with it. Either way, I was getting paid for this gig, so I might as well do it right.

I snuggled down into my dad's big chair. The house was nice and quiet. Jenny was at school and dad was out running errands.

"Oh, whatever," she giggled. "You're funny."

"How am I funny?" I asked.

From what I could tell this chick must never get approached by guys. That was strange considering she was kind of a pretty girl—she'd be hot if she just lost a little bit of weight, but hey, some guys like that kind of thing. I'm just not really into that.

"It's just funny...anyway, what are you up to today?"

"I'm done with work and now I'm lounging around trying to figure out what to do with the rest of my day. Exciting huh?"

She laughed a little. "It could be worse...you could be stuck at a boring jewelry store with me."

"Sounds like torture...being stuck somewhere with a beautiful woman all day? Just kill me now," I joked.

She giggled uncomfortably. "You're silly."

We talked like that back and forth. We talked as she left the café and went back to work. We talked while she was at work, and while Shannon, who apparently is her roommate/coworker/best friend, put in her two cents in the background. I realized after a while that I was actually enjoying our conversation.

She wasn't like most chicks, all flirty and boring. She actually talked to me and asked me questions about myself. Not the normal stupid giddy female questions, but actual questions about my family and work. It was kind of nice to talk like that. It was comfortable, maybe because I didn't feel like I needed to impress her. Now that I think about it, it was kind of strange. I didn't feel like I was talking to someone I barely knew. We talked like old friends.

By the end of our three hour conversation I learned so many things about her. She talked about her and her mom's shitty relationship, which was uncomfortable considering I had already met her bitchy mom. She told me about her dad that lived in California and how she never really saw more than his back and briefcase when she was growing up. She told me about going to an all-girls school, which let's face it...was really fucking hot! The point is, I could tell from our conversation that she was kind of raised alone—no brothers, no sisters, and really no mom and dad.

It made me appreciate my crazy ass dad and goofy little sister. Yeah, we sometimes argued and sometimes my little sister tried her hardest to make me choke her, but at least we were a family. We were a family who laughed together and worked together to make it through this crazy life. I'd do anything to keep my family's life afloat. I know I should feel bad about what I was doing to Lilly, and in a way I did, but I couldn't regret the fact that doing this was going to pay the bills.

My little sister came bursting through the door about the time that I was about to hang up with Lilly.

"Who you on the phone with?" she screamed across the house while the refrigerator door was being slammed.

She came busting into the living room with a coke and a bag of chips.

"Did you hear me, Dev? Who you talking to?" she continued to loudly yell, while shoving a handful of chips into her big trap.

Lilly started to laugh through the phone.

Jenny's name should've been Benny because everything about her screams male teenager. She's fifteen, soon to be sixteen, and is in tenth grade. She has long, dark hair that she keeps tied up in a low pony tail and big, green eyes that match my own. When I sit and think about it, there really isn't a girly thing about her. She dresses like a boy, burps like a man, walks like a dude, and fights like a pit-bull. The last part is thanks to me, of course. Even her bedroom is covered with car posters and blue and green bedding.

"Hey, I'm gonna let you go, OK? My loud ass little sister is home. I'll be by to pick you up after work tomorrow, OK?"

"Okay sounds good. See you tomorrow."

I hung up the phone, rolled my eyes at Jenny, and then got up to leave the family room.

"That wasn't Renee, was it?" Jenny smiled back at me like she had just caught me red handed.

"It's none of your business, nosey," I smirked back.

"Oh my God, you cheater!" she laughed and bits of chip flew out of her mouth. "Thank God! It's about damn time. You know I never liked that bitch Renee."

"Would you watch your mouth? And no, it wasn't Renee, but keep that between you and me, OK? Seriously, Jenny, it's important, OK?"

"OK, cool! So...when do we get to meet her?"

"Never!" I laughed, as I poked her on the tip of her nose when I walked by.

"Ah, come on. No fair, Devin!"

It would never go that far. I would date her, get my money, and then never see her again. Yeah, it would last about three months, but there was no way in Hell she'd be meeting my family, especially considering my dad would see right through me and the situation if I ever brought her around.

Oh well, I got a date tomorrow. It's all in a good days work.

That night, after dad got home and we ate dinner, I relaxed in my bed and had a sudden guilty feeling. Would I be able to do what needed to be done? Would I be able to lie in Lilly's face? Most people consider me a heartless bastard and honestly I kind of made it that way myself. It was, in a lot of ways, my wall. It kept people from getting close to me, which in turn kept me from getting close to people. A psychologist would call it my defense mechanism. I call it being smart.

The reality of it was that I wasn't a heartless bastard. I didn't want to hurt this girl, and by lying to her and making her think that I was interested in her, I was hurting her without her knowing it. Honestly, she was kind of sweet. I could see me hanging out with her and being friends. Maybe that's why I felt so damn bad about what I was starting with her.

I barely got any sleep that night. I tossed and turned, and when I finally did sleep I had horrible nightmares about the day my mom left and never looked back. I woke up at five thirty the next morning drenched in sweat and hyperventilating. I didn't even bother going back to sleep.

By the time dad came out to the garage to open I was already mostly done working on Mrs. Bennett's old Cadillac and had already changed out the tires on Ralph's new Chevy. Dad stopped in his tracks and stared at me like I had suddenly grown two heads. I swiped at the greasy sweat that was draining down my forehead with the back of my hand.

"What?" I asked.

"Nuttin'...if you keep workin' like this we're gonna run out of work. We're already ahead. What's going on with you? You've been acting funny the last couple of days. You OK?"

"Yeah, I'm good. I'm just trying to stay busy. We got to make this money. I don't know if you forgot, but we got eight thousand dollars to pay in a couple of months."

"No, I ain't forgot, but you sure you're OK?"

"I'm fine."

I really had to be careful around my dad. The man didn't miss a thing and he wouldn't approve of what I was doing.

I finished up around the garage and then headed inside to get a shower and to get ready for the night. I needed to pep myself up big time, and I needed to figure out exactly where I was going to take this chick. She was rich and I didn't know if I could afford to take her to the places that she was used to. Hopefully, after this first date, her mom would give me that first installment. That would help out a lot.

Seven

A Date with the Devil

I spent most of Thursday afternoon shopping with my mom. As much as I complained about it before, I needed her expertise in finding something to wear on my first official date. I ended up with a very low-cut black top and a sexy pair of slimming boot-cut jeans. We finished it off with a cute, black necklace that almost touched my cleavage and dangly earrings. Mom tried to convince me to get my hair done, but I refused.

"Are you going to tell me about him or not?" Mom smiled an unnatural-looking smile as we sat at her favorite ritzy restaurant.

"There's not much to tell really. He came into the store. Then I saw him later at the café and he just asked me out."

"Oh come on, Lilly. More than that happened. Don't you know anything about dishing with the girls about guys?" she laughed.

"OK, fine." I sloshed my straw around in my drink. "He's really hot, like, super-hot, and he has the most gorgeous green eyes I've ever seen. You probably wouldn't like him though. He's not rich, but I like that about him. He works at his dad's garage and yes, he still lives with his dad, but they kind of own everything together."

Mom didn't flinch, which I found extremely unnerving. She should be going on and on about dating a poor guy and how he was probably only after my money. I pushed harder to try and break her silence.

"He doesn't wear expensive clothes or anything and if I'm not mistaken he drives an old car. Like, really old...I think, but money isn't everything, right? I mean, as long as he's a nice guy."

"Whatever makes you happy, honey, and you're right, as long as he's a nice guy, that's all that matters."

I stared back at her like she had just shot fire out of her ass. Something was definitely up.

"What's wrong, mom?"

"Nothing's wrong. Why?"

"Come on, now. What are you playing at?"

"I don't know what you're talking about."

"Please! By now you would've already been going crazy about me dating some penniless guy and blah blah blah. You know, the usual we're rich and above him comments. What the hell?"

"No, I know you're lonely, Lilly, and if this guy makes you happy, then I'm happy. Now, can we please order something? I'm famished. What kind of wine do you want?"

Maybe mom was going through menopause or something. I'd have to be sure to Google the symptoms when I got home. I'd never heard her speak so level-headed. People change, though, and maybe my mom was going through some emotional changes. It's not necessarily a bad thing.

We ate dinner in an almost silent state. It was really odd. She didn't comment on anything except to say that she thought I looked really nice in my new outfit and that I was sure to make him drool. I laughed at that one. Why would anyone drool over me?

*****

On date day, the hours seemed to stand still. I couldn't wait until he picked me up and took me out. This whole thing was so new to me. It's been way too long since I felt excited about a new development. It was always the same thing over and over again for the last year or so. I was slowly becoming a hermit who only came out for work and the occasional girl's night out.

At about six thirty, I went into the store bathroom and refreshed my hair and makeup. Shannon agreed to close up and drive my car home for me so I didn't have anything to worry about, except looking my best. I was in the middle of applying a fresh coat of lip gloss when I heard the little bell over the door jingle followed by Shannon calling my name.

I shoved my powder compact and lip gloss back into my little black purse and then patted my hair down one more time. As I walked out behind the counter Shannon turned to me and mouthed, "Oh my God—hot!" I couldn't help but smile.

That's when I saw him again.

He was leaning against the counter all sexy looking with a pair of loose fitting jeans that hung from his hips and a black Henley shirt. He turned to look at me and I could swear I saw something in his eyes that said, "Wow." I blushed and looked down at myself one last time. He held out a single white rose and I took it from him and held it to my nose.

"Thank you...it's beautiful." I smiled up at him.

"You're very welcome." His eyes dropped to my cleavage.

"If you want, I can put it in some water when I get home. That way you don't have to leave it to die in the car," Shannon said.

I handed her the flower and then smiled back at Devin. My very first flower from a guy, you know that bad boy is getting dried and crushed between the pages of my journal.

"I know roses are kind of typical, but I figured you've probably gotten like a million lilies in your life," he said.

I chuckled to myself on that one. If only he knew. No lilies for Lilly!

"You ready to go?" he asked in that creamy, mocha latte sounding voice of his.

I know I know! Stop with the food already!

"Yes, I'm ready."

I ran over closing with Shannon real quick to make sure she didn't forget anything and then followed behind him to the door. He held the door open for me and as I was passing by I heard Shannon yell.

"Have fun, kids. Don't do anything I wouldn't do, or better yet do everything that I'd do!" she laughed out loud at that.

I rolled my eyes and felt my face turn red. Devin chuckled softly to himself.

On the walk to his car, he placed his hand on my lower back and I suddenly felt like all my skin was melting off of my body. The heat from his hand went through my shirt and straight into my spine. It was such a sweet moment in time and I was kind of sad when we finally got to his car. I felt his hand leave my back as he opened the car door for me.

"It's not much, but it's mine," he said apologetically before he closed my door and ran around the front of the car to the driver's side.

Before he could get into the car, I whispered out loud, "It's perfect."

It was perfect to me. It wasn't a brand new vehicle, but it had character and small touches all over that reminded me of him. I had seen enough flashy cars in my life and this, as far as I was concerned, was a real car. Just like my old Honda, a real car, with scratches and dents—a car that had lived, and if I wasn't

68

mistaken, it *was* an older sports car, just like I had said before. Nail on the head baby...nail on the head.

Remembering the day in the café when he had asked me out made me wonder again why he wanted to take me out. I couldn't for the life of me see this incredibly hot guy being attracted to me. Me! Large Lilly, the fat girl in class, the loser who hid behind mommy and daddy's money—at least that's what the kids at school used to say. I had to stop thinking these things. I wasn't in high school anymore. I wasn't large Lilly anymore. I just needed to remember that...even repeat it to myself all night if I had to.

After jumping in and starting the car, he turned to me and smiled as he revved the engine. I felt my cheeks heat up, and for a second I worried that maybe this date was bad for my blood pressure. Lord knows I was feeling a little flushed just looking at his sexy smile.

"I believe I was correct about the old Mustang named Bertha," I said, as I hoped for a sudden change in mood.

"Nope, her name's Lucy and she's a Camaro." He smiled sweetly as he caressed the dash of the car like it was an actual female.

I'd never wanted to be a car more in my life, if that's what it took to have him softly caress me that way. I silently wished to be a car—I was big enough to be one. I wanted to imagine myself purring every time Devin got inside me and took me for a ride. Unfortunately, all I could see was me drunk with chocolate

69

smeared across my face singing the Transformer's intro "Robots in Disguise!" into Shannon's broken box fan.

"So, where do you want to go? I was thinking dinner and a movie, but it's completely up to you if you wanna do something else instead."

"A movie sounds fun. I wonder what's playing."

We stood out front and looked at all the movies playing. There really wasn't much to choose from. There was a sappy chick flick, which I'm sure any other girl would choose, but that I had absolutely no desire to see. Then there was the new slasher film that was supposed to be super gross with lots of blood, sex, and action...I was dying to see it.

"It's up to you, but I don't mind blood and guts in case you're wondering." I shrugged, as I hoped he'd man up and pick the slasher flick.

There was no way I was going to admit that I wasn't like every other normal chick he's been out with. So instead, I just hinted that I'd rather see the scary movie.

"It's OK if you wanna see the scary movie instead of the chick flick. To be honest, I'm glad. I hate chick flicks." He laughed and I felt myself relax.

"Yeah, me, too. No girly tears and drama for me."

"My kind of girl." He winked. "Come on, let's get the tickets." He grabbed my hand and I followed him to the ticket line.

His hands were warm and hard, and they made my chubby hands seem small. I liked the fact that he was so much taller than me and his hands were so much larger than mine. Again, he made me feel small and I loved feeling small for once in my life. Callused rough spots rubbed against my soft hands and instead of turning me off, I imagined how nice those rough spots would feel against different soft parts of my body.

He *paid* for the tickets and then we went inside where he *paid* for the popcorn and the drinks. I felt awful. Here I was loaded, with more money in my personal bank account than he'd probably make in his whole life, and yet he was paying for everything. I didn't say anything. He'd probably hate it if I offered to pay. He was entirely too proud for that and the last thing I wanted to do was make him feel like he was poor or something.

Soon we were settled into the movie theater with our popcorn and drinks, watching the previews. I wasn't as nervous anymore, but I couldn't help but notice the few females who kept looking at Devin. It made me feel like they were looking at us and I couldn't help but feel like they were wondering what the hell he was doing with me.

We sat and watched the movie. I felt like a dumbass every time I jerked when the scary killer jumped out of nowhere. Whenever I'd jerk, he'd reach down and squeeze my knee. I loved it. It was like he was reassuring me that he'd protect me if the killer jumped out the screen. I'd never had anyone treat me that way before. It was a small action, but it was huge for me.

His deep chuckle vibrated my shoulder as I covered my eyes when things got too bloody. Don't get me wrong, I love a good scary movie, but some things are too much.

There was one point when we stuck our hands in the popcorn at the same time. I pulled my hand back like the popcorn container was full of snakes and he flashed his "I know you want me" smile.

When we got up to leave he held my hand and I felt like I was in high school again. Holding hands isn't something I'd ever experienced before tonight and it made me sad to think of all the things I'd missed as a teenager. I'd be sure to make up for all those lost things now, though.

He opened the car door for me and I slid in. He smiled before shutting the door and making his way around to the driver's side.

"OK, so where to now?" he asked.

"Where ever is fine with me," I answered.

"Are you always this easy?" he asked, before he busted out laughing. "You know what I mean...not like that. I mean so easy to get along with."

It took me a minute to catch on to what he was saying before I started laughing, too.

"I know what you mean. OK, fine—um—what about putt putt?"

"Now that's more like it! Be prepared, I'm the putt putt king!"

The rest of the night was a blur. We had so much fun. I was so comfortable with him. We laughed and picked at each other. He ended up not being very good at putt putt after all and that was comedic in itself. He spent most of the night being a complete gentleman: Holding fences open for me, getting me something to drink, holding my putter while I pulled my hair out of my face. It was amazing.

Later, after I'd won like three rounds of putt putt, we decided it was getting late and left. We talked the entire drive back to my apartment. He asked me questions about myself and I could tell that he actually cared about the answers—he wanted to get to know me.

He answered my questions as well.

"What grade's your sister in?"

"Jenny's in tenth grade. She's a hand full that's for damn sure. I swear she's got the mouth of a forty-year-old sailor. Just the other day she got in trouble at school for calling her math teacher an old bitch."

I laughed. He had no idea how lucky he was to have a sibling that he was so close to. Something about having a baby sister around really appealed to me, even if she did act like a boy.

"Tell me about your dad. Are you guys close?"

Apparently, his dad, Herald, could charm the pants off any lady in town and fix an engine with his eyes closed.

"Sounds like you're a lot like your dad," I smiled.

"No...I'm not." He didn't smile back.

73

I dropped the subject of family when he seemed to get tense and changed the subject to classic cars. I watched as he very animatedly talked about his favorites. He was absolutely adorable when he was accidently being himself and not the sexy playboy.

All in all, it was one of the best nights of my life. I was sad when I saw that we were parked in front of my apartment. I didn't want the night to end.

Eight

An Accidental Attraction

I spent most of the night staring at her tits like I was some wet-
behind-the-ears punk. This was *not* working out in my favor so
far. I was supposed to be the one seducing, but her innocence
was making me wild. Biting her lip was her nervous tick and I
swear to God every time she did it I wanted to bite it, too. It
made me uncomfortable as shit and that never happened to me.

Another surprising thing about Lilly...she was a blast. I
was shocked by how much fun I had on our little "fake" date.
There was no alcohol, drugs, or sex involved, just good ole
friendly fun and it was throwing me off my game big time. I
laughed more with Lilly than I had with any other girl and I
mean real laughter, not the bogus shit I'd throw out to appease a
girl before I fucked her.

She had to be one of the coolest chicks I'd ever been out with. The fact that she loved slasher flicks was good enough for me, but she was a badass at putt putt, too! You can't beat that shit with both hands. Most girls would whine about sitting through a dude movie, not Lilly. She smiled and did the cute little jerking thing every time the killer jumped out. I used those little jerks as a reason to reach down and touch her. Damn, she was growing on me and it sucked ass.

The things we had in common were unreal. I never thought in a million years that I'd be so comfortable with a chick so fast, and while her tits were fucking amazing, I wasn't thinking about banging her every five seconds. I actually enjoyed her company. It was kind of sad that we couldn't stay friends after all this was done and over with. This was never supposed to end well...I knew that when I started. She'd hate me when I just suddenly never talked to her again...that was expected. She wasn't my friend, she was a job.

When we pulled up to her apartment I got out and opened her car door for her. The seat belt had pulled down her low cut top and a hint of light pink bra peeked out. Not the black, lacey, zebra bullshit like the bras Renee and the other skanks wore, but just a soft baby pink that suited her so well.

She must lotion her hands like ten times a day. That was the only explanation for hands as soft as hers. I could only imagine how soft the rest of her was. This was my thought process as I held her hand up the side walk to her door. I felt a hint of sadness when she pulled her hand away to dig through her purse for her keys.

She pulled them out and fought with the lock for a few seconds. Her hands were shaking so bad that the keys were actually jingling. The poor thing was a nervous wreck. She probably thought I was going to kiss her goodnight since that's what happened on normal dates. At least that's what I've heard...I've never dated.

At the beginning of the date, she was nervous, and it was cute, but after she got comfortable with me her nervousness melted away. Once she started having fun, she was more than cute. Her happy smile illuminated her face and she glowed. I really liked that glow. I hated that she was nervous again and for some uncomfortable reason, I wanted her to smile...I wanted to make her glow.

I reached out and put my hand over hers to stop them from shaking. I let my fingers linger over hers longer than needed as I slowly took the key from her and unlocked her door.

"Thank you," she said as she looked down and tucked her hair behind her ear.

When she looked up again she smiled and her blush made *me* feel warm. Realizing that I was losing track of the situation, I shook myself.

"You're welcome. I had a lot of fun tonight. I hope we can do it again."

"Me, too," she said.

I was about to tell her goodnight...maybe kiss her on the cheek and make a run for it, but again she surprised me.

"You know...my roommate's still out if you want to come in for a few." She peeked up at me through her dark bangs and nervously nibbled her bottom lip.

I unconsciously licked mine with the thought of nibbling on her lip, too. She looked so innocent and sweet with her flaming cheeks. My throat suddenly felt coated with a strange thickness as I swallowed hard.

Did I really want to go inside her apartment? What was she offering anyway? And if she was offering herself, would I be able to say no? Did she realize that by asking me into her place she was practically saying she wanted to do it? Probably not, she was way too innocent for that.

"Sure," I blurted out.

I stepped into the apartment and was surrounded by a homey down-to-Earth place. I'm not sure what I expected to find—maybe an oversized palace with crystal chandeliers? Instead, there were big comfy couches and pictures on the walls. It screamed 'home sweet home' and I found myself relieved that she didn't live in one of those ritzy apartments that were so perfect you were scared to sit on the couch and fuck up the throw pillows.

"Make yourself at home. I'm gonna run to the bathroom real quick. The remote's on the coffee table, turn on whatever you want. I'll be right back."

I sat on the big fluffy couch and relaxed for a few while flipping through the hundreds of channels. Damn, what I'd give for the expensive cable.

Finally, I made it to the Discovery channel and a really cool heart surgery caught my eye. The narrator was walking me through the entire process as the chest was opened and the heart was exposed. I watched half disgusted and half amazed.

It wasn't long before she came back dressed in a cute pair of pink and black flannel pants and a black razor back tank. It covered her completely and really there wasn't anything sexy about the outfit, but those pink bra straps were really visible. For some reason I didn't fully understand, I was turned on.

I shifted on the couch and used a pillow to cover my crotch...just in case.

I'd never in my life found a big girl attractive, but Lilly was a different kind of big girl. She was thick in the right places and had the most beautiful long hair. The desire to run my fingers through it followed me around all night. At one point during putt putt, she pulled her hair up into a messy bun so she could see to play and I wanted to beg her to let it down again.

Her hair was swept up right now and I wanted to ask her to please take her little hair ribbon out. The thought of that long hair lying on her shoulders and those pink bra straps peeking out was doing it for me.

"Find anything good on?" she asked as she sat beside me on the couch and propped her fuzzy slipper covered feet on the coffee table.

Since when were fuzzy slippers fucking hot? Damn, I need to get laid in the very near future.

A horrified expression crossed her face when she realized what I was watching on TV. Apparently, she only liked fake blood and guts.

"Oh my God...what are you watching? Eww turn it, turn it now!" she covered her eyes.

I jokingly pulled at her hands and laughed.

"Oh come on, Lilly! I thought you liked blood and guts?" I continued to playfully pull at her hands.

She fell back onto the couch to get away from me and I followed her as she plucked the remote from my hands. I tickled her to get it back. Once I got it I leaned back and held it out of her reach. She unknowingly squashed her tits against me as she attempted to get it back. I enjoyed it almost as much as I enjoyed picking at her. I was laughing like I was twelve years old again, back when my life was simple. Real heartfelt laughter, like before, and it felt good.

During all the playing and tickling, I'd managed to pin her down on the couch. I held her arms above her head by her wrists and once she realized that she was good and captured she stilled beneath me. Her breathing was hard and deep as she smiled innocently up at me. She felt amazing—all soft and welcoming...sweet. I wasn't sure if it was the playful fighting or the fact that I was lying on top of her, but my breath quickened.

We were so close I could feel her heart beating against my chest. I moved in and rested my forehead against hers while I breathed her in. Vanilla and cherries—the mouth-watering scent matched her sweetness. I bet she tasted just as sweet as she smelled. This close, her skin looked even softer than I originally thought, and I felt the sudden need to touch her. I released one of her wrists and stroked her dimpled cheek with my thumb.

I'd thought before that kissing her wouldn't be an issue. I was never more wrong. I wanted to...badly. This realization sent me into a mini panic attack, but instead of giving in and freaking out I focused on my thumb against her amazing skin and calmed myself. My reaction to her was scaring the shit out of me and it didn't make any sense. I wasn't technically attracted to her, but I was. I was attracted to her, not her tits or her ass, even though they were truly luscious, but her. This had never happened to me before, and I wasn't sure I liked it. Actually, I fucking hated it.

She made me feel different. I didn't want to be asshole Devin, I wanted to be sweet. Like one of those pussy-whipped men you see following their woman around and buying tampons and shit. I almost laughed at the absurdity of my situation. I didn't want to pretend to be a nice guy for Lilly...I actually *wanted* to be one. Not for any other reason, but she deserved all the sweetness I could give.

I fought with myself internally over kissing her, but somehow with her I was winning and losing at the same time. Puffs of warm breath struck my mouth as she breathed in and out. I looked down at her lips and my inner struggle increased. Just the thought of touching those plump lips with mine gave me an immediate reaction. Before I could stop myself I brushed my lips across hers. She sucked in a deep breath and held it.

I'm not a rocket scientist, but I know females, and this girl wanted me to kiss her, probably more than any other girl I'd kissed. She wanted me, and instead of being aggravated by it, I liked it. Her responsiveness to me was a major turn on as it stroked my ego.

What is it about this crazy, carefree, chubby girl? She's nothing like the usual girls I screw. For one, she's not blonde, or blue eyed, or tall and skinny for that matter. Except this one, this one girl's slowly breaking all my rules and instead of dropping my boxers, I wanted to drop a few Devin walls for her—I wanted to let her in.

I took a deep breath and went in for the kiss. I was so close I could feel the warmth of her lips against mine when she stopped me.

"Wait," she whispered against my lips.

Whispering had never made my skin burn before. This girl was making me insane. It had to be because she was forbidden. That was the only reason I could come up with. She was off limits and for a man like me who had no limits with women, it was frustrating. To think, I had actually laughed when the subject of kissing had come up with her mom. What a dumbass I had been.

I waited, perched on top of her and ready to feel her mouth against mine. With her eyes still closed, she spoke in the most seductive whisper I'd ever felt against my skin. Her lips brushed against mine with each word, making my groin muscles tingle.

"I know I'm probably ruining what could possibly be the most perfect moment in my life, but please..." She stopped and opened her eyes.

I fell into her deep brown pools and nearly drowned. I held my breath as I waited for her to finish her sentence.

"Don't do this unless you mean it," she finished.

I wasn't sure what she was asking me for. I wasn't sure what I meant. I just knew that I wanted to kiss her. It wasn't going to *mean* anything. A kiss is a kiss. It's not my fault that women turn such meaningless things into big dramatic issues, but the fact of the matter was, Lilly wasn't kissed often, if at all, and this *was* going to mean something to her.

She would probably remember this moment for the rest of her life, meanwhile, in three months when all was paid and my car had a new paint job, I'd never think of her again. What kind of man would I be if I kissed her knowing these things? Then again, since when do I give a rat's ass about things like consequences? Especially consequences for some chick I'd never have to see again soon.

That was my final thought before I gave in, closed my eyes, and pressed my lips to hers.

Her mouth was every bit as soft and sweet as it looked. She let out a little moan that made goose bumps cover my arms. I pressed my body closer to hers as I slid my arms behind her shoulders and pulled her closer to me. The kiss got deeper as our bodies got closer. I opened my mouth and ran my tongue along the seam of her lips, urging her to open her mouth. She did without even one question and I slid my tongue in.

The sweetness that engulfed my mouth was nothing short of amazing. No woman should be allowed to taste so delicious. I couldn't get enough, so I let go of her shoulders with one hand and slid it up the back of her neck, digging my fingers into her hair and pulling her face closer to mine. I tilted my head to the side and before I knew it we were in an all-out spine melting kiss.

I couldn't think of anything but the fact that I wanted her. It started out as an innocent kiss that I wanted, but now I had to have her. I broke the kiss and both of us took a much needed deep breath. I pushed her legs open with my knee and then fitted my body between them as I repositioned myself on top of her.

I know what I was doing was against the rules, but all the best things usually are. I kissed her again and then moved away from her lips and pressed soft kisses down the side of her neck. Vanilla and cherries filled my senses.

"You smell so good and you taste even better. Damn, baby, you feel so good," I whispered against her neck.

Sweet talking isn't my thing, but the words seemed to come on their own. She's turned me into some blabbering romancer.

Her innocent responses and delicate touch were too much. My cock was so hard that it was beginning to hurt and that tiny ounce of pain brought a little bit of common sense back to me. I had to stop. If I didn't, I was going to ruin my shot at the money before I even got started.

I pressed my hips against her one more time just to get one more feel of her through our clothes before I pulled away. At least I thought I was going to pull away, but as I was about to, she slipped her hands down my back, grabbed my ass and pressed my hips deeper and harder against her. She let out a little sound that made me throb all over.

I hate clothes, but I love them because if it wasn't for our clothes I would very well be having sex with this woman. I could not under any circumstances let it come to that. For the first time in my life I prayed that a female would stop me. I needed her to say no, because quite honestly stopping wasn't something I was capable of anymore.

Thankfully, before I could start removing any clothing, Shannon, her roommate, came crashing through the front door. I sat up quickly pulling Lilly up with me, neither of us able to catch a good breath. Shannon, my savior, couldn't have come home at a better time.

"Holy shit! I'm so freaking sorry!" she yelled out, while covering her eyes. "I'm going straight to my room, I swear." She fumbled through the apartment with her eyes covered and knocked over a floor plant.

I took that opportunity to make a break for it.

"No, Shannon, I was actually about to leave."

I looked over at Lilly and gave her my best sorry look before I jumped up off the couch. I'd never let it go this far with her again. Leaning down, I gave her a quick impersonal kiss on the lips before walking toward the front door. It was the least I could do considering I was practically dry humping her less than a minute ago.

I had to get away—she was too much for me right now. As if her glazed-over bedroom eyes weren't enough to get me going, those luscious lips waiting for me to kiss them definitely were.

I looked back at her before opening the front door. I couldn't miss the confused look on her face.

"I'll call you tomorrow, OK?" I said

I didn't even wait for her reply. I walked out the door.

Nine

Jeopardy Theme Song

I'm a slut. Not just an ordinary slut, I mean a dirty, nasty, get-freaky-on-the-first-date kind of slut. This is a shocking realization for me considering I technically had my first kiss tonight, as well as almost lost my virginity. I was totally about to let him have his way with me. Actually, I was practically begging him to give it to me. I just met him a week ago for freak's sake! Who does that? Apparently, me!

The sad part is I liked being a slut, which puts me on a whole other level of slutdom...a slutty slut. I blame hormones.

Meanwhile, I had the best night of my life. Devin's everything that I could ever dream of. I really hope he asks me out again. That is if I didn't scare him off with my looseness. I can't even believe how I responded to him. Talk about embarrassing!

Shannon says it's completely normal. I say I'm a horn dog on the loose...a horn dog that was starving after he left. I'm not sure why I was afraid to eat in front of him on our date. The man can look at me and clearly see that I eat everything that isn't bolted down. Yeah...that was dumb of me. I should have stuffed my face. I wouldn't want to give off false advertisement or anything.

Now, it was time to play the waiting game. Either he'd call or not—I'm sure as Hell not calling him. I already looked like a crazy sex fiend. I'm thinking adding desperate bitch to that title isn't a great idea.

In any case, the ball's in his court on this one and every part of me, including my deprived girl parts, are praying that he plays.

I spent the day after our date replaying the whole night over and over in my head. I should've done this differently, I shouldn't have said this, and I wonder if he meant this when he said that. Oh my God, talk about pure Hell.

Shannon's been laughing at me because I've been stuck in Devin dreamland all damn day. I even gave in and went shopping—me...the bitch that loathes shopping, but I wanted to be prepared. I wanted to sex myself up just in case I get a chance to run into Mr. Dead Sexy again.

Shannon picked a sexy red top that barely covered my boobs and a pair of black pants that, I had to admit, made me look two sizes smaller. Anything that makes your ass shrink is a good thing when you're a solid size twenty.

I picked out a cute pair of strappy black shoes with a two-inch heel. Then we spent the rest of the day getting our nails and hair done. My mother would have died if she knew.

By the time we got back to our apartment we had bags and boxes galore, new hair, and huge smiles on our faces. We did a quick cleaning job on the apartment, threw together a quick, unhealthy dinner followed by something smothered in chocolate, and then spent the rest of the night in front of the TV.

I spent the entire time checking my phone to make sure I had signal or that my battery wasn't dead. My phone was fine and yet there was still no phone call.

That night I barely slept.

The following day, Sunday, I opened the store for Mrs. Franklin and spent the day stuck to the front counter with my phone beside me. I was getting pretty pathetic, and by the end of the day I decided to give up on the thought that he might call. It was a fun night and that's all it would ever be. I decided to let it bounce off of me and forget about it him and his mind-blowing green eyes or his soft kisses or...

"OK, you're doing it again, Lilly!" I said out loud to the empty store.

Valerie, Mrs. Franklin's niece who comes over twice a week to go over the books, came from the back of the store.

"Did you say something, sweetie?" she asked confused.

"Just talking to myself," I said as I swiped my bangs from my eyes.

"Gotcha...want to go grab some lunch?"

I couldn't even pretend like I had an appetite.

"Nah, I'm good—rain check for next week?"

I spent the rest of the day selling jewelry when and if we had a customer. If it wasn't for me randomly buying expensive pieces of jewelry every now and again I think Franklin's Jewelry store would've closed months ago.

It's worth it to me and I'm sure the children's charities that receive anonymous expensive diamond rings and necklaces are happy about it. I always send to children's charities. Maybe it has something to do with the fact that I can't have kids.

I remember how sad I was when the doctor told me that I'd never bare children. *Apparently*, if you get kicked repeatedly in the lower part of your stomach by a bunch of angry teenage girls it causes internal bleeding as well as affects your ability to reproduce. The memories of that day six years ago still stung.

I thought I'd made some new friends when in reality they called me to their little meeting in the woods to let me know that they didn't like me very much. I'd never been called so many horrible names in my life and after a while I didn't even feel the kicking anymore. I should have known then that something was wrong.

"I'll sue those little bitches for everything they have!" My mom was irate when she found out what had happened.

"Mom, they're a bunch of teenagers...they don't have anything at this point in their lives. Just let it go."

That's exactly what I did. There was no way in the world I'd let those girls know what they'd taken away from me. Instead, I switched schools and never saw any of the girls ever again. Yeah, it was the coward's way out, but if I had said anything I would've been hated by the entire student body for the last three years of my high school life for getting rid of half of the cheerleading squad.

It's a memory that I keep hidden in the back of my mind, but I'll always be reminded of that day every time I see a cute little baby smiling back at me. I get sad just thinking about how lonely I'm going to be when I get older. I dream of having a huge family with tons of kids that I can love who'll love me in return.

The girls, and Randy, say I could always adopt. Honestly though, who in their right mind would give a single woman a child? No matter that I'm a secret millionaire—a child should have a family, a mom and a dad. At least that's the way it is in normal families. Then again, I grew up with a relatively "normal" family and look how shitty I turned out.

The following night we all met at McCrady's, the Irish pub close to my house. They were having karaoke and I tried really hard to have a good time even though all I could think about was how stupid I was to think that I stood a chance with such a good looking guy like Devin.

Deep down, I wished that I'd never even gone on the date in the first place. At least then I wouldn't be sitting around wondering if I said or did something wrong. Or worse than that,

I wouldn't be sitting around picking out all of my flaws and cursing my fat ass.

Even with my craptastic mood, I couldn't help but laugh hysterically when Randy got on stage and sung "Like a Virgin." Not only was it funny because, well... he's a guy singing Madonna better than Madonna sings Madonna, but Randy was so far from being a virgin that it just wasn't even right.

That night I managed to get some sleep thanks to the few beers I drank while out with the girls.

Soon, it was Tuesday and I had pretty much forgotten about Devin. I was planning on spending my wonderful day working at the store. I had this whole "rearrange the store" day planned. The store was in need of a mini makeover, plus it was time to start putting out seasonal stuff.

Since today was Shannon's day off, I'd have the entire store to myself. Even though I wasn't supposed to I turned the radio station to something that wasn't boring and then sang softly to myself as I decorated the store.

I was standing on the stepping stool behind the counter putting up the fall decorations when the little bell on the front door opened. I turned to see who it was before getting down and lost my balance when I saw Devin staring back at me.

Ten

Dr. Devin

It had been four days since I'd talked to Lilly.

Did I feel bad about it? Yes.

Was it the right decision? Hell yes.

She's a good girl and she didn't deserve to be manipulated. We needed that money something serious, but I didn't have it in me to do what Mrs. Rich Bitch was asking me to do, not to Lilly. Caring about someone else's feelings wasn't really my thing, but doing that to her was the equivalent of kicking a kitten. I hate cats, but I'm not that much of a bastard.

I finished up an oil change and then went over the books for the garage. It was bad...really bad. It wouldn't be long before we'd be packing up everything and living on the streets.

I sensed the evil in the room before I looked up and saw the she-devil herself standing in the middle of the garage. By her expression you would've thought we were standing in a pile of dead animals and maggots. I pushed myself away from the broken-down metal desk and walked over to her.

"What can I do for you?" I asked.

I didn't want to seem too familiar with her in case Dad popped up outside.

"Oh, you've done quite well already. I'm just here to give you your first installment. A deal's a deal, right?" She held out a check and from afar I could see the long line of zeros.

I shook the bad thoughts out of my head and mentally flicked the little asshole devil from my right shoulder.

"I don't want that. I'm not doing it."

I saw raw anger flicker in her gaze before she quickly plastered a false smile on her thin lips that never reached her eyes.

"What do you mean you're not doing it?"

"She's a nice girl and I don't feel right about it, OK?" I turned to walk away before the check could draw me any nearer. It was a like a tractor beam pulling on my back.

"I talked to Mr. Schaefer the other day, you remember him, don't you? He was the man that had you arrested. He's agreed to help you as long as I give my word. I guess it's true what they say...money talks."

"Look, lady, I said I can't do it."

"You're a little too close to losing everything to suddenly develop a conscious, don't you think?" she growled. "Don't be stupid. Take the deal I'm offering you. You'd be the most selfish man alive if you didn't, your poor little sister and dad living on the streets when you could've prevented it. Trust me, I know my daughter. She'd approve if she knew how close you were to living in that thing you call a car."

Her words attacked my brain waves and then started to seep in. As much as I hated to admit it, she was right. I *had* to do this, for my family more than anything. Maybe she was also right about Lilly. She'd understand after she got over the hurt, right?

"Let's get this over with before your father gets anymore dirt on my BMW. At least I assume that's your father outside drowning his sorrows in that can of beer out front."

I looked outside and she was right, my dad was out there running his grimy fingers down the side of her expensive car. He was definitely drunk. I guess he was giving up just like me, except now I refused to give up. There's no other way. I reached out my hand to her.

"Give me the damn check," I said dryly.

"There's a good boy," she smirked, before turning and walking away.

"What a bitch," I said out loud to myself.

Two hours later I was outside of Franklin's jewelry store again. I shook the tension out of my shoulders and checked my clothes. What the hell kind of excuse was I going to give her for not calling for four days? I reached out my hand and pushed the door open. Guess I'll just have to wing it.

I saw her standing on a stepping stool of some sort behind the counter. She was hanging fake swags of yellow and orange fall leaves and flowers. She immediately turned toward the door as I came through it and I watched as she lost her footing and fell. She disappeared behind the counter when she hit the floor. Running over to the counter, I jumped over it quickly. The bright red blood all over her leg and floor was a direct contrast to the gray carpeting behind the counter.

"Are you OK?"

It was a stupid question since seeing that her pants and her leg was ripped open she was most definitely *not* OK.

She looked like she was fighting back tears while she reached down and very slowly rolled what was left of her pants leg up.

"Ouch!" She jerked her hand back. "I think I caught the edge of the glass top counter there," she hissed. "Apparently, it's pretty sharp."

I ran into the employee bathroom in the back of the store and grabbed as many paper towels as I could.

"Here, let me help you," I reached down to help clean the blood.

She jerked away quickly like she had been burned. This let me know she was seriously pissed off at me and I couldn't blame her. I'd be pissed, too, if I were her.

"I got it, thanks." Her words were clipped and not once did she look at me.

I watched as she wiped up blood from her leg and the floor around her. She wouldn't let me help no matter how many times I insisted, but when she almost fell trying to get up, I reached out and held her up regardless of her complaining. Once we got her settled into a comfortable chair she let me move the napkins and look at the huge cut down the side of her leg that was still pouring blood.

"We gotta get you to a hospital. I hate to tell you this, babe, but you're gonna need stitches."

She still looked like she was about to cry, but no tears ever came.

"It's just a scratch," she said. "It'll be fine—I'll just have to put a lot of band aids on it."

The expression on her face as she looked down at her bleeding let me know she knew she was going to need stitches as well. I recognized the exact moment that she resigned herself to a hospital trip. She shook her head and tried to get up from the chair.

"I need to lock up first."

She stood up to get the store locked and hissed loudly at the pain from her leg.

"I'll do it. Just tell me what to do," I offered.

She talked me through locking the front door then I pulled down the closed sign. While I was doing that, she called the owner of the store and told her that she needed to leave and explained why. I heard the lady on the other end of the line going crazy with worry.

I finally convinced her to let me take her to the hospital and soon we were on the way. There were no words spoken between us once we were in my car. The talkative giddy girl from our date was nowhere in sight and with her wincing in pain every couple of minutes I figured now wasn't the best time to lie about why I disappeared off of the face of the earth. I was going to have to be something good—something that tugged on her heartstrings.

When we got to the hospital they took her straight back. She didn't say anything when I followed.

"OK, Mrs. Sheffield, I'm going to need you to remove your pants so I can get a better look at this." The ER doctor looked younger than us.

She peeked over in my direction, still not looking me in the face then took a deep conflicted breath. Instead of taking her pants off in front of me like the doctor asked, she reached down and ripped her pant leg off from the knee down.

I watched as the doctor cleaned the wound and was really surprised by how big it was. It was going to leave one hell of a scar, that's for sure.

"Yep, we're definitely going to have to stitch you up. Let's get you numbed up first," he said, as he pulled out a needle.

"Don't numb me...just stitch me up, doc," she hissed, as she turned her leg.

The doctor looks surprised for a second. "Are you sure, sweetie? This is going to hurt."

"I'm sure."

"OK, well you may want to hold your boyfriend's hand."

A soft blush covered her cheeks and I covered a smirk.

"He's not my boyfriend."

She peeked over in my direction once more; again her eyes never reached my face. I wanted to make her look at me.

I watched as she flinched and gripped the sides of the hospital bed. Gritting her teeth, she made tiny hissing noises every time the needle went into her skin. She was in horrible pain, but not once did she cry—her eyes didn't even water.

I lost count of the many stitches she received. I was too busy trying to stay in my seat. Part of me wanted to hold her hand and be there for her, but the tiny anti-Devin sign she was wearing kept my ass in my chair. I had the feeling I'd get bitten if I went anywhere near a wounded Lilly.

They gave her crutches and pain medicine and then I was helping her to my car. The ride back to her apartment seemed to take forever. I had to break the silence soon, this was crazy. I'd never had any problems talking to a female. Fixing cars aside, smooth talking the ladies was always easy for me.

I turned the radio down.

"Lilly, I'm sorry I didn't call. I know you're pissed off at me and...," I started.

"I'm not mad—I understand."

That stopped me. How could she possibly understand? Did her mother tell her?

"You understand?"

"Yepper deppers," she slurred.

"Are you OK?" I asked.

She ran her fingers through her hair causing her bangs to slide over her eyes. Her head bobbled a little before finally falling back against the headrest. I watched as a strand of her dark hair fell down her cheek and onto her neck. I suddenly felt like I was driving a drunk chick home from a party.

"Thy drugs are quick," she slurred a quote from *Romeo and Juliet* before she laughed hysterically. "I should've probably mentioned that I have zero tolerance for pain meds, huh?" she spewed another burst of laughter.

There was no way in the world she'd take me seriously now. She was high out of her mind—glazed-over eyes and all!

Once we got to her apartment, I had to practically pull her out of my car. She laughed the whole way to the door while trying to maneuver one crutch and my arm at the same time. I caught myself laughing, too. The simple fact was she was a cute druggie.

If I were any other guy, I could take full advantage of this situation. I could bang her back out and she would have no idea about it in the morning. If I were any other guy that's probably what I'd do. Instead, I took her key, opened her door, and then helped her to the couch where she collapsed in laughter, pulling me down with her.

I felt her arms go around my waist and my entire body reacted. The sensation shot straight down my abs and into my thighs. My jeans went tight in the crotch just that quickly and I freaked. As fast as I could, I pulled back and tried to get up to close the door.

"Don't leave," she slurred with her eyes closed. "I don't want to be alone—I'm so tired of being alone."

She looked up at me with unfocused, sad eyes before her head fell to my shoulder. She was out like a light.

I laid her back and then propped her legs up on the couch, careful not to touch her cut. I got up, shut the front door, and then contemplated whether or not I should leave her or wait until her roommate got home. I decided to wait and sat on the loveseat watching TV for what felt like hours.

Her last words before she fell asleep lingered in my mind. She was tired of being alone. Maybe when this is all over with I'd find her a nice guy who could appreciate her. All things considered, she was actually kind of great. Too damn good for a disconnected piece of shit like me. My own mother didn't want me, why would that sweet piece of woman lying on the couch want me. I'm not good enough, but there was some dude out there that was and I'd find him if I could. It was the least I could do considering what I was doing to her.

I looked over and watched as she slept peacefully on the couch. She looked angelic... all innocence and I was the devil. I was the horrible fiend who was swooping in to attack. I suddenly felt a little sick to my stomach.

"I have to do this," I said to no one, as I changed the channel and hardened my heart.

Finally, I felt myself getting tired and before long I was sleeping, too. I don't know how long I slept, but I woke to someone saying "ouch" over and over again. I looked up to see Lilly limping towards the kitchen. I jumped up to help her.

"What the hell are you doing?" I asked.

"I'm thirsty," she was breathing hard.

"Why didn't you wake me up, I'll get it for you. Here sit down before you bust your stitches." I helped her back to the couch and then went digging through the nicely decorated kitchen.

I found a coke in the refrigerator and took that to her.

"You want anything else. Are you hungry? I could make you something."

"No, but thanks," she rolled the coke can in her palms nervously. "You can go. You don't have to sit here and babysit me. I really appreciate it, but I can call my mom and have her come over until Shannon gets home," she winced in pain, as she put her leg back up on the couch.

"I don't mind, I like being here with you." I said it to make her not so weary of me, but once the words came out I realized that I actually meant them. "Besides, what kind of gentleman would I be if I left you here all by yourself? Just sit back and let doctor Devin take care of you."

She giggled finally and then stopped suddenly as she gripped her leg in pain.

"Do you want me to get you another one of your pain pills? Enough time has passed...you can take another one if you want."

"No, I'm OK. I don't usually take pain medicine and I still feel kind of groggy from the dose I took earlier. Thanks anyway."

"You're crazy. If you're in pain you should take it. I still can't believe you let him stitch you up without numbing you first. You're a tattoo artist's dream. Most girls would have cried."

"I don't cry," she said blandly.

"What do you mean you don't cry? Like ever? You never cry?"

That was the craziest thing I'd ever heard, women cry—that's what they do. It's, like, programmed in their DNA to be whiney and emotional. I don't think I've ever met a woman that didn't whine and cry about something or another. Even my little sister Jenny, who was a total hard ass, still cried occasionally about something.

"Never," she sounded raspy.

"Not even when you were a kid?"

"The last time I cried I was fifteen. It's been years since I've shed a tear and I don't plan on starting again anytime soon," she smiled tightly.

I didn't say anything else on the subject. Something seriously traumatic must have happened to her. Her little confession changed something. There was a brief moment that I saw a broken Lilly. I know broken when I see it. But just as quickly as it slipped off, her giggle girl mask was firmly placed back on.

She was hiding something...a darkness that only another broken person could see. Suddenly, I felt a manly streak of protection run through me. It took everything I had not to growl and paw at the ground. It was a demented situation. Here I was... the delivery man of hurt and yet I wanted to beat the shit out of anyone who even considered bringing this girl pain.

I was shocked by how protective I felt towards her. It was a strange feeling considering the only female in my life that I've ever been defensive over is my sister. She's the only female in my world that I give a shit about.

We watched a few sitcoms before she asked me to help her to her bed. Her room was exactly as I pictured it. Very Lilly... that was the only way I could explain it. First of all, there was no pink, which I silently gave thanks for. Her room was a neutral color with palm trees everywhere. It was like being stuck on an abandoned island. There was a huge king size bed that looked like fluffy clouds and beside the bed there was a night stand covered in books.

She limped into the bathroom and was in there for a while before coming out with her hair piled on top her head and a pair of sleep pants covered in cherries on. It was fitting since she naturally smelled like vanilla and cherries. I shouldn't know that...I shouldn't care to know that. I mentally punched myself in the balls.

I helped her into her bed, gave her the TV remote, and then got prepared to leave. Her huge room suddenly felt very small.

"I'll call you tomorrow... if that's OK?" I said, as I started to leave the room. "I'll make sure the door is locked and if you need anything before Shannon gets back just call my cell."

"Devin," she whispered.

"Yeah," I stopped and turned to face her.

"I really hate to ask this, but could you stay until I fall asleep? I don't wanna seem like a big baby, but I don't really want to be alone right now."

The room began to shrink again. I shook my head yes and started back towards the bed. My words were literally stuck in my throat. The last time I was alone like this with Lilly we almost had sex. I swore I'd never get into this position again. Yet here I was, climbing into bed with her.

I slipped onto the bed and sat up against the headboard. She snuggled up under the covers with her eyes closed while I flipped through channels trying to find something to watch.

I don't remember falling asleep. I just know that I slept better than I had in many years. I don't know if it was her plush, expensive mattress or the fact that she snuggled up to me all night long. All I know is when I woke up the next morning I felt a warm body pressed up against me in all the right places.

Half asleep I pulled that body closer to me and pressed my hard on against the soft warmth. I heard a little moan, which in my mind was a bright green go sign, so I kept pressing myself against her.

I pushed some thick sweet smelling hair out of my way and began kissing the back of her neck. I felt her turn in my arms and soon her lips were pressed against mine and I was grabbing a handful of ass and pulling her closer.

I kissed her deep and hard and her little sighs drove me harder. I slipped my hand inside of her shirt and felt her tense

105

against me. She didn't say anything so I just kept going. With my eyes still closed, I pushed her onto her back and fit myself between her legs. I didn't need to see...I know my way around a female body. I pressed up into her thigh and it felt so amazing I thought I might unload right there, but I must have hit her stitches because she let out an ungodly scream that knocked me out of my sleepy, horny daze.

I jumped up and shook my head trying to get myself together. She pulled back the covers and started checking under her wrappings to make sure I didn't accidently bust her stitches open.

"I'm sorry," I said roughly, as I ran my hands through my hair pulling on the ends.

"It's okay."

Her hair was all ratted up and her eyes were heavy with sleep. Her lips were moist and red from my hard kisses as she nervously nibbled on her bottom lip. The strap to her tank top was pushed to the side revealing a little peek of side boob. She looked so tempting. All I could think about was climbing on top of her and burying myself into her hard and deep.

I shifted my hips and adjusted myself to relieve some pressure from my jeans against my hard cock. This shit wasn't getting any easier. It was getting harder...literally. Like any harder and I'd be popping a button on my loose fitting jeans.

It pissed me off just thinking about it. This was complete and total bullshit. This is *not* me and I'll be damned if some chunky virgin was going to turn me into some little bitch over sex. I wasn't about to let that happen. I would play this off, get my money, and get the hell out.

"What is it about you?" I heard myself ask.

"What do you mean?" she asked nervously.

"I can't seem to keep my hands to myself around you," I laughed sarcastically to myself, as I ran my hands through my hair again. "Which is why I tried to stay away from you, but there's just something about you. I'm sorry. From now on I promise I won't touch you anymore."

I couldn't even bring myself to look at her as I spoke. I was embarrassed that I was even feeling this way. I was pissed off that I even had to apologize for myself. I'm a man and I liked to fuck... end of subject. I shouldn't have to say sorry for that. It's who I am.

I've always prided myself on the fact that I never lost control with any woman and yet here I was always losing my self-control with this girl. This chunky girl who I kept telling myself I wasn't physically attracted to. It was a cruel joke from God.

When she finally spoke, I had to force myself to leave.

"I like it when you touch me," she whispered.

She was brazenly looking at me and I watched as a pink blush covered her skin. It took a lot for her to say those words.

"I gotta go. I'll call you later."

Then I did what I was best at... I left a girl in bed begging me with her eyes to stay. I didn't even wait for a reply. I had to get out of that room before I jumped into that bed and screwed her brains out.

I passed Shannon on the way to the front door and I thought for a minute that her eyes were going to pop out of her head. I closed the front door behind me, but not before catching the smirk that Shannon threw my way.

Eleven

Party Time

And so fatty fell. In front of the God of lust, too, which made it ten times better. I was never one to do anything half-assed. I couldn't have just fallen. Oh no, not me. I had to fall and rip my calf open and I had to do it in front of Devin. Not Shannon, not alone so that I had to drag my fat ass across the floor of Franklin's army style to the phone. Oh no...Devin *had* to be there.

.   After days of waiting for him to call me he popped up at the store only to watch me make a complete fool out of myself. I couldn't just stop at busting my ass right in front of him. I then proceeded to sit the rest of the day in the emergency room. He stayed with me the entire time, probably because he felt like he had to or it was the right thing to do.

Then, like the stupid bitch that I am, I accepted the pain medicine that the doctor gave me because... DUH...I was hurting so damn bad. That was another one of my big, bright ideas! There's no telling what I said or did while I was drugged up.

Then I slapped a big, fat cherry on top when I pretty much begged him to stay the night with me. Begged...like a dog...big puppy dog eyes and all. I was still under a small influence of pain medication by that point, but that's no excuse.

You'd think I'd stop there. Oh no, not Lilly! I then proceeded to rape him the next morning only to realize that he was still asleep when he was kissing me and responding.

This is good because it further lets me know that I'm a complete and total ass-face! This is also good because if he comes back around after all the times that I've practically thrown myself at him, it means it must truly be meant to be.

What the hell is wrong with me? My hormones are all jacked up. Maybe I should stay away from him? He did say one thing before he left that kind of threw me for a loop. He said that he was having a hard time keeping his hands off of me. Me! That's just crazy! No one's ever said anything like that to me.

Of course he was running for the door when he said it. Running for his life...I'm sure he was afraid to be eaten alive.

After he left, I spent the entire next day in my bed. My leg hurt so bad that I could barely stand it. Mrs. Franklin sent over the biggest bouquet of flowers I've ever seen in my life and then called a million times to check on me. Shannon said something about how afraid she was about me suing her. If only they knew.

If Shannon ever took the time to balance her check book, she'd see that I never cashed any of her checks for the bills. I'd say she had quite the checking account going on for herself. I wasn't looking forward to the moment when she finally realized that she was living with me completely free. She's no squatter and I can already imagine the wrath that she was going to let loose on me for that one. Just the fact that I never mentioned that I was filthy rich was going to be enough to piss her off.

I had to explain over and over again what happened the day before while Shannon and I played twenty questions about Devin. After lunch, Devin called me to check on me, which made my day.

"Don't leave that bed, young lady!" he joked.

I couldn't stop smiling for the rest of the day. I finally crawled out of bed and got a shower at almost dinner time and that helped me feel better. I hobbled out of the bathroom and into my bedroom, trying with all my might to keep the towel wrapped around me. I was still in so much pain and Devin was right, this thing was definitely going to leave one hell of a scar.

Later that night, he called again and asked if I'd be interested in dinner this weekend. As if I'd say no.

"There's this really nice restaurant I wanna take you to. It's the least I can do since I've been pawing at you like a wild beast," he joked.

If only he knew how badly I wanted him to unleash his beast on me. He thought I was offended by his touches and kisses, meanwhile I've had to change my panties three times all day just thinking about it. If anything, he was raising my metabolism because every time he came near me or any time I even thought of him, my heart rate increased. High Metabolism equals weight loss. Thank you, Devin Michaels!

I took the rest of the week and the weekend off from work. I spent most of my days hanging out around the house. Soon, my stitches weren't hurting as bad as before and I could manage to walk without leaning against something. My mom stopped by and freaked out over my stitches and how bad it would scar. Of course, she went on and on about how I needed to quit my job and blah blah blah. I don't remember the rest. I zoned her out as usual.

At night I sat in my bed and talked on the phone with Devin, who was being so sweet I could hardly stand it. We stayed on the phone until I couldn't keep my eyes open every night.

Soon, it was Friday and I was getting dressed to go out to dinner. I put on a dark purple v-neck top and a black skirt that Shannon told me I *had* to wear. I'm not usually a skirt person, but anything rubbing against my leg caused it to burn and itch.

I did manage to wear a pair of tall boots that didn't stick to my leg. They were just tall enough to cover the bandage. Not long later, I had my makeup and hair done and I was nibbling on the inside of my mouth as I waited for Devin to ring my doorbell. When my doorbell finally did ring, it wasn't who I was expecting.

"Well, well, Lilly, aren't you all dressed up?" my mother smiled knowingly. "Got a hot date tonight?"

She walked around me and threw her very expensive bag onto my couch.

"Mom, what do you need? I actually do have a hot date and he'll be here any minute so could you make this kind of snappy?" I snapped my fingers for emphasis.

"Oh, so now I need a reason to want to see my lovely daughter?" she smirked.

"Mom, you never come over here this late. I know you and you would've just called. What do you want?"

The doorbell ringing stopped her reply. I ran to my room to get my purse, and then I ran back. I wanted to get out of my front door as quickly as possible. The last thing I wanted was for my mom and Devin to run into each other. I did *not* want them to meet. I couldn't let that happen right now, not if I ever wanted to see him again.

When I came out of my room, I stopped face to face with Devin. He had a really weird look on his face and for a minute I thought he was going to cancel our date and say that he never wanted to see my fat face again.

"Aren't you going to introduce us, Lilly? Don't be rude, I didn't raise you to be rude." She smiled sweetly at Devin, but I knew what was on the other side of that smile.

I rolled my eyes and blew out my deep breath.

"Mom, this is Devin. Devin, this is my overbearing, bossy, thinks she owns my apartment building, mother." I smiled sarcastically and sweetly back at my mom.

I could feel Devin's nervousness radiating toward me. Poor guy.

"Devin, you look familiar. Have we met before?" my mother purred.

His entire body went stiff and for a minute something seemed...off.

"No, ma'am, I don't think we have, but it's nice to meet you. Lilly, are you ready? I hate to be rude, Mrs. Sheffield, but we have dinner reservations for thirty minutes from now."

"Not at all, Devin, you kids have fun."

The way she said his name made my stomach turn.

She snatched up her bag and went to the front door. "I'll call you tomorrow, Lilly."

Then she was gone. I turned to Devin with an apology in my eyes.

"I'm so sorry."

"For what?" he asked.

"I didn't arrange for you to meet my mother or anything like that, she just popped up and I was in the process of trying to kick her out when you..."

He reached out and grabbed my hand, stopping all words from leaving my mouth.

"No worries, it wasn't that bad. Stop apologizing to me all the time," he smiled. "Let's go, I'm starving."

Once we were at the restaurant, I spent the first few minutes looking over the menu and trying to find a not so expensive meal. I wanted this meal to also be small. I wanted the meal to say, "Hey this chick *really* doesn't eat *that* much."

Later, after we left the restaurant, we stopped off at a gas station really quick and I sat in the car while Devin pumped gas. He apologized like a mad man for not having gotten the gas before the date. I laughed at him. Like I cared whether or not he got gas. I was out and about with him and that's what mattered to me at this point. It didn't matter if we were at a nice restaurant or at a ratty old gas station.

I ran inside for a pack of minty gum and was on my way back to his car when I noticed him talking with another guy.

"Lilly, this is my friend Matt. Matt, this is Lilly." He looked nervous as he tucked his hands into his pockets and looked away from me.

"Nice to meet you," I said.

The million dollar question...do hot boys run in packs? Was it like a secret society that no one knew about, because Matt was hot! He was just as tall as Devin with black hair and sea blue eyes. I wanted to stick my pinky finger in his little dimple as he smiled back at me. His eyes brazenly moved up and down my body and I suddenly felt naked. I had to stop myself from covering my boobs with my hands. Heat infused my face as I started to blush.

Was he wondering what Devin was doing running around town with the fat girl?

"It's *very* nice to meet you, Lilly."

He exaggerated the L's in my name which resulted in his tongue being flicked at me before he sucked his bottom lip in and ran his teeth across it.

And then I saw it... a look that I instantly recognized. It was the same look Devin had given me that very first day in the café, the same look I get from Devin all the time. Matt was checking me out. He was smiling and talking to me all flirty like.

What the hell was going on around me? Was I suddenly secreting some female hormone that I never had before? And did this secret female hormone attract sexual man beasts? I seemed to be surrounded by them lately. I'm not complaining, but what the hell?

I looked over at Devin and almost laughed out loud when a scowl developed across his face.

"So, Lilly, what the hell are you doing out with a punk like Devin. You could be out with a real man like me," he winked and nodded.

Typical playboy moves...I think. At least that's what they do on TV.

I laughed nervously and tucked a piece of hair behind my ear.

"That's enough, Matt," I heard Devin say. "What are you getting into tonight?"

"Headed over to a party on the docks. Y'all should come. It'll be fun."

"That sounds fun." I smiled sweetly at Devin. "Wanna go?"

Devin didn't look too happy about it, but he agreed.

Within the hour, we were at some strange house with a bunch of laughing, drunken people. It was pretty exciting. Technically, it was my first house party.

Matt handed me a fruity drink before leaving me and Devin alone. I watched as he made his way through the room and socialized with random women.

"He's a dog, you know?" Devin spoke as his sipped on his soda.

I thought it was really cool that he wasn't drinking so that he could drive.

"What?" I asked.

"Matt, he's a good friend. Don't get me wrong, but he's a man-whore. He flirts with everyone. I just wanted to let you know before you run off with him for the rest of the night." He shrugged and looked away like he could care less.

"Whatever," I laughed and playfully pushed at his hard chest.

I met so many different people, some were friends of Devin's, some were friends of a friend, like me. I felt very welcomed and comfortable. It was nothing like high school that was for sure.

Before long, I had quite the buzz. I'm not sure how many drinks I had, but I thought for sure that my bladder would explode in a matter of minutes if I didn't find the nearest bathroom.

The music was muffled once I was in the bathroom. I tried to reapply my makeup and look a little more presentable. I laughed at myself when I realized that I actually looked drunk. My eyes were glazed over and my cheeks were flushed. I even noticed myself leaning a little more onto the bathroom counter than I usually would.

"No more drinks for you, Lilly," I said to myself with a little chuckle.

I left the bathroom and was making my way down a long, empty hallway that led to the party when I met Devin. Like the drunken person that I was, I gave in and leaned against the wall.

"Stick a fork in me. I'm done!" I giggled when I heard myself slurring. The giggle was followed by a hiccup.

He laughed.

"Do you want me to take you home?" An adorable smile spread across his face.

"Yes, please." I pressed my cheeks against the cold wall and closed my eyes.

The hallway seemed to be shifting under my feet and I knew that I had definitely over done it in the drinking department. A soft moan escaped my lips as I switched cheeks against the cool hallway wall.

Suddenly, I felt fingers in my hair. I turned toward the hands and enjoyed the feel of it. He worked his fingers through the strands and tucked stray pieces of hair behind my ear. Soon, I felt his soft lips against mine. His kiss was so soft and sweet. I let him take my lips. I heard myself making little noises, but it was like the alcohol had washed away the filters in my brain and I was free to say whatever I wanted.

"That feels amazing," I slurred.

"You feel amazing," he whispered in my ear.

My sexual tension snapped and I turned and kissed him. I used my palms to push him up against the wall as I attacked his mouth like a starving woman. I felt like I could do anything. I had no fear whatsoever about being rejected. I kissed him harder and faster as I pinned him to the wall with my body. He delved his hands into my hair and turned my head to get deeper into the kiss.

Liquid bravery...I'd been taking shot after shot of that shit all night and now I could do anything I wanted. I reached down the front of him and grabbed his hardness through his jeans. He was turned on and the noises he made once I was touching him were making me even more courageous.

I had no idea what the hell I was doing, I just knew I wanted to touch him everywhere. I started to move my hand up and down and I felt his body go tense as he let out a little growl. I moved closer to him and continued to kiss him like the deprived woman that I was.

I moved away from his lips and nibbled at his ear before I moved to his neck. More little noises were pulled from him. His breathing got hard and fast as I continued to run my hand over the front of his pants over and over again. He whispered my name and it drove me harder.

"Lilly, stop," he rasped against my mouth.

I continued touching him and kissing him.

"Please, Lilly, this is wrong. You have to stop."

119

His voice was soft and inviting. He didn't sound like a man that wanted me to stop. He sounded like he was begging me to keep going. The whining sound in his voice let me know that he definitely did not want to stop.

I didn't. Instead, I reached down inside his jeans and grabbed him.

"Yes," he whispered into my mouth. "Fuck yes, touch me, baby."

I moved my hand up and down the best I could since his belt was cutting into my arm. He was so hot to the touch and while he was hard as a rock, he still managed to feel soft to the touch.

Before I realized what was happening he pushed me up against the opposite wall of the hallway. I felt his hot hands against my outer thighs as he roughly pushed my skirt up. I heard the jingling of his belt and the sound of his zipper. He lifted my leg up and around his hip and tugged my panties to the side. He looked back up at me and the look in his eyes was raw... dangerous with need.

I gripped at his shoulders and prepared myself for the shot of pain that was supposed to come with your first time.

I felt hot hardness against my inner thigh and his breath against my ear when he leaned forward. He gripped my ass with one hand and lifted my leg more with the other as he pressed against me. Then as quickly as it started, everything stopped.

He let go of my leg and he moved away from me. I let it slowly drop to the ground while he reached down and pulled my

120

skirt to cover me back up. Finally, he looked me in the face and the wild passion was gone. Instead of the feral man he was just seconds before, he looked like a scared, unadulterated little boy that had just woken up from a horrible nightmare.

"I'm so sorry, Lilly. I don't know what came over me," he shook his head.

"It's OK. I don't want you to stop," I breathed.

"No," he snapped. "This can't happen."

He looked away from me and put his clothes back together. The jingle of his belt and his zipper sounded again, reminding me of what almost just happened.

"Did I do something wrong?" I asked.

I still felt like my knees were going to give out on me.

"I can't let that happen. We can't have sex."

It took a minute for his words to register. This continues to happen—me throwing myself at him and him wanting me, and then suddenly pushing me away. I was getting blue balls and I didn't even have balls! I felt like every girl part I owned was about to pop if something, anything, didn't get released soon.

What man in his right mind turns down a ready and willing woman? I mean seriously!

Then a thought crossed my mind.

"Oh God, Devin. Do you have something? Like an STD or something?"

"What? No! Why the hell would you even ask me that?"

"I just assumed since you keep saying we *can't* have sex that there must be a really important reason."

121

"No, that's not it. I can have sex, "he jabbed himself in the chest. "Just not with *you*."

The way he said it made me think of all the high school boys who used to talk about me. He sounded like he was completely disgusted by me. I felt like I'd been punched in the face. All this time I was throwing myself at him and he was disgusted by me. That should've been my first thought. Duh, Lilly! Men want beach bodies, not beached whales!

Oh he was a sexual creature who wanted sex alright— just not from *me*. Me. The fat girl. Me. Lilly. He didn't want me.

I pushed him away and started down the hallway. I felt tears sting my eyes, but there was no way in Hell I was going to cry. I hadn't cried in years, there was no way I would let him make me cry. I cursed myself for even allowing my eyes to water that little bit.

I heard him call out my name, but I kept walking. I passed through the crowd of party-goers in the living room and I heard his friend, Matt, call out my name as I went out the front door. The cool air rushed over me and cooled my hot, embarrassed skin.

"Hey, sexy girl," Matt said with a slur. "Did ass-face leave you stranded? Wanna ride me? I mean...do you want me to give you a ride?" He said on purpose with a smirk.

"Yes, please take me home."

I didn't care that he was being a big drunk pervert. I didn't care that he was drunk at all. It was stupid on my part, but I needed to get the hell away from the party and Devin as fast as possible.

I don't really remember the drive home. I was completely heartbroken and drunk. When I got home Shannon was on the couch with Erin and Gabby.

"Are you drunk?" Shannon shot off of the couch and followed me to my room. "Lil, what's wrong? Did that bastard do something to hurt you?"

"No, I'm fine!" I called out before slamming the door in her face.

I wasn't trying to be mean and I know she'd forgive me tomorrow, but I just wanted to go in my room, wash my face, and go to sleep. I never, ever, wanted to see Devin again!

Thirty minutes later, after I was settled in bed with night clothes on, I heard a tap on my door. I knew it was Shannon and the girls trying to be nosey.

"Not now, y'all!" I called back. "I just wanna go to sleep. We can talk about what's bothering me tomorrow. Goodnight!"

I turned my back to the door and was in the process of getting comfortable when I heard my bedroom door open.

"Shannon, I don't want to talk about it. I don't need a power to the fatties pep talk. I just want to be miserable. Please, just let me dwell in my unhappy fatness tonight, OK? Please." I turned my head into the pillow.

"Don't say things like that about yourself," Devin said in a sharp tone.

I sat up like lightning to see him standing beside my bed.

"Get out," I hissed before turning my back to him.

"I'm so sorry." I heard him take a deep breath.

The alcohol was slowly leaving my body and the little bit of numbness I felt earlier was beginning to melt away. I was starting to feel the pain of tonight—and my past was slamming into me. Not to mention, my damn leg was starting to hurt again.

I couldn't take another apology. Not tonight. Not ever. As far as I was concerned, he could take that apology and shove it right up his sexy ass. I grabbed my pillow and hurled it at him.

"Get out! Just leave me alone. You don't want me that way, then fine! I get it, OK? So quit torturing me. I've never done anything to you. Why do you insist on driving me nuts? I'm done with this crap, so leave me the fuck alone!"

I never dropped the F-bomb unless I was really emotional. I'm pretty sure this qualified as an overly dramatic emotional moment.

He didn't say anything else.

I turned away from him again and soon I heard the soft click of my bedroom door when he left. I fell into a deep, drunken sleep.

Twelve

A Hardened Heart

It's been three days since I've heard from or seen Lilly. She isn't answering any of my phone calls and the one time that I stopped by her apartment Shannon said she wasn't there, yet her car was. I'm pretty much being ignored. I know this game well since I've played it many times in my life, except this time I'm on the receiving end and it sucks monkey balls in hell.

I've never had a female ignore me before, and it's driving me bat-shit crazy. I know it's nothing less than what I deserve and in a strange way it's kind of setting me straight. It's a taste of my own medicine and it's coming from the most unbelievable source. If I had told any one of my friends that an overweight chick was ignoring my phone calls they'd shit.

It's an awful place to be...the receiving end. I can't even say it's because of the money. I'd be lying if I said I even thought about the money even once since the night of the party. I know we still need it and everything, but I spend my days thinking about her and my nights waiting with my cell phone close by just in case she misses talking to me as much as I miss talking to her. I even started doing something that I've never done before, which is worry about another guy.

All I can think about is the fact that my man-whore of a friend, Matt, had taken her home and had at least twenty minutes alone with her. Matt would have no problem what-so-ever with throwing her up against a wall and fucking her senseless. Me on the other hand, I had to suddenly grow a conscious.

I'd kill him if I find out he even laid a finger on her.

What the hell is happening to me?

Later that day, Jenny and I did some grocery shopping. Well, Jenny grocery shopped and I pushed the grocery cart around.

"What's going on with you, Devin? You've been in la la land for the last couple of days. You're not on drugs are you? I'll kick your ass if that's the case," Jenny blurted out.

"Would you watch your mouth? You're too damn young to be running around cussing like a sailor, and no I'm not on drugs. Just got a lot on my mind is all." I bumped into a small display table almost knocking everything over.

"Dad says you act heartbroken. Are you?" she said with a huge grin. "You know I think I might like this new girl you're talking to."

"I'm not heartbroken," I said, and then quickly tried to change the subject. "You want spaghetti on Wednesday night?"

I started to pick through the different kinds of spaghetti sauces like it was my one true calling when I heard Jenny once again curse.

"Oh shit," she whispered.

"Jenny, I said enough already with the cursing!" I stopped when I stood face to face with Renee. "Oh shit."

"Hi, Devin." She smiled at me smugly as she crossed her arms and worked her neck. "What do you know? I guess you *are* back in town? Funny thing is—I found out that you never left! What the hell, Devin? I got people calling me all day telling me that you were at a party last night with some fat girl and now you got the nerve to stare back at me like you don't know who the hell I am! Why haven't you called me or answered any of my calls? I can't believe you! I have half a mind to break up with you."

Great...it was exactly what I needed. Now she wanted to go all psycho girlfriend on me. What is it with women and marking their territory? Renee was perfectly fine being a fuck buddy until she thought that someone else was moving in. She was acting exactly like I thought she would and I was about three seconds from telling her to go straight to Hell, but Jenny spoke before I could.

I saw that angry spark hit Jenny's eyes and I knew it was going to be bad the minute I saw her hand come up and the outraged look on her face.

"OK, first of all, don't you ever yell at my brother like that because I will climb your tall lanky ass like a tree! Second of all, nobody even likes you, so the best thing that could…"

I cut her off by grabbing her arm.

"Jenny, let me deal with this," I said as I turned back to Renee. I almost laughed at the shocked look on her face.

"Are you gonna let her talk to me like that?" Renee asked in anger.

"Renee, whatever we had going on is over. The only reason I let it go on as long as I did was because you were a quick and easy lay," I said calmly. I turned toward Jenny. "Come on, let's go pay for this and get out of here."

"Wait a minute! You're not serious!" Renee called out. "*You* are breaking it off with *me*?" She stabbed herself in the chest with her too long fingernail. "Oh. My. God. This is epic! *You*, a dirty old garage boy and *me*, the hottie with a body! This is so funny I can't even…"

Her next words never made it out of her mouth and for once I didn't punish Jenny for acting like a boy. Renee never knew what hit her. I taught Jenny how to throw a punch and I'll be damned if she didn't throw one that landed right in the center of Renee's face.

She covered her bloody nose with freshly manicured fingers. Bright red blood covered the white tips of her long nails.

"You broke my nose you little dike!" Her cries were muffled.

I had to pull Jenny back as she went in for another hit. She wasn't having it, so I lifted her and carried her out. She fought and cursed the entire time.

We slipped out as store employees came to help Renee. After an hour of shopping, we left our buggy full of groceries in the aisle.

Later that night, I got a shower and then relaxed in my bed. My life was going straight down the shitter. We were about to lose everything, I had just broken it off with my semi-girlfriend/side piece, and now the one female that I actually enjoyed being around didn't want anything to do with me. The shitter.

There was a light tap at my door that broke into my deep thoughts.

"Yeah," I called out.

Jenny walked in and handed me a Twizzler.

"You OK?" she asked as she snapped off the end of her Twizzler with her teeth and started to chew.

"Yeah, I'll live."

"So...this new girl that you won't let me meet, is it because she's overweight?"

"What?" I started to panic.

Alarms went off. How the hell does Jenny know anything about Lilly's size? Does Jenny know what I've been up to?

"Renee said you were at a party with a fat girl and I just kind of figured that maybe that's why you won't let me meet her.

Devin, you know me and dad don't care about stuff like that. I think it's great."

I felt a sudden burst of relief. The last thing I wanted was for my sister and my dad to know what a complete and total ass I *really* was.

"Yeah, she's a little on the plus side, but that's not why I haven't let you meet her. We just aren't in that zone, yet. Technically we aren't in any zone anymore because she won't talk to me."

"Send her something nice. I'm not the most girly-girl in the world, but I know I'd like for a guy to send me something nice, especially if he did something to piss me off. When Josh does something, he sends me candy." She held up her Twizzler. "He accidently broke my Gameboy today at school," she shrugged.

"Josh cares about you, Jen." I shook my head and laughed at her enlarged eyes. "I'll think about sending her something nice. Go get in bed, you got school tomorrow. I'll see you in the morning, OK?"

I watched as my little sister, who now seemed so grown up, walked out of my bedroom. I jumped up and immediately went to my dresser and snatched up the little jewelry box that I got from Franklins Jewelry store the day I met Lilly.

I popped it open and stared down at the little locket. It really was perfect for her. I smiled to myself.

A week later, there was still no communication between Lilly and me. Of course, I'd given up on calling her. I knew the best thing for me to do was to just forget about her. That whole date someone for money thing was a bad idea to start with, not to mention it kind of backfired in my face considering that I was starting to really like Lilly.

I got an expected visit from Lilly's mom. I wasn't living up to my end of the bargain, and at this point, I didn't care anymore. I was already starting to think of new options. Maybe after we lost the house we could rent a place for a while or maybe move to Georgia and stay with some family until dad and I got back on our feet. I had already started looking for a better paying job while still helping to maintain the garage, just in case a miracle occurred.

"A deal's a deal, Devin. My daughter's miserable. What did you do and how are you going to fix it?" She picked at a piece of lint on her perfect coat.

"I didn't do anything. She hates me. She should hate me after what I was attempting to do. The deal's off, and I don't care if we lose everything. I can't do it."

She took a deep frustrated breath and pinched the bridge of her nose like I was causing her a headache.

"Look, her birthday's this weekend. There's going to be a big party at my house—I can't believe I'm about to do this, but please come to the party."

"I *can't* do this, it's wrong and she's really a nice girl, I just don't..."

"Twenty thousand," she said. She was now rubbing her temple.

"What?" I almost choked on my own spit.

"I will personally hand you a check for twenty thousand dollars if you do this, that doesn't include the money I've already given you."

"You're fucking nuts, lady!" I ran my hands roughly through my hair in frustration. "Let me think on it."

Wrong. Wrong. Wrong. Why? Why? Why?

She pulled out a card and handed it to me. I looked down and it had her name and address on it.

"Call me when you figure out whether you want to be a man and take care of your family or not."

Then she was gone.

I made that decision later that night. After a hard day of work in the garage, I ran into the house and saw my dad sitting at the kitchen table. I could tell by the slump of his body that he was drunk as a skunk, but the tears on his cheeks are what really did me in.

"What kind of man am I, Devin?" he slurred. "I can't even take care of my own damn family. We're gonna lose it, all of it, and it's my own fault. I'm not a man, I'm a drunk. She made me this way, your momma. She made me this way. I was a good man, Devin, I was, and she made me this way." He pressed his forehead against the table and cried until he passed out.

Jenny helped me drag his limp body to the couch.

It's been years since I've seen my father cry, not since right after mom walked out on us. In that moment the wall around my heart hardened immediately. Seeing him that way gave me a fresh new outlook and reminded me what women were capable of. I couldn't allow Lilly's innocent attack on my senses to take over. She was a woman...they hurt you and they leave you. They were only good for one thing and I would *not* be doing that one thing with Lilly. I'm not some wet-behind-the-ears pussy boy. I'm Devin Michaels, the playboy of the south, and it's about damn time I started acting that way. I don't know why I ever doubted myself to begin with. I knew what needed to be done and it was time I manned up and did it before my family lost everything.

I barely made it into my bedroom before I pulled the card out of my pocket and grabbed my cell phone. I dialed the number and waited. It rang twice before she picked up.

"I'll do it," I said before rudely hanging up.

Thirteen

Birthday Wishes

I stuffed another spoon full of cookies and cream into my fat trap. Ice cream makes me happy, I wasn't happy, hence the ice cream. Is it even possible to really be that into someone after such a short period of time? He's all I can think about. Does that make me crazy? Like, should I reach someone at the local mental health institution? I felt like I was losing my mind.

I haven't been this depressed since I was a miserable teenage punching bag. I guess realizing that I wanted something that Devin didn't want brought back too many old memories— memories and emotions I thought I buried so many years ago.

"Put down the ice cream, Lilly. A customer's coming in and he's *sexy* with a capital S," Shannon said as she tried to get a better peek at the new customer.

The bell above the door rang out. I sat down my life force of cookies and cream, wiped my mouth and headed to the front of the store. I stopped dead in my tracks when I was met with a pair of dazzling blue eyes.

"Hey there, sweet cheeks, fancy meetin' you here." Matt smiled his slanted smile.

I can only imagine what my face looked like in that moment. I adjusted my shirt and stepped up to the counter.

"Hey, Matt. It's good to see you again. What can I do for you?"

"Ah, how sweet...you remembered my name. I didn't think you would've remembered anything with as much as you had to drink that night," he joked.

Shannon cleared her throat.

"I see you have this taken care of, I'll just be in the back if you need me," she said as she left to go to the back of the store.

"You're looking good today, Lilly. Did you do something different with your hair?" He tilted his head and worked that mind-shattering smile.

He's good, but Devin's better.

I could feel my face starting to burn as I cleared my throat nervously.

"Um—is there something you were looking for?" I tried to change the subject back to his purpose at the jewelry store.

"Nope, I came here looking for you."

The butterflies in my stomach were having one hell of a party and for a minute I couldn't think of a response. He knew

135

what he was doing to me, I could tell by his satisfied expression. He ran his eyes down my body and then back up before smiling. He sucked in his bottom lip and then ran his tongue across his top lip.

It was shameless and kind of tacky. It was different from Devin's smooth seductive manor. Matt was trying too hard...Devin didn't have to try.

"Well, here I am, now what can I do for you," I repeated.

"You can go out with me this Saturday night," he cocked his perfectly shaped eyebrow at me.

"Excuse me?"

No way was this happening. Just weeks ago I was approached by Devin, who is probably the sexiest man I've ever seen, and now today the second sexiest man I've ever seen is standing in front of me asking me to go out with him. I must have heard him wrong.

"I want to take you out, unless of course you and Devin are still..."

"No! Devin and I aren't anything," I said too quickly.

Great now it was probably obvious that I was totally falling for Devin. What can I say? I'm a master at being calm, cool, and collected. Not!

"I actually have something I have to do this Saturday night. I'm sorry, maybe some other time." I mustered as nicely as possible.

Sure he looked tastier than that pint of cookies and cream that was probably melting in the back of the store. Sure, the way he eyed me made me want to throw myself at him and beg him for things that I have absolutely no clue about, but my achy girl parts were thanks to Devin, not Matt, and there was no way in the good name of Ben and Jerry's that I was going to take that road again.

I don't know why, but for some crazy, unknown reason hot men were throwing themselves in front of me. Thanks, but no thanks. I'd rather spare myself the drama. I may not know what the hell Devin wanted, but I know exactly what Matt the muscular man-whore wants and I think I'll pass on my turn to take a spin on that tilt-a-whirl.

At least that was my plan. Apparently, Shannon had other plans.

"Lil, why don't you invite your new friend to your birthday party Saturday night?" She wasn't really paying any attention to us as she started to stock things behind the counter.

For that reason she missed it when I gave her our secret shut up look. You know the bug-eyed tight mouth look that everyone gives to their not so smart, speak before they think, friends.

"I *love* birthday parties," Matt said.

How is it possible to make a single sentence, like that one, sound like a sexual invitation? Where does one learn a skill like that?

"You—you do?" I stuttered.

"Oh yes. So, are you gonna invite me? I'll make sure to give you something *really* good for your birthday," he whispered.

137

Needless to say, I now had a date to my birthday party Saturday night. Thank you very much loud-mouthed Shannon!

Even though I prayed that the time would go slowly, Saturday rapidly approached and I was getting dressed for the big, unnecessary birthday party. Honestly, I'd rather hang out with the girls watching movies all night. I have no desire to spend the night of my birthday in a room full of people who only consider me a friend because they *think* that my mother's rich.

The doorbell rang and then I heard muffled voices.

"Lilly! Matt's here!" She called through our small apartment.

I finished getting dressed and then threw on my shoes. I checked the mirror one more time. I grabbed my bag and made my way into the living room. Matt's eyes lit up when he saw me and for a minute I let myself enjoy the compliment his eyes gave me.

"Wow, you look hot," he blurted out.

I smiled and blushed.

We walked to his car. He opened the car door for me and closed it once I was seated. The inside of his car smelled like a brand new car. Hell, his car *was* brand new. I'm not sure what kind of car it was, but who cared? I found myself missing the old rusted Camaro and the smell of motor oil. Devin.

When we pulled up to my mom's house I had a sudden burst of nerves. Not that I mind being the center of attention in a room full of friends, but even though my friends would be there, it was still mostly a room full of my mom's ritzy acquaintances. Joy!

Matt grabbed my hand on the walk up the marble front steps to the front door. I wanted to pull my hand away from him, but I figured that would be rude. His hands were hard and cold. Devin's are firm, but warm, another difference between the two. I already know before I make it to the door that I'm going to be comparing all night. I don't know what it is, but something about Matt just doesn't seem right.

Soon, it was an hour into the party. I'd survived this long without any long term damage, plus, I'd already had a few glasses of champagne down my throat so I was a little more relaxed. I even let Matt pull me into the middle of the enormous room, which was decorated in pink and black. There was some slow song playing and I let myself relax against Matt as he led me around.

I felt him pull me a little closer and for a minute I contemplated walking away. Instead, I relaxed my head against his shoulder. Bad idea!

"You smell good," he whispered into my ear.

"Thank you," I said.

"Vanilla and cherries, that's what you smell like," he said as he ran his mouth against my ear.

I watched my arm as the goose bumps formed. I couldn't help it. I hated my reaction to him, but Devin had my body primed for sex and it's all I could think about anymore.

Please, let this night be over with soon.

I closed my eyes for a minute and imagined it was Devin I was dancing with. I'm well aware of the fact that Matt is hot, but he's not warm. I don't mean physically warm, but warm inside. It doesn't make any sense. I kept my eyes closed for just another few seconds and enjoyed the thoughts of Devin.

Finally, I brought my head back up and looked around the room. The green eyes that stared back at me caught me off guard. The man of my imaginings was standing across the room from me and everything about Devin was right. The relaxed fit jeans he was wearing, the black buttoned up shirt he was wearing, and the smile that he should've been wearing would've been perfect as well. The only problem was he wasn't smiling at all. The problem was he looked completely pissed off.

Fourteen

The Party Crasher

I showed up late to the party. I figured better late than never. Also, it took me at least two hours to persuade myself to go through with it. With a hardened heart and a mission, I walked into the secret lair of the she-devil. There were so many people there that I had to slip and slide through the crowd just to make it to the main room.

I looked around at the richly dressed people and then down at my jeans. Oh well. I grabbed a glass of something from a man that was walking by with a tray and then slowly made my way through the room. It didn't take long for me to spot Lilly from across the room. She looked so pretty and I had a sudden urge to be near her. My hardened heart slowly softened at the sight of her. *Lilly...my Lilly.*

I smiled at the warm feeling that spread through me.

She was dancing with some guy and I didn't want to approach her until she was alone. Suddenly, I realized just who that guy was and my smile quickly disappeared. I watched as Matt let his hands rest against her hips. He was leaning down and whispering something to her. I have no clue what he was saying, but Lilly seemed to be enjoying it.

She must have felt my gaze on her because she looked up and straight into my eyes. I wanted to go over and rip her out of his arms. I wanted to take him by the neck and choke the life out him, but more than anything I wanted to be the one she was dancing with. Seeing her there with his hands all over her literally knocked the breath out of me.

I impatiently waited until they were finished dancing and then made my way over to where they were standing. Matt turned around and smiled at me before I grabbed his arm and pulled him closer to me.

"What the hell, Matt?" I hissed.

"Dev! What's up, bro? I didn't know you were gonna be here. It's a nice party, huh?" he smirked, letting me know he was doing it on purpose.

I looked over at Lilly in question. She stared back and our eyes caught before she put her head down. I turned my attention back to Matt. I could feel my pulse in my temples and the heat on my face.

"Can I talk to you for a minute?" I asked as I tugged on Matt's arm again.

He pulled his arm back and gave me a strange look. He turned back to Lilly and grabbed her hand. I watched as he lifted her hand to his lips and kissed her fingers. I wanted to rip his face off. The flirty smile he threw at her made my stomach turn. I knew exactly what he was up to and there was no way in hell I'd let that happen.

"I'll be right back, sweetheart," he whispered to Lilly.

A pretty little blush covered her face and my anger spiked. I practically dragged him to the other side of the room and out of Lilly's hearing range.

"You better start talking," I growled.

He pulled his arm out of my iron grasp.

"What the hell's your problem, Devin?"

"Why are you here with Lilly? Better yet—why are you even here at all?"

"I was invited. I'm her date."

"The hell you are! You stay away from her. I'm serious, Matt. You stay the hell away from her!" I yelled a little too loudly.

A few of the guests turned and looked our way. Thankfully the shitty music they were playing helped to drown out some of what we were saying. Matt leaned in so that no one could hear.

"Look, man, you blew it. Get over it. Just stand back and watch the master work."

Even though I wanted to knock him the hell out, I knew I couldn't, not there, not at Lilly's birthday party in front of her friends and family. I wasn't going to give those snooty bastards a reason to look down on me any more than they already did.

"You need to go. You need to leave now," I said as calmly as I could manage.

"Oh come on, Devin. Don't act like you weren't trying to get in her pants. I know you, dude. We're cut from the same mold. Of all people, don't even *try* to play *me*. I know the way the game is played," he chuckled.

I was on my last thread. It took all the self-control I had to keep from busting him in the face with my fist. I took a deep breath and then turned my attention to where Lilly was standing.

She stared back at me with innocent brown eyes and I knew that no matter what I did, I'd make sure to keep Matt away from her. I also knew that no matter what, I wouldn't fight at her birthday party. I wouldn't ruin her night or embarrass her. The next words he uttered crushed those plans.

"You know... fat girls have low self-esteem," he slyly whispered. "Lilly's a pretty girl, if I play my cards right, I could be in that tonight," he leaned away and laughed at his joke.

Fuck it!

I don't remember what happened next, I think I blacked out from all the anger that crashed into me. All I know is when I finally came to I was standing over a bleeding Matt and there were four strange men pulling me away from him. I tried desperately to break away from their hold so that I could kill him. Another man came over and helped to keep me back.

I could hear them telling me to calm down. Some woman was telling me to leave. There were hushed whispers all throughout the room. All I could think about was killing Matt with my bare hands.

"I'll kill you!" I heard myself growl.

Females appeared from all around with towels to help control the blood that was pouring from Matt's nose.

"You broke my damn nose!" I heard him sputter.

I tried again to break through the men holding me. My anger just wouldn't go away. I'm usually calm and laid-back, but for some reason, Matt's words just made me snap.

"I'll break more than your nose when I get close to you again, you son of a bitch!"

Suddenly, Lilly appeared in front of me with disappointment in her eyes and I instantly stopped. Her friend Shannon was next to her staring at me like I was some kind of monster.

"Devin, what's wrong with you?" Lilly whispered in a rush. "Please, stop."

The begging look in her eyes brought reality back to me. She was embarrassed. Her face was red and she was cautiously looking around the room at the people who were staring at the scene playing out in front of them.

"Please leave—please, just leave," she asked softly.

She looked up at me and the softness in her eyes calmed me even more. In a daze, I nodded and I felt the arms holding me back loosen. Before I left, I leaned over her so that only she could hear me.

"Get away when you can and meet me outside, I'll wait all night if I have to. I miss you so much," I ran my fingers down her cheek.

I'm not sure why I did it. I needed something to hold me in place, and her face seemed to be the only thing I could focus on without flipping out again. The softness of her cheek against my rough fingers kept me in check.

I gave her a pleading look and then turned and walked away.

I didn't realize until I was outside leaning up against my car that I actually meant what I'd said to her. I did miss her. Seeing her all hugged up with Matt let me know it. It also let me know how much I cared about her. I didn't want her to get hurt by me or any other asshole around here.

Seeing Matt with his filthy hands on her made me sick, and hearing him talk about doing things with her made me irate, madder than I've been in a very long time. That kind of anger hadn't washed through me since that day in the bank when the bastard of a bank manager down talked my family.

No one talks badly or hurts the people I care about. When they do, I see red, and that's it. Maybe I'm more fucked up than I thought.

After sitting outside for about thirty minutes, I watched from afar as Matt left the house, got into his car, and then left. It took everything I had not to go over and beat the hell out of him again.

It felt like forever, but soon I heard the front door open again and I watched as Lilly stepped outside and looked around. She spotted me and then walked toward me with an angry stride.

She looked so nice all dressed up with her hair curled. Once she was close enough I could smell vanilla and cherries, and I smiled to myself.

"You think this is funny?" she asked, outraged.

She used a finger to jab me in my chest and it turned me on. I liked that she wasn't afraid of me. She poked me again and I grabbed her small hand in mine.

"Well, do you?" Her angry eyes flashed.

"No."

"Then why are you smiling? I could smack that smile right off of your face, you know that?" she huffed, and then blew her bangs out of her reddened face.

The thought of her being angry enough to smack me was making me hard for some reason. She was a lioness, a tiny lioness, but a fierce one still.

"You smell good."

I watched as her blazing eyes softened.

"Don't change the subject," she said as she broke our eye contact.

"What were you doing with Matt? You know what he's about, Lil. He's after one thing and one thing only."

147

"I don't know," she sighed as she ran her fingers through her hair. "It just kind of happened. I didn't invite him, Shannon did. Why do you even care, Devin?"

Good question. I ran it through my head over and over again. There was only one answer and that was the truth. The moisture in my mouth disappeared. I tried to swallow and almost choked on nothing.

"I care about you, Lilly." Those tiny words seemed to take all of my oxygen as I spoke them. I suddenly felt like I couldn't breathe, like saying things that involved feelings would be the death of me. "I don't want to see you get hurt and if you keep playing around with men like Matt, you will."

Her shoulders relaxed a bit. "You mean men like you?"

"Yes, definitely stay away from men like me," I chuckled softly.

If only she knew how serious that sentence was. Stay away from me. I wanted to scream at her all the things that were blatantly obvious to me. I was bad for her. I was going to hurt her in the near future and I knew that coming into this gig, but I had no choice. There was nothing else I could do.

She smiled at me and it was such a sweet, heart-shattering smile. For a second, I couldn't do anything but smile back at her.

"I missed you, too," she whispered. "And I'm sorry about that night at the party. I think I may have had too much to drink. I mean—I understand if you don't see me that way and I'm sorry for throwing myself at you like that. It's so embarrassing." Her face was blazing with humiliation. I watched as she awkwardly tried to think of something else to say. "So... friends?"

She held her hand out for me to shake on it.

I almost laughed out loud. She was so far from the truth that it wasn't even funny. First of all, the fact that *she* was apologizing when I should be the one apologizing completely threw me for a loop. Secondly, she obviously had no clue how I really saw her. I thought she was sexy in her own little, sweet way and as a person she was amazing. Yeah, she's a little chunky, and yeah, a month ago that really wasn't my thing, but now she's beautiful to me, inside and out.

I grabbed her hand and slowly pulled her to me.

"I'm the one that should be sorry," I said as I wrapped my arms around her.

"Why should you be sorry?" she whispered in that innocent, tempting kind of way that I can't explain.

I could feel her nervously shaking against me and it pushed me harder. Although I knew that I shouldn't, I had to. I couldn't take it anymore! She was too close and she smelt so good. She felt good in my arms and I missed her like crazy, like really, really missed her.

"I'm just sorry. Do me a favor and say you forgive me."

I knew what I was asking her for. I was asking her to forgive me for what was to come. I just needed to hear her say it.

"I forgive you," she smiled up at me.

I leaned down and kissed her without a care for anything. There was no shop and home loan that needed to be paid. There was no devious, rich-bitch mom on my back. There was just me and my sweet Lilly, and right then, in that moment, it was all I needed.

When I broke the kiss I looked down at her. Her eyes remained closed.

"Happy birthday, baby, I'm sorry I kind of ruined your party," I said as I placed soft kisses on her cheeks and nose.

It was a new low for playboy Devin and I liked it.

"You didn't ruin it, you made it perfect," I felt her arms get tighter around my neck.

I kissed her again and for just that moment, decided to forget about everything but her.

Fifteen

Meet the Michaels

"Are you gonna be like this all week or are you gonna snap out of it soon?" Shannon asked with a smile.

I continued to stare out of the store window and daydream of Devin. It had been two weeks since my birthday party and things couldn't be more perfect. We spent hours on the phone every day and when we weren't on the phone or at work, we were together.

Some nights he would come to my apartment and we'd watch movies all cuddled up on the couch. Sometimes we'd go to dinner, some nights we'd stay in and make a mess in my kitchen cooking things we had no clue how to cook. I'd never smiled so much in my life. I'd never laughed so much in my life. I've never been this happy... ever.

On game night I included him and he fit right in. My friends adored him. Randy drooled over him and later told me that he thought Devin was a hot piece of ass.

After everyone left and Shannon suspiciously got too tired to stay awake another minute, Devin and I cleaned the messy apartment. He looked so cute loading the dishwasher with a little dish cloth slung over his shoulder.

"What a good little maid you are," I joked.

He smirked at me with his all-too sexy self. All the crazy "I want to jump his bones" feelings came crashing over me. Over the last couple of weeks there were lots of smiles and jokes. There was tons of tickling and cuddling and even though we both pretended it wasn't there, there was so much tension. No matter what, I didn't want to seem like I was throwing myself at him in any way and even though he never said it, I could tell that he was trying especially hard to keep his distance.

It didn't make any sense to me. We were both adults and I can look at him and tell he was experienced. I never asked how many women he'd been with, but it was obvious from his mannerisms that the man knew his way around a woman's body, no map needed. He had his own inner sense of direction and I'd love nothing more than to let him find his way through my valley.

When all was cleaned I walked him to the front door.

"Text me when you get home and let me know you made it safely," I said.

"OK," he yawned.

"If you're too tired, you can crash here. I can get you a blanket and you can sleep on the couch if you want."

"Nah, I need to get home. I've got a busy day tomorrow at the shop and I wanna get an early start. Goodnight. Sweet dreams, baby," he whispered as he gave me the traditional kiss on the cheek.

His lips warmed the side of my face and I felt his breath against my ear. The man was making me crazy. Without thinking, I reached up and rested my hand against his cheek. I ran my thumb across his lips—his light mustache tickled the tip of my thumb. His eyes connected with mine and all time stopped.

All too soon I snatched my hand away.

"Goodnight," I said.

When he left I closed my door, made sure everything was off, and then got ready for bed. Thirty minutes later, I was snuggled up in my bed when I got a text. I picked up the phone and read it.

I'm home, but I wish I was with you.

I did indeed have sweet dreams that night.

It was exactly a week later that Devin took me to his house for the first time. We were out and about when he realized that he'd forgotten his wallet. He didn't seem too happy about having to go all the way back to his house, but we made the thirty minute trip from Charleston to Walterboro anyway.

It was a cute little country house. The huge, screened-in front porch took over much of the front yard. There was a short driveway that met what looked to be a converted garage and overgrown gardens with broken garden statues. Sure it could use some maintenance, but it felt comfy. It felt like a home should feel. It was everything I imagined it would be.

Behind the house, led by a long gravel road that ran beside the house, was a massive garage. There were a few broken down cars waiting to go in and old tires lying around. I could smell the motor oil and rubber from the front yard and it instantly reminded me of Devin. It was weird to see where he worked and lived, but it somehow made me feel closer to him. I liked it.

There wasn't anyone home, so I didn't feel so nervous when he asked me if I wanted to come in for a minute. His house was welcoming and warm. I followed him to his bedroom and stood in the doorway while he searched his room for his wallet.

I couldn't help but smile. The room was so...Devin. There was a big bed in the middle of the room with green bedding. There were car pictures on the wall and a pin up calendar that I couldn't help but notice. I wanted to hate the skinny sex kitten that stared back at me from the calendar, but she was just too damn pretty to hate.

Devin noticed what I was staring at and for a second I thought I saw him blush.

"Ah, here it is!" he said as he held up his wallet.

He spun around to face me and no matter how hard I tried I couldn't wipe the goofy smile off my face.

"What's so funny?" he asked.

"Nothing, it's just this room is so...you. It's exactly how I pictured it in my mind."

"You've pictured my bedroom in your mind?" he asked with a smirk.

He tilted his brow, questioning me in his all-too sexy way that drives me crazy.

I felt my face heat up. Devin walked closer and stood in front of me.

"Have you?" he asked again and his voice was lower, darker.

He reached up and tucked my hair behind my ear and then let his fingertip run down the side of my neck.

"I—I—don't," I stuttered.

I could think of nothing else to say. Once again I was knocked speechless. Real nice! I might as well tell him that I've imagined him naked in his bed at night.

He cupped the back of my neck and moved a little closer.

"You have, haven't you?" He moved closer like a predator on the prowl. I had never felt so small, as his large frame overwhelmed me.

"Tell me," he whispered against the side of my mouth. His lips tickled before I felt his hot tongue run along the seam of my lips.

"Yes," I blurted out.

My eyes fluttered shut and I knew I was a goner. Man he was good at this stuff. I was way out of my league with this sex crap.

"When you imagine my bedroom, am I in my bed?" I felt his other hand work its way up my side.

"Sometimes," I squeaked.

"Well, sometimes, when you picture me in my bed, am I alone or are you with me?"

"I'm with you." My voice sounded foreign.

I softly nibbled my bottom lip.

"Am I naked?"

Again he teased my mouth with his tongue and I released my bottom lip from my teeth. Softly, he sucked the spot on my bottom lip where my teeth had been digging in seconds before.

I never gave my answer. Instead, I gave in and pulled him closer to me. I pressed my lips against his and kissed him. He responded immediately. He pulled me farther into his room and shut the bedroom door behind us. I felt my back against the door when he slowly walked me backward.

His tongue slipped into my mouth, causing me to purr out loud. I met his tongue with mine and he shocked me as he sucked the tip of my tongue and pressed his body harder against mine.

I was coming undone. Every part of my body was tingling and I needed something, anything, to happen at that point.

Out of nowhere, there was a loud rumbling noise coming from outside that scared me. I pulled away.

"What's that?" I asked.

He inhaled then exhaled deeply while leaning his forehead against mine.

"That would be my dad out in the garage. The loud rumbling noise would be an old truck that we've been working on for the last week. My guess is... it's fixed."

I didn't meet his dad that night. Instead, we left quickly and spent the rest of the night out.

After that night, I was taken to his house more often. Every time we went there no one was ever home. He gave me a tour of the garage out back and showed me a few of the cars he was working on.

Through all of it, I could never figure out what it was that we were doing. Were we friends that dated or were we a couple that acted like friends? Needless to say, I was completely confused. There were moments when Devin acted like he could barely keep his hands off of me and then there were moments when he treated me like one of his buddies.

It wasn't long until I was wondering exactly what he would label us as and no matter how many times I'd heard from friends that it was a bad idea to ask him, I couldn't help myself. I wanted to be involved with Devin... I wanted it more than anything. The walled-in parts of me wanted to peek around the corner and pull him into my world completely, but I couldn't do it, not until I was sure that he was in the same place emotionally as me.

I decided to leave work early. I thought it would be a good idea to stop by Devin's house and have a talk with him. It needed to be done. I was rapidly falling hard for him and I really needed to know if I should allow these feelings to blossom, or nip them in the bud.

I turned my radio up and kept psyching myself up. This was it, I had to do this. I had to talk to Devin. I needed to know exactly what we were doing. I know all girls want things clearly defined for them and that scares guys to death, but now, for the first time in my life, I understood exactly how much that definition meant. Were we just friends or were we more?

I mean seriously, we *are* adults. I should be able to just ask Devin where he sees this whole thing going, right? Whatever he said wouldn't matter. I just needed to know how much to invest into this whole thing and if by some chance he just wanted to be friends then I'd be the best damn friend he ever had.

I pulled up to the garage instead of his house since I knew he'd be working. He must have heard my car because he walked outside looking all sweaty, greasy, and just plain sexy. Dear Lord, please have mercy on me. I silently prayed for the strength to keep my hands to myself.

I didn't turn my car off. Instead, I stepped out and closed the door behind me. I didn't want to get all comfortable just in case he was too busy to sit and chat for a few.

"Hey, baby. I didn't know you were coming over. I would've cleaned up a bit." He attempted to clean some of the dirt and grease from his clothes.

If only he knew how hot he looked all covered in grease.

"Do you have a minute to talk? If you're busy, it can wait. I know I should've called but I really need to talk to you about something kind of import...."

"Ssshhh," he cut me off.

He had a confused, questioning look on his face as he stared off into space.

"Is something wrong? Devin?" He cut me off again when he held up his finger, telling me to be quiet.

He walked around to the hood of my car.

"Pop your hood, sweetie."

"What? Are you listening to me?"

"Yes—well, not really, but I will. First, pop your hood."

I walked back to the driver's side door of my car, opened the door, then reached down and popped the hood of my car.

"Happy?" I asked sarcastically with a smile.

He lifted my hood and then started digging around.

"What *are* you doing?" I leaned down over the open hood where he was digging.

"You need a tune-up and an oil change. Don't you hear that?" He turned his head to smile at me and a lone streak of grease on his cheek caught my attention. I almost reached out and wiped it away. "Pull your car into the garage and I'll take care of it."

"What? No. Devin, I came here to talk not to get my car fixed. It's fine, I'll take it and have it fixed somewhere later."

"Like hell you will! First of all, I can talk and change the plugs and oil at the same time. Second of all, what kind of man

159

would I be if I didn't take care of my girl's car? I *am* a mechanic, you know." He smiled sweetly at me.

His girl.

He jumped into my car and shut the door. I watched as he pulled it into the garage and started jacking it up. I couldn't say or do anything. I was his girl. What the hell does that mean anyway? Shannon's my girl, but that doesn't mean I want to have sex with her. Don't get me wrong, she's pretty and all, but she's not really my type.

His comment left me even more confused than I was before. Damn him and his confusing everything! That and his sexy everything and damn his seductive everything. Just damn him!

I followed him into the garage. I couldn't very well bring up the whole "what the hell are we?" subject now that he called me his girl. That could mean anything. I could be his female friend that he'd hook up with his fat buddy named, Bubba, or I could be his girlfriend that he'd do naughty things with at night and daydream about all day.

I'd prefer the latter.

I watched as he worked on my car. He had on greasy jeans with an even greasier red rag hanging out of his back pocket. The black tank top shirt he was wearing was so wet with sweat that it was sticking to every cut and corner of his body. I couldn't help but stare. His tanned arms were flexing and stretching and the shiny oil on his skin made his tattoos look

160

extra sharp. One day I'd get a better look at those tattoos. One day I'll outline those babies with my tongue.

He was so fine and I was getting so very hot and bothered.

He climbed under the car and grabbed at different tools. It was like watching an artist at work and I could tell that he truly loved what he was doing.

"So, what did you wanna talk about?" he asked from under the car.

"Huh? Oh, um—I don't remember. I'm sure it was nothing important."

He pulled himself from under the car, the little rolling bed thingy made a creaking noise. I watched him stretch his perfectly shaped body as he got comfortable.

"You OK, Lil? You look funny. Are you feeling OK?"

It took me a minute to peel my eyes off of his chest and dirty jeans to look at his face.

"Huh? Oh, I think I'm coming down with something. I feel like I might have a fever."

My face had to be bright red. I couldn't think about anything but him and those thoughts weren't very pure. At night I had dreams of him doing and saying things to me. During the day I had daydreams about him touching me certain ways and making me feel things I've never felt before. I couldn't focus on anything at work. Even Shannon commented on how out of whack I was lately.

161

He jumped up from the rolling bed thingy and walked over to me. He pulled the red rag from his back pocket and wiped the grease from his hands before softly laying the back of his right hand to my forehead. Chills went through my entire body, yet I felt hot all over.

"You don't feel warm, but you do look a little flushed. Stay here, I'm gonna run in the house and get you a soda, OK?"

"OK."

I watched him run across the yard and into the back door, the screened door slamming loudly. I sat down onto a fold out chair next to my car and waited for him to come back. I heard a car pull up and then watched as a young boy in a baseball hat jumped out and headed toward the garage. He was half way to me before he noticed I was sitting here.

"Hey, is anyone here to help you?" he asked as he pulled off his hat and a mess of a brown ponytail was revealed.

I suddenly realized that it was a young girl, not a young boy, and I knew right away that it was Jenny, Devin's little sister.

"Yeah, I'm actually waiting on Devin to come back. He went to get me a soda."

Her eyes lit up.

"Are you Devin's new friend? The one he's always on the phone with?"

"Um—I think so? My name's Lilly. You must be Jenny?"

First of all, Jenny was the cutest little thing I'd seen in forever. Yeah, she was dressed like a boy and yeah, her hair was a

162

hot mess all pulled up in a low ponytail, but other than that, she was gorgeous. She had Devin's pretty green eyes and a tan that girls pay good money for.

Her smile was wide and white and her face was unblemished. She had the flawless skin of a girl who didn't contaminate her face with makeup every day. She was short with a small frame, so absolutely adorable.

I had to smile at the torn up jeans and big black ACDC t-shirt, but I could tell that beneath it all there was a beautiful young girl.

"That's me! It's so nice to meet you. You're so much prettier than Renee!" She blurted out.

"Renee?"

"Yeah, she was a major bitch. He didn't tell you about Renee? Oh well, I don't blame him." She waved it off. "No one likes her. I don't even think he liked her very much. She was just a piece of ass. You know how those things go. "

I didn't, not really, but apparently this teenage girl did. Not to mention the awful sinking feeling that attacked my stomach at just the mention of Devin with this girl Renee. Was Renee his girl, too?

I was about to ask more about this Renee person when I heard the screened door slam again and I knew he was coming back.

He walked up to me with a huge smile on his face and a coke in his hand. Looking at them, I could say that if there weren't an age gap between the two, they could pass as twins, other than the fact that he's tall, dark and handsome and she's petite, tan, and gorgeous.

I watched his smile disappear when he saw his little sister was standing next to me.

"Jenny. You're home early," he suddenly looked nervous as he handed me my coke.

"Yeah, today was an early out day. Remember? I told you that last night. I told you that I'd help you out at the shop today. What's up with this Honda? Is this your car, Lilly?" She turned her attention back to me before walking over to the car and looking under the hood.

"Yep, that's my baby. I haven't named her like your brother named his, but I will at some point. I was thinking something along the lines of Barbara or Bertha."

Jenny laughed with me. Devin still didn't say anything; he just kind of walked back over to the car and started working on it again.

The next thirty minutes were awkward. Jenny and I sat and talked the whole time. We laughed and giggled about school and a few girlie things. For someone who was such a tomboy, she still had a hint of teenage girl in there somewhere. Throughout all the talking and car work, I couldn't help but notice how quiet Devin was being.

After my oil was changed and the tune up was complete, Jenny invited me to dinner the following Saturday at their house with her, Devin, and their dad. I looked to Devin for a response, but when he didn't look my way I decided to make the decision for myself.

"Sure that sounds fun. Should I bring something?"

"Just yourself," she smiled.

Not long after that Jenny went inside and left me and Devin all alone.

"Is everything OK?" I asked.

"Everything's cool. Well, your car's all better now. You'll need another oil change in about three thousand miles. I'm going to go inside and get a shower, I'm covered in grease. I'll see you at dinner this weekend?"

He wasn't looking me in my face at all. Something was wrong.

"If you don't want me to come, I won't. I wasn't, like, plotting and planning to meet your family or anything. I should've called before I came. I'm sorry for intruding, and I understand if you don't want to do the whole meet the family thing. Call me later."

I tried to sound as if the fact that he may not want me to be around his family didn't bother me. Plus, there was all this stupid Renee talk. How would she feel knowing that there was another chick coming to dinner at his house?

There was no way he knew how heartbroken I felt by the tone of my voice or the expression on my face. I turned and started to get into my car when he grabbed me by my wrist and pulled me to him. The next thing I knew his warm mouth was moving against mine.

I responded immediately and threw my arms around his neck. He began backing me up until I felt my back against my car. He pulled away a bit and nipped at my bottom lip before moving to my neck.

"You always smell so good," he whispered against my neck.

A deep moan was my answer. Words were beyond me at this point. I pulled him closer to me and tilted my head to the side to give him more space to work. His mouth felt so amazing. He felt so amazing. The car was pretty much holding me up. My legs sure as Hell weren't holding me up anymore.

The sound of someone clearing their throat made us jump apart from each other. My legs still felt like rubber, yet somehow I managed to stand.

"Dad, this is Lilly. Lilly, this is my dad," Devin sounded out of breath.

The older man standing across from us smiled back at me like we shared some great secret. He was just as greasy as Devin, except he wore an old, light blue workman's shirt with a name patch sewed on and dirty, old, navy blue pants.

He was an older Devin with a scraggly beard and a twinkle in his eye. He radiated calm and warmth and I instantly felt comfortable around him.

"Nice to meet ya, little lady. So, you're the one taking up all my boy's time."

He pointed to Devin using the fishing pole in his hand. The other hand carried a case of beer. I could feel the burn in my face and all I really wanted to do was jump in my car and haul ass.

"I'm sorry," I whispered.

"Ah, hell honey, don't be sorry. It ain't a bad thing. I'm glad he finally got him a real woman. That one gal, what was her name again? Oh yeah, Renee. She was a snooty little thing. She wasn't nothin' but a little rack of bones. Good to see ya got yourself a lady with some meat on her," he said to Devin. Devin's face turned seven shades of red. "Don't you be a stranger, ya hear? And don't you be calling me Mr. Michaels, either. Around here, it's either Harold the Handsome or Dad." He winked at me as he walked by.

I stood there a minute trying to figure out if that had really just happened or if I was having a horrible nightmare. There is no way that I just met my Devin's dad for the first time, after he busted us making out up against my car.

Well, that was just a great first impression. I'm sure he thinks I'm just another one of Devin's little sluts. Hell, I guess technically I *am* just another one of Devin's little sluts. I'm surely acting like one.

"Oh. My. God. That was so embarrassing," I said.

My voice was shaking.

"Lilly, about Renee—I'm sorry I didn't..." I cut him off.

"Don't worry about it; you don't have to tell me everything about your life, Devin. It's not like we're getting married or anything like that. You're free to do whatever you want. I'm not

167

your warden." I tried to act like the mystery of Renee wasn't bothering me.

"We're not together anymore...I mean, we kind of never were. It doesn't matter... we don't anymore. We don't do *anything* anymore."

I knew what he was trying to tell me and I'm glad he did. Nothing else was said about it even though I wanted to ask a million questions. I kept my mouth shut. I didn't want to seem like a psycho girl, but I suppose now I know who got the really great necklace I picked out at Franklin's Jewelry store the first day I met him.

When I got back to my apartment, Shannon was lounging on the couch. The moment I walked by her she began laughing hysterically.

"What's so funny?" I asked.

"Somebody had a good day." She continued to laugh.

I stared back at her, confused.

"As a matter of fact I did, but how do you know?"

She busted out laughing one more time before pointing at my pants.

"There are big black greasy handprints all over your butt, Lil." She laughed harder.

"OK, so I had a great day." I stuck my tongue out at her as I made my way to bedroom.

That Saturday was the day of the dinner with Devin's family. I got to Devin's house early and we hung out in his room while his dad put the finishing touches on dinner. I picked up a box of pictures that he had sitting on his dresser and started picking through them.

There were pictures of Devin and Jenny when they were just kids that we laughed at. He was such a cute kid. There were family pictures of cousins, aunts, and uncles. There were pictures of Devin at his high school prom and pictures of him and his friends. Suddenly, I came across a picture that made me gasp.

Staring back at me was a picture of Renee Roberts, the ring leader of the twelve girls who had kicked and beat me. She was a viscous girl who cared for nothing or no one but herself. She had ruined my life and laughed about it.

I silently prayed that this wasn't Devin's Renee. I begged God to make it not so. Could he have been sleeping with the girl who single-handedly plotted the high school attack on me? Was it the same bitch who left me in the woods bleeding internally?

I could still hear their laughter. Years of therapy got me through it, but there were still occasional nights when I'd wake up with the sheets stuck to me and a scream for help on my lips. I never wanted to feel that helpless again. Seeing her face brought back those terrible feelings.

I dropped the picture quickly and went to put the lid on the box, but Devin must have seen my response to her picture. He picked it up and looked at me kind of strange.

"Do you know her?" he asked as he held up the photo.

"No, who is it?" I pretended to not know who she was.

"No one," he said as he balled up the photo of Renee and threw it into the trash can next to his dresser.

I instantly felt relief in knowing he no longer had a connection to such a cruel girl and I prayed that I'd never have to see her face again.

Sixteen

Puzzle Pieces

After hanging out in my room with Lilly for a while, it was time for dinner and we were all sitting around the little table in the middle of the kitchen.

"I don't need a math tutor! Come on, dad, that's crazy! I already spend way too much time in school and now you want me to get a math tutor? This is bullsh...," she stopped immediately.

Dad glared at her.

"You keep it up with that filthy mouth and I'll hire a lady to teach you how to act," Dad said as he winked at Lilly.

Of course my family would spend this time arguing in front of a dinner guest. I love them, but couldn't this wait until we were alone?

I looked over at Lilly and watched as she played with her spaghetti with her head down. She looked really beautiful, but I could tell there was something bothering her. I'd have to remember to ask her what was wrong later when we were alone.

Not that it mattered, but with the clothes she was wearing I could tell that she was slimming down a bit and I silently hoped she wouldn't get too slim. Those thoughts made me smile to myself.

I'd come a long way from the tall and skinny girls that used to appeal to me. Lilly wasn't skinny and she wasn't tall, but she was slowly becoming everything I could ever want.

She pushed her hair behind her ear revealing her neck and for a minute all I could think about was putting my mouth there. I don't know how it happened or when it happened, but every minute I spend around Lilly was pure Hell for me. There were moments when we were around each other that all I could think about was holding her close to me. I pictured her smile just after I'd kissed her good and hard. I imagined the softness of her skin.

Sometimes, I imagined doing things to her with my mouth and hands, things that would make her say my name over and over again, things that she was probably clueless about.

I won't get to be the one who introduces those things to her. Some other man who deserved her would have that luxury, but I'd always have tiny moments like this one. Moments where I watched as she played with her food without knowing my eyes were on her. I'd always have the memory of her smile and the sound of her laughter. It would have to be enough.

Hopefully, once all of this shit was done and over with, I could move easily back into my old role and be myself again.

Hopefully, I'd be able to forget about Lilly, with the exception of a few tucked away memories that only I knew existed.

She must have felt my stare because she looked up. She didn't say a word, but I could see it in her eyes. She was thinking about me, too. Maybe not those exact things, but something that made her blush since her sweet face was the same color as the spaghetti sauce on her plate.

She wanted me—I could see it every time she looked at me. You don't know Hell, until you're near an untouchable woman that makes your blood boil; a woman you knew would do anything you desired, if you were allowed to touch her. Hell.

I felt myself hardening and panicked. Before realizing what I was doing I jumped up from the table. The chair skidded around the kitchen floor and the table shook. Dad and Jenny stared at me like I'd lost my mind. Lilly quickly looked back down at her plate of food.

"I'll be right back," I blurted out.

When I made it to the bathroom in the hallway, I stared into the mirror and counted from one hundred backward. It was always something different every time I got around Lilly. Today, it was counting backward. Yesterday, I recited the pledge of allegiance three times. There's no telling what I'll do tomorrow to take my mind off of sex with her.

Ten minutes later, I was ready to join dinner again. The rest of the night flowed smoothly. We talked and laughed throughout dinner and then we ate the strawberry cheesecake that Lilly made for dessert. It was delicious, of course. My dad was his usual humorous self and Jenny went on and on about school and her friends.

During the conversation, Lilly even somehow talked Jenny into going to some school dance and had somehow managed to convince her to wear a skirt. Dad and I both laughed out loud at that one. Jenny blushed and Lilly gave us both the bug-eyed, "stop that" look. She patted Jenny's hand and whispered something about men and how ignorant we were. We all continued to laugh. This house hadn't seen this much joy in a very long time.

Through it all, I could tell one very important thing, Lilly fit. My family adored her and she loved them. I could tell by the way she smiled at my dad or laughed with Jenny. She fit perfectly in my world. She was like a missing puzzle piece for us and that was probably the scariest realization ever.

After dinner we all sat in the living room and watched a movie. Dad passed out in his chair twenty minutes in and Jenny, who was lying on her stomach on the floor in front of the TV, didn't even know we existed. I had no clue what the movie was about, all I could do was think about how nice it felt to snuggle on my couch with Lilly. It felt so right.

These were things I shouldn't be thinking. These were the thoughts that were not allowed to run through my brain at any point and time, but I couldn't stop them. I was falling for her and I wasn't sure if that was a good thing or really bad thing.

When it was time to leave, I walked Lilly to her car. I wanted to ask her to stay with me. I wanted her in my bed for the rest of the night whether we were snuggled up sleeping or enjoying each other, either way sounded great to me. I never said a word about her staying, though. As far as I was concerned, that was just another illegal thought.

"I adore your family," she said as she dug through her purse for her keys.

"They love you." I couldn't take my eyes off her.

She giggled and then pulled her keys out.

Please stay with me. Please stay.

"I'll call you tomorrow." My voice sounded raw, like I'd spent the night eating gravel.

"OK. Goodnight." She leaned up and kissed my cheek.

The warmth of her mouth made the entire right side of my face tingle.

"Goodnight, sweetheart."

I stayed on the front porch and watched as she drove away. Her tail lights were completely gone before I finally went in.

"I like her, Dev," Jenny said on the way to her room. "Like, I really like her. I think she's a keeper."

"Yeah, I like her, too. I don't know about the keeper part, though," I grinned.

"Oh shut the hell up! You ain't foolin' nobody. Me and dad saw you eye fucking her at the table."

"Jenny!"

"What? I didn't say balls." She laughed as she shut her bedroom door in my face.

That night I had the most vivid nightmare about Lilly. It started out like any other dream I had with her involved. We were kissing and touching, you know, the usual guy dream, but this time in the middle of the dream she started to disappear. I kept calling out for her to stay, but she just smiled and backed away from me while slowly disappearing. Before she disappeared completely, her face transformed into the face of my mother. Then she was gone.

I woke up in a cold sweat with Lilly's name on my lips. Needless to say, it was a sleepless night.

Seventeen

Breaking Rules

We developed a routine after that. Lilly came to my house for dinner often and brought Dad a different dessert each time. Occasionally, I spent the night at her place and slept on the couch. That only happened on late nights when I was too tired for the long drive home, and *only* when Lilly insisted on it.

I even saw her mom a few times, which was horrible, but I just kept pushing it into my head that it was the most important thing I could ever do for the most important people in my life. The only problem was, Lilly was rapidly becoming one of those important people.

As hard as I tried to keep the relationship light, I couldn't help it. Being with Lilly was like second nature and the sexual tension was starting to kill us both. We stayed that way for weeks until finally I snapped.

We had spent the night watching movies and eating take-out Chinese at her place. It was just like any other normal night and as bad as I wanted to stay cuddled on the couch with her, I knew I had to go.

"OK, baby, I gotta get going," I said as I stood and stretched.

These late nights and early work days were starting to take a toll on me. No matter how much sleep I was getting I always felt tired. It was sleep, but it was a restless sleep.

"Stay," she whined as she stood and wrapped her arms around my waist.

"I can't, babe. I gotta be up bright and early in the morning."

She looked up at me and poked her bottom lip out. She looked so damn cute that I couldn't resist laughing.

"Alright, alright, I'll stay, but only because you gave me the puppy dog face. It has absolutely nothing to do with the fact that I'm completely addicted to you," I pulled her closer to me and she wrapped her arms around my neck.

"You're addicted to me?"

"Oh yeah, I'm in need of serious intervention." I gave her a quick peck as she giggled. "I'll just go get a blanket and pillow. It's not going to freak Shannon out when she comes home and I'm crashed on the couch again?"

I started toward the linen closet in the hallway and grabbed for an extra blanket and pillow. When I turned around Lilly was standing in front of me.

"That won't be an issue because you're not sleeping on the couch tonight."

She pulled the blanket from out of my arms and stuffed it back into the closet. I started to protest when she covered my mouth with her hand.

"Devin, I want to fall asleep in your arms. I haven't had a decent night of sleep in weeks and I'm tired. I know the only way I'll sleep well is if you're lying next to me, so come on."

She slipped her hand into mine. I did nothing to stop her as she pulled me the rest of the way down the hall and then into her bedroom. What could I say? Those were my thoughts exactly, and if she wanted to sleep in my arms as badly as I wanted her to, then I knew I could control the situation. I could be a gentleman just one last time before all of this was over.

I knew deep down that I'd have to be honest with Lilly at some point, preferably after I had the money in my hands, and I also knew she'd never talk to me again.

I held her close to me and rested my cheek against the top of her head. It wasn't long until I felt myself losing my battle with sleep. I was almost gone when I felt her finger against my lips. I popped my eyes open and there she was smiling back at me.

"Sorry, I can't help myself," she smiled. "I love your mouth."

The sleepy feeling went away instantly as she ran her finger across my bottom lip. I wanted to suck it and nibble the tip, but I didn't.

"My mouth loves you," I responded.

I laid there while she traced my lips. Her touch did so many things to me. I looked into her eyes, my favorite thing to do, and wondered to myself how she got into my world. How did she get in my head?

She ran her fingertip across my brow and I closed my eyes as she softly touched my eye-lids. When I opened them to look at her again, she ran her fingers around my eye socket.

"I love your eyes," she whispered.

I swallowed hard. "My eyes love you."

Other words were on the tip of my tongue. I wanted to say so many things, but I felt like my mouth was full of dry sand. I had to quit ignoring what my heart was repeating with every beat. I had to stop denying it. I was slowly falling in love with her.

She was so much fun to be around. I felt happiness just being near her. I was always smiling and it felt great. She made me *feel* again and that was, in itself, wonderful.

"I love your cheeks," she said as her finger moved down my cheek.

Speaking wasn't an option for me. I just watched and allowed her a freedom that I'd never allowed anyone else. She had complete control of me.

"And I *love* this," she said as she ran her finger through my goatee and mustache, circling my mouth.

I softly kissed her finger-tip when it stopped on my lips.

Then a thought hit me. This would all be over soon. I'd have to leave her. What was I thinking? There was no way in Hell I'd ever tell her the truth. It was cruel and unneeded. I'd do the honorable thing and just walk away. I'd end it as soon as I could and I'd walk away and never look back.

I was a horrible person. I did it all for money and it bit me in the ass. I was falling in love with her. Karma was having her way with me, whips and chains style without a safe word, and I could do nothing to stop her.

Lilly deserved a good person. She deserved someone who loved her because she was the most wonderful woman in the world, inside and out, not some broke mechanic who accidentally fell in love with her because he was being paid to date her. I knew what would come in the next couple of weeks, and it was probably a good idea for me to start preparing to mentally back away. It would be easier for both of us if I did that.

"What did I do to deserve you?" she sighed.

Exactly! What had she done to deserve me? She didn't deserve me—a horrible person who worries more about himself than anyone else. Well, that wasn't entirely true—I was doing it for dad and Jenny. More for them than for me, but still, it didn't excuse the fact that I let this poor girl fall for me. Leaving her behind was going to hurt like a bitch. She deserved better, period.

She leaned up and kissed me sweetly. The more and more we did this, the harder it was for me to leave. I'd come over to her house or she'd come to mine, we'd get close to having sex, and I'd either take her home or I'd leave. It wasn't right, but I couldn't help it. The time I had with her was so precious to me and her touch felt so damn good.

After all the women I'd been with, this girl could touch me and bring me to my knees every time. Her skin was so soft, she was so soft. It wasn't like being with Renee or any of the other skanks. Lilly was caring and gentle in everything she did. She touched me like she loved me, and for a boy whose mother walked out on him, a boy who hadn't felt worthy of any form of love, it was huge for me. Having to resist that time and time again was breaking me down.

I kissed her back, pulling soft moans from her. She tugged me closer and I thought I was going to catch on fire when she put her hand up my shirt and began to rub my stomach up and down. Lower and lower, closer and closer to the top of my jeans. I assumed she was a virgin, but she knew what the hell she was doing and it made me wonder.

"You make me so crazy," she murmured in my ear. "Everything about you makes me so..."

She cut off and starting kissing me again. OK, so this time she was sweet talking me, too. It was definitely going to be hard to walk away this time. I just kissed her back, deep down praying to God that I could refrain this time around. I always prayed when we got to this point.

When I didn't think it could get much worse for me, she grabbed my hand and forced it up her shirt and pressed my palm against her hard nipple. I was so totally wrong about it getting worse.

"I want you, Devin," she whispered in my ear.

I sat up quickly and snatched my hand back like a rattle snake was nestled inside her shirt.

Why did she have to say things like that to me? I pulled her shirt down and then mine while lying back beside her.

"I think I should probably just go home, Lil. Dad's got tons of work for me to do tomorrow and I'm gonna to need to be there early," I said quickly, stumbling through all the words. "You gonna walk me to the door?" I tried to act unaffected.

Holy shit I was affected; about to cum in pants affected, which is just crazy because all I did was touch her tit like some fourteen-year-old copping a feel.

"Don't leave me, please," she whispered. "You always leave when we get to this part and I...I just don't think I can..."She stopped.

"What?" I asked.

"I don't think I can stand another night alone in this bed, especially with you on my mind. You always leave me like this and I can't do it anymore, Devin. You're making me crazy, mentally and *especially* physically. I just need to know, is there a reason you keep stopping this? Is it me?" I watched her throat work up and down as she swallowed hard. "I know I'm not a skinny girl and I promise to be understanding. Just tell me the truth, are you not attracted to me sexually? I can take it, you know. I'd prefer the honesty."

183

I couldn't believe what I was hearing. She thought I didn't want her. She thought I wasn't attracted to her. She had no idea of the list of sexual things my body begged me to do to her.

How do you tell the woman who haunts your dreams every night that you can't have sex with her, ever? No matter how much I fantasized about it, no matter how badly I wanted to rip her clothes off and bury myself deep inside of her, I couldn't. I wanted to connect my body with hers in a way that only the deepest parts of my soul could understand. I was in agony, and it fucking sucked.

How do I tell her that the reason I won't have her is because it would be wrong? It was wrong because the whole relationship started out as a lie. Technically, it still was a lie. Even though over the last couple of weeks Lilly had beat down every metaphorical wall I had and was now wrapped tightly around my heart, I was still taking her mother's money. I was still lying to her.

There's no way she'd ever understand how I felt. She'd never do this to another person. Her heart's too good for mine. She's too good for me.

"I guess I just got my answer," she said.

"What do you mean?" I asked.

"I asked you if it was me and you didn't say anything," she sighed loudly. "Go ahead and go, I won't be upset, I promise."

She turned her back to me and curled up on her side like she was about to go to sleep.

"Please make sure and lock the door before you leave."

I was making her unhappy, and I hated it. I kept screwing things up so bad. Maybe that was why my mom left me. Maybe I was too fucked up for her to love me, just like I'm too fucked up for Lilly.

Fucked up or not, I refused to give in. I refused to take her first time away from her like that. It should be special and not with a man who's being paid to be near her.

Leaving her that way was probably the hardest thing I'd ever had to do, but I'd never be able to tell her that. As much as I wanted to be completely honest with Lilly, she could never know how this all started.

It's not that she wouldn't understand, it's more than that. I know that if she ever found out, it would kill her. To find out that her mother plotted behind her back, to find out that I would've never noticed her had it not been for her mother's money, and knowing how much she despised money, I don't think she'd ever be the same. I never want to hurt her that bad.

I slipped closer behind her, spooning her and taking in all her warmth. I just wanted to hold her for a minute before I left. Every time I leave her it always feels like it's the last time I'll ever see her. Deep down I know it's the guilt.

She pressed her ass against me and then started to grind against my crotch.

"You can't keep doing that," I whispered hoarsely in her ear.

That must have done something to her because before I knew it, she had rolled over to face me and was reaching down the front of my pants grabbing and stroking me. Like a girl freaking out on a handsy guy, I grabbed her arm and tried to pull her hand away from my cock.

"Holy shit, Lilly, you have to stop," I practically yelled. "I need to go...oh shit...I need to go." Her hand felt so good.

"No!" She growled though her teeth as she rolled me onto my back and straddled me. I love it when a girl takes charge and having Lilly do it was fucking hot.

"Tell me you don't want this, Devin. I want to hear you say you don't want me. Say it, and I promise I'll never touch you again."

She began to move back and forth like a pro. The friction was too much to bear.

"I can't...I don't..." The words were stuck in my throat. Nothing I wanted to say would come out.

"I can feel that you want me," she said as she pressed her body down against my hardness. "Just tell me that you don't want this and I'll walk away right now."

There was something different in her voice. There was some sound I'd never heard before. I couldn't put my finger on it, but it was definitely different. I reached up with both hands to touch her face. The wetness beneath my fingers told me exactly why she sounded so different.

"Are you crying?" I asked. My heart stopped and all the blood left my brain.

"I don't cry." She swiped roughly at her face. "You know that better than anyone...you know *me* better than anyone," she whispered. "Devin, you need to leave. I don't want to do this anymore. I'm tired of trying. No matter how close I think I'm getting to you, you just seem to keep pulling away from me, so before what I feel gets any worse, maybe we should stop hanging out so much."

Panic slammed into my chest and not because of the money. The thought of not being around her suddenly made me sick to my stomach.

"What? Why? I'm sorry, baby. I just...I want to be around you," I said in a rush.

"I'm just trying to save myself," she sniffled.

"Exactly! That's what I'm trying to do, too. You just make it so hard for me to..."

She sighed in frustration. "No, that's not what I mean. I'm trying to save myself, but not the way you think."

"I don't understand. Am I doing something that's hurting you?" I swallowed hard.

If only she knew.

"No, well, kind of." The room became quiet. The sound of our heavy breaths filled air. "I think...I think I'm in love with you, Devin."

Everything stopped, my chest felt heavy. I couldn't breathe. Why couldn't I breathe? This was the part where I should get up and run for my life, but I couldn't move. She said the words that a man like me dreaded. She meant them too, I could tell.

Renee once told me she loved me during sex, but when Lilly said those words it gave me a physical reaction. It literally felt like my heart was trying to burst out my chest, like it was trying to return to its rightful owner...Lilly.

"I shouldn't have said that. The last thing I want to do is scare you off." She started to try and take it back immediately.

No way in Hell was I letting her take it back. Not when it soothed every painful experience I'd ever had in my life.

I covered her mouth with mine; kissing her like I never had before. She loved me. Me. The horrible, lying, no good, son of a bitch that I was, and she loved me. God knows I didn't deserve that love, but I needed it.

I wrapped my arms around her and turned her onto her back, positioning her beneath me. I pulled my mouth from hers and starting kissing her neck. She moaned a deep, husky whimper and I gave in completely.

Her announcing her feelings for me did something to me. I don't know what, but I couldn't stop myself. I didn't want to fight it anymore.

From this moment on things would be different. I'd be tortured and pulled in two different directions. I had my family to get this money for and then I had Lilly, who I never wanted to hurt. No matter what decision I was going to make someone I cared about was going to get hurt. I was fucked no matter what I did.

Her hands were everywhere. She was touching my face, running her hands down my chest or up my back. It was driving me mad, but I knew I had to take it slow. No matter how bad I wanted to rip her clothes off and screw her brains out, I knew I had to go slow. Lilly had never said that she was a virgin, but I kind of assumed she was. The thought of being the first to claim her made me grow harder.

"I want you so bad. Are you sure you wanna do this?" I asked.

I wanted to give her another chance to back out of it. Lord knows I was beyond stopping myself at this point. I helped her as she peeled my shirt off me before she started to kiss my neck and shoulders.

"I've never been more sure about anything in my life."

I moved to the side of the bed and turned on the small table lamp. I wanted to be able to see everything; every facial expression and every moan. I wanted to see all of her skin. I moved back on top of her and started to unbutton her shirt. She went completely tense and that's when I noticed the scared expression she was wearing.

"What's wrong?" I asked.

"Do we have to have the light on? I don't really feel comfortable...I don't want you to see me naked," she finally blurted out.

I smiled. She was worried about me seeing her naked. She thought I wasn't going to like what I saw. Well, it was too late for that. I'd already felt her against my body so many times that I could picture her naked and I knew I was going to love every single part of her.

"I wanna see you, baby. Please, let me see you," I kissed her softly.

"But..."

"No buts," I whispered. "You're beautiful. I should've told you that a million times already, because it's the truth. I wanna kiss you." I kissed her lips. "And lick you." I licked her lips. "All over your body and I can't do that unless you're lying in front of me completely naked."

The thought of her lying in front of me naked like some kind of perfect sacrifice that I didn't deserve made my cock swell harder.

"Please, let me make love to you, Lilly."

"OK," she whispered.

I started to unbutton her shirt again.

I took my precious time undressing her, unwrapping her like the gift that she was. I kissed and enjoyed every part of her that became visible. The noises she made stirred my insides.

Once she was completely naked I got up on my knees and stared down at her. She attempted to cover her breasts, but I quickly brushed her hands aside so that I could admire every part of her body. Every curve, every little dimple, every piece of her warm, soft flesh called to me.

"Oh my God, baby. Never hide your body from me again. You're so sexy and soft and warm," I ran my hands up her sides toward her breasts and once I got to them I ran my thumbs over her perfectly round perky nipples. "And these are perfect."

I leaned down and replaced my thumbs with my mouth and tongue. The sound she made caused my entire body to throb. I took my time tasting and sucking her like she had never been tasted before. Her fingers played through my hair and at times pressed my mouth harder onto her. Mine, was all I could think. She was mine and I was never going to let her go. She moaned softly and kept telling me not to stop. I wasn't stopping, I was just getting started.

Eighteen

The Release

I resisted the urge to cover myself every time he looked down at my body. I still couldn't believe that I was lying here naked while he pretty much looked at and touched every part of me. No one had ever made me feel so comfortable with myself. No one had ever made me feel so beautiful and sexy in all my life. I knew that after tonight I'd never let him go.

I had never in my life felt something so wonderful. Everything Devin was doing to me made me feel good all over and I was to the point where I couldn't control the sounds that were spilling from my lips. I wanted to feel his skin against mine. I wanted to feel him all over. His skin was softer than I imagined it would be and he was so hot, like, he physically felt hot against me.

"Yes, touch me," he groaned against my body.

He slowly started to move his hand down my stomach toward the part of me that cried the hardest for him. I could hardly wait for him to touch me. I was starting to ache so bad that it was becoming uncomfortable and I could feel the slide of moisture between my legs every time I moved. Finally, he pushed his hand between us and ran his finger across my clit. I thought I was going to jump out of the bed. The sensation that ran up my body caused me to cry out without any regard for what I would say.

"You're so wet for me," he whispered against my lips.

He ran his finger up and down just inside the lips of my most vulnerable parts, moving my moisture all around and causing me to breathe in little pants. No matter how hard I tried, I couldn't get a good breath. Then his finger slowly moved inside of me and I thought at that moment I'd never feel something so good ever again.

Slowly, he moved his finger in and out and I slammed my eyes closed and arched my back for more. I sank my teeth into my bottom lip and tried to quiet the animalistic sounds that were coming out of my mouth. When he slid a second finger into me I thought I was going to die from the pleasure of it. He continued to move his two fingers around in ways that caused waves of sensation throughout my belly. I felt tingly all over.

"You're so tight and soft inside," he breathed against the side of my neck.

He started using his thumb against my sensitive hot spot again while still moving his two fingers in and out of me and I thought I was about to explode. There was a build up like I had never felt before. It was making me squirm and pant, and I couldn't even be embarrassed by my reaction. I couldn't worry about how my body looked—all I cared about was making the ache between my legs stop.

"Do you ever touch yourself like this?" he asked softly.

There was no embarrassment, just the sweet ache.

"Yes," I moaned.

"That's so hot. I love it when a woman touches herself." His fingers moved faster. "Have you ever made yourself cum?"

I shook my head no.

"We should do something about that, shouldn't we?" he said breathlessly.

"Yes, please," I begged.

I couldn't even open my eyes. I was so close, I could feel it. So close. He stopped everything and pulled his fingers from me. I heard myself protest the sudden stop.

I wanted to cry.

That's when I heard the zipper on his jeans and then the sound of rustling clothes. When I felt his hot hardness next to my thigh, I finally opened my eyes to look at him. This was really about to happen.

"Tell me you want me, Lilly. Tell me you want me inside of you." He kissed me slowly as he positioned himself between my legs.

I could feel the tip of his heat against me, hard and pressing, and I wanted to thrust my hips for more. I wanted him deep, hard, and now!

"Please, Devin...," I heard myself say as I started pressing myself against him.

"Say it, baby. Tell me you want me inside you—I need to hear it,"

"I want you, Devin, inside of me," I whimpered.

"I don't have condom, but I'll pull out, OK?"

I had no idea what he was talking about, but I didn't care.

"Uh huh," I mumbled.

It burned and rubbed my ache when he slowly entered me. It felt so good, yet it stung as I stretched to accommodate his size.

Once he was in completely, he became suddenly still.

"Look at me, Lilly." He sounded strained.

My eyes connected with his.

"Is this OK?" he asked. "Does it hurt?"

"Just a little."

"Do you wanna stop?"

"No, please don't stop."

He leaned down and started kissing me as he slowly withdrew and then plunged inside of me again. It caused the nerves in my stomach to flinch. Funny noises that I didn't recognize spilled from my lips.

In and out, over and over again and it was amazing. His breath in my ear and the smacking of our two bodies coming together was all I could hear. He seemed to slide into and touch every part that begged to be touched. He was so good at it and part of me knew that he was holding back for me.

195

"You feel so good, so tight. It's been so long and you feel amazing, baby." He said as he moved inside of me over and over again.

His pace changed and while he was still deep, he was moving faster. My breathing changed as I sucked in little bits of oxygen. The ache and tingle was slowly working its way up into my hips and down into my legs. There was something just out of my reach. I was pretty sure that I was about to have my first orgasm.

"Don't stop," I said desperately. "Please."

I bit down on my bottom lip as the ache and tingle made its way into my lower stomach and sat and simmered. It snaked around my body and slowly started to dissolve. There was a rise...up and up and up and even though I'd never felt the fall before, I knew it was going to be wonderful.

"Oh my God, baby. I think I'm gonna...don't stop," I knew I was being loud, but I didn't care who heard me.

I latched onto his ass and pressed him harder against me. I was so close I couldn't take it anymore. Up and up some more, the rise kept going and I didn't know how much higher I could get.

"Fuck. I have to stop now, Lilly." I heard him say.

He sounded out of breath and in pain.

There was no way I was letting him stop. I was about to fall. Everything inside of me was about to melt into something miraculous.

Instead of letting him pull out, I latched on tighter and pressed him deeper. It was right there. Oh God, it was right there.

"I have to stop," I heard him say louder.

"No! Don't stop! I'm..."

I grabbed him and held on tighter as I made noises I'd never heard myself make. My body took on life of its own as the ache and tingle that was simmering in my lower stomach slowly dissolved into pure intense pleasure that poured out of my body. I felt myself tightening around him over and over again as each spasm of delight ripped through my body. I was dying! At least I felt like I was dying and it felt so damn fantastic.

"Yes, baby. That's right, let it out." He strained above me.

Then he was cursing himself.

He sped up which only intensified my release. I barely heard him saying something and making his own noises when finally, he let out a loud growling noise. His body jerked as he slammed himself hard and deep into me. Then everything stopped.

He held onto me like his life depended on it and I felt his whole entire body shaking. My legs were shuttering like crazy as a few more ripples of pleasure rolled through me.

We were breathing like we had just run a marathon. He lifted his face from my neck and a tiny bead of sweat dripped from his forehead and landed on my chest. Time stopped as he stared down at me like it was the first time he'd ever seen my face. He studied my face so critically that I was beginning to wonder if I'd transformed into someone else during my orgasm. I sure as Hell felt like a new woman.

He stayed on top of me and inside for a few seconds longer, before finally pulling away. I instantly felt his loss and I wanted to hold him to me, but instead he jumped up and started putting on his clothes. Suddenly, I felt too exposed and the embarrassment started to set in. I grabbed at my blanket to cover myself.

"What's wrong? Did I do something wrong?" I asked when he grabbed for his shoes.

"I said I needed to stop!" He growled at me and it made me jump.

He had never yelled at me and now he was mad. How could he be so mad after something so wonderful had just happened? I still felt tiny hints of spasm and delight and yet he was standing in front of me putting on his clothes like there was a fire and yelling at me.

"I'm sorry, I...," I started.

"What if I've knocked you up?" He jerked his shirt over his head. "I said I didn't have a condom, but you just kept pushing me to keep going!"

"But, Devin, I can't...," he cut me off again.

"Do you think I wanna get stuck with *you* like that?" He pointed at me and I caught his disgusted face as he bent down to tie his shoes.

In that moment a tiny piece of me died.

Pain shot through me, his words cutting so deeply that I was positive I was bleeding to death.

I didn't even have time to tell him that it was impossible for me to get pregnant before he grabbed his keys and ran out my bedroom. I heard the front door opening and then I heard it slam shut... just like my heart.

I'd never in my life felt so used and disgusting. The look in his eyes at the thought of being "stuck" with me, it was tragic. Here I was, spilling my heart to him and giving myself to him in every way I could, and he was obviously pushing me away the entire time. I threw myself at him, and a man's a man, they can only turn it away for so long, right?

He didn't want me, but I was there and I was ready and what kind of stupid asshole would turn down a wet and ready female?

I fell back into my pillows and cried like I hadn't cried since I was fifteen. I cried like it was freshman year all over again and I was being ridiculed for being the fat kid. I cried like I swore I'd never cry again and I made a promise to myself in that moment that this would really be the last time. I was done, done with everyone, especially Devin. I would never let myself get this hurt again. Never!

Nineteen

Heartbroken Heartbreaker

It had been three days since I last saw or spoke to Lilly and I was miserable. I missed her. I've never really missed anyone before, well except my mom, but I think the hate I had for her got me through. I don't hate Lilly. I love her. I can say that to myself now. I'm in love with Lilly and it fucking sucks.

I don't know why I freaked out on her like I did, I wasn't even mad at her. I was mad at myself. I was mad at myself because for the first time in my life I lost control with a woman. I've never in my life done that. My only excuse is that sex with Lilly was amazing. She was amazing.

Every time I closed my eyes I could still see her squirming beneath me with her eyes closed and her mouth open in pleasure. I could still hear her moaning my name and panting as she, for the first time, experienced an orgasm, an orgasm that *I* gave her with *my* body. Just thinking about it got me turned on and so for almost two days I walked around rock hard daydreaming about Lilly. I hadn't jacked off that much since I was thirteen.

I was in the middle of one of those daydreams while trying to change the oil in a little four-door Honda, which reminded me of Lilly, when, like a dumbass, I was suddenly covered in all the old oil that was inside the car.

"Damn!" I pulled myself from under the car to find my dad laughing down at me.

He handed me a rag and I started wiping the oil off of my face and arms. What the hell was the matter with me?

"You know you need to just break down and call that gal. You been screwing up things around this garage for two days now. I can't afford to keep ya around, boy." He smiled his secret smile.

"I don't know what you're talking about." I started throwing around nuts and bolts and cleaning up the oil.

"It's OK to admit that you miss her. Don't be an ass like I was. What'd you do anyway?"

"Why do you automatically assume that I did something? Don't you have any faith in me?"

"Oh come on, boy, that girl couldn't hurt a fly. Matter of fact, she's pretty damn close to perfect, ain't she? Shoot, I'd scoop her up before someone else did, that's for damn sure. Don't be a fool, Devin." He walked back to the truck he was working on and didn't say another word.

He was right. He usually was, but I couldn't do it. I love her and I have to make it go away. It was my way of protection. Never again would I be left the way I was when I was young. Never again would another female leave me heartless the way my mother did.

There's no other way to it, women leave. They love you and then they leave. I can't let that happen. So, I'm leaving Lilly alone, before she breaks me down even more.

"Dad, I'm gonna take off for a few days. Maybe head down to spend time with Alex in Jacksonville. I just need some time to think. You think you could hold it down here while I'm gone?"

"I held this place down for many years before you came along. I might be old, but I think I can handle things around here without you." He huffed and went back to work. "But you can't outrun it, no matter how fast you run."

I ignored him and went inside to get a quick shower. Right after that I was on the phone with my cousin, Alex, who I hadn't seen in three years, followed by packing a few things in my black-suit case.

An hour later, and after telling Jenny I'd be back in a few days, I was out the door and in my car on the interstate headed to Florida. It might seem extreme, but I needed a vacation. I needed time to think about what the hell I was doing.

I drove in silence until I was half way through Georgia. I turned my cell phone on silent and just drove. So many things went through my mind. So many things kept eating at me: Losing the shop, the only home I'd ever known, and Lilly, the only woman to ever steal my heart. Without even doing anything, without even realizing it, Lilly broke my heart and it wasn't even her fault. It was my fault.

I've left many broken hearts in my tracks and honestly I never thought twice about it. Now, for the first time in my life I was sorry for the things I'd done. I was sorry if I'd ever made anyone feel any kind of pain. The worst part was that I took something from Lilly I could never give back. I took her virginity when I didn't deserve it. I was a thief! I was a sick, perverted, selfish man who *deserved* all the pain I felt right then.

I made it to Alex's place in no time. I brought in my black suitcase and then we grabbed a quick bite at a small restaurant. The small family reunion of just me and Alex was continued at a bar down the street from his apartment. I drank so much that I don't even know how we made it back to his place.

I woke up the next morning with the worse hangover I'd ever had in my life. I couldn't even get off of the couch. I had relaxed there for about an hour with a pounding headache when I started to smell bacon.

"Hey, Dev! You up, bro? I'm cooking a quick breakfast!" Alex yelled across his small one-bedroom apartment.

Each syllable banged inside my head causing the ache to get worse. I rolled off the couch and suddenly felt nauseated. It made me wonder how the hell Dad did it every day.

I dragged myself into his kitchen and fell into a chair.

"Could you not yell anymore, please?" I rubbed my temple.

Alex sat a beer in front of me and the smell of it made my stomach roll.

"Bite the dog, bro, it's the only way."

I pinched my nose and downed the beer as quickly as I could. Then I devoured the greasy bacon and eggs that Alex threw on a broken plate for me.

"So—to what do I owe the honor?" Alex asked as he relaxed against the kitchen counter.

"Just needed a break," I bit off another piece of the bacon, which was surprisingly settling my stomach a bit.

"A break, huh? Seems to me you were doing more than taking a break last night. I know my family, and I'd say you were drowning some sorrows, and I do mean drowning. I don't think I've ever seen anyone drink that much in my life."

"I wasn't drowning anything, just having a few with my favorite cousin. So, how's Aunt Peggy?" I changed the subject quickly.

"She's OK, I guess, same ole mom. How's Uncle Herald and Jenny? She still a ball buster?"

We continued to catch up. I never mentioned the fact that we were about to lose everything and I never said anything about Lilly, even though she stayed on my mind the entire time.

I couldn't help but wonder if she was OK. Did I hurt her? Does she hate me? Fuck it. I hope she hates me! Maybe it will make it easier to let her go. This bipolar inner monologue continued for hours.

I checked my phone constantly to see if I had any missed calls. I wanted her to call so bad, but at the same time I hoped she wouldn't. I wanted to hear her voice. I wanted to tell her I was sorry and beg for her forgiveness, but I could never speak to her again. It was that simple.

That night, while sleeping on Alex's horrible broken down couch, I had another nightmare about Lilly turning into my mother and leaving me. I woke up at two in the morning more hell bent on cutting all ties with Lilly than I was before I went to sleep. It would be hard to do. When I told Lilly that I was addicted to her, it was the truth, but she was one habit I was determined to break.

Twenty

Flashbacks

"Lil, what's up with you?" Shannon asked.

"Nothing I'm just tired." I rolled back over to attempt to go back to sleep.

After Devin literally loved me and left me, I cried, got angry, took a shower to wash away the disgust, and then I got in my bed where I had been ever since.

"Mrs. Franklin's really worried about you, Lil. You *never* miss work, and if I'm being honest, if you don't start eating soon, I'm going to call your mother."

"Please don't torture me more by calling her. I'll eat in a while. I just really need some sleep."

She said something else, but I just ignored her and went back to sleep. When I opened my eyes again it was dark outside. Someone was ringing my doorbell and banging on my door like a crazy person. I kept waiting for Shannon to answer it, but apparently she wasn't there.

I wrapped my blanket around myself and dragged ass to the front door. I slung it open and was surprised to see Jenny standing there.

"Dayum! You look like ass, Lil. Are you sick?"

"No. I'm just tired. Is something wrong?"

The minute I saw her standing there I thought instantly of Devin. I suddenly had a horrible thought about something bad happening to him. Even though his name was like fire in my throat I had to ask.

"Are Dad and Devin OK?"

"Oh yeah, everyone's fine. Dad's at home and Dev went to Florida."

Oh my God! Did he move to Florida? Am I really never going to see him again?

I started to panic.

"For good?" The words squeaked out.

"Hell no! He just went to visit our cousin, Alex. He should be back in two days."

I was pissed at myself for being so relieved.

"Well, what's up?"

"I got a date!" She squealed like an actual teenage girl.

"What? Come in, come in! Tell me everything!"

I pulled her into my apartment and for the first time in days I felt normal as she proceeded to tell me about this guy named Justin who asked her to the school dance.

"I know it's last minute, but could you please help me get dressed. I have no idea what to do," she shrugged innocently.

"I'd love to! Call Dad and make sure it's OK for you to sleep over and then we can spend all day tomorrow shopping and getting you ready. What time is *Justin* picking you up?"

"He'll be at my house at six."

Jenny called and of course Dad was OK with her crashing at my place for the night. Shannon came home soon after that. We had Chinese delivered and then spent the night watching chick flicks. I tried with all my might not to talk about Devin or much less think about him. I failed horribly at the last part. I kept thinking about his spontaneous trip to Florida and if it had anything to do with me. I kept wondering if he was even thinking about me.

I went to sleep that night feeling a little better. For some reason, Jenny being with me made things easier. It was the next best thing to having Devin there.

The next morning we got up early, had a quick breakfast, and then headed to the mall. This shopping thing was getting more fun every time I went. We got our hair and nails done and finally, when we were about to give up, we found a gorgeous emerald green knee-length dress that Jenny agreed to wear.

When we walked into Devin's house I thought Dad was going to have a heart attack when he saw Jenny. She looked beautiful. Her hair and make-up were perfection and the green of her dress brought out her eyes beautifully.

Dad and I met Justin, who seemed like a really nice kid, and then, like a proud older sister, I watched as he gave her a pretty corsage and opened the car door for her. I was so proud and sad at the same time. I looked around me.

I watched Jenny go and looked over at Dad. I shouldn't have been there. Once the cute couple was completely out of sight I told Dad I was going to head back home. I had no idea what he and Jenny knew, but since the excitement of Jenny's moment was over, I felt out of place.

"You can stick around, Lilly. Maybe have some dinner with an old man." Dad said as he took a quick swig of his beer.

"I'd love to, but I really gotta get home. Me and Shannon have some plans tonight and it's getting late." I tried to come up with a quick reason to leave.

Being there, in that house full of pictures of Devin when he was younger was making me crazy. The desire to go to his room, lie in his bed, and cry was too overwhelming. As sad as it sounds, even the smell of the old house was depressing me.

"OK, honey. Don't be a stranger."

"I won't," I lied.

I reached up and gave him a quick hug. I knew I'd probably never see him or Jenny again. Sadness filled me, and before I started to cry and made myself look like an idiot, I quickly turned to leave.

"He misses you," Dad called after me.

I stopped.

"What?"

"I just thought you should know. Devin misses you."

Crying was becoming a regular thing for me these days. I cried the entire way back to my apartment. When I got home Shannon finally forced me to tell her what was going on. She hugged me while I cried on her shoulder.

With swollen eyes and an achy throat, I fell asleep in my bed.

At around eleven that night my cell phone started to ring. In a sleepy haze, I almost didn't answer it in time.

"Hello," I answered half asleep.

"Lilly! It's me, Jenny! Could you please come and get me?" She was in a panic.

I sat up quickly and rubbed my foggy eyes.

"Where are you?" I asked quickly.

I could tell by the sound of her voice that something was definitely wrong.

"At an after party. There's a bunch of coked out older people here and some fucker grabbed my tit. Justin's drunk and can't drive. Please come and get me," she begged.

I got directions as I tied my shoes and threw my things in my purse.

"I'll be there in twenty minutes. Don't move!"

I was out the door and at a house full of people my age in no time. I got out of my car and made my way through the crowd on the front lawn. The music was so loud I could barely hear myself think.

When I got inside of the house I went up to a few girls and asked if they knew where I could find Jenny. No one seemed to know who I was talking about. I saw Justin passed out in the corner then, after searching the entire first floor and breathing in entirely too much second-hand smoke, I took the stairs two at time.

I threw open every door I came to searching for Jenny. The music seemed to follow me and I still couldn't hear anything, but out of nowhere the sound of a screaming girl seemed to pierce through the loud rap song that was playing.

I ran toward the scream and ended up in front of the very last door in the long hallway. Without a second thought, I slammed the door open. There struggling on the bed was Jenny and three older men. She was fighting them off with all of her might as they ripped at her pretty green dress.

Memories of that day in the woods when I was being attacked by the malevolent cheerleaders ran through my mind. I could hear my screams in my mind, I could hear myself begging for them to stop beating me, and then Jenny screamed again and it pierced my memories and brought me back to the moment. They were trying to rape her. I only had a second of shock before I went in for the attack.

"Get away from her!" I screamed.

I picked up a huge, red vase and slammed it against the head of the first guy I came to. It shattered as he fell to the floor out cold. The other two attackers swung around on me and I saw Jenny's terror-filled eyes as she struggled to get off the bed.

Her dress was ripped and her hair was a mass of tumbling curls. Black mascara ran down her face with the tears that were rushing down her cheeks.

"What the hell?" one of the guys said.

"Who the hell are you? Look, Eric, it's a baby hippo!" They laughed.

More memories of being taunted in high school slammed into my mind, all the horrible names, all the bullying and teasing.

"Just let her go," I tried to sound as calm as possible.

"Why don't you go downstairs and find something to eat. I'm sure you'd much rather be stuffing your fat trap than worrying about other people's business."

"Oh fuck that. I got something I can stuff in her fat trap." They laughed again.

With a growl I threw myself at the guy closest to me, but he was stronger than he looked. He pushed me against the wall and I watched as his fist came up. In slow motion it came down against my face.

My cheek exploded and I tasted the blood instantly. I reached out and dug my nails into whatever skin I could find. I could hear Jenny fighting with the other guy in the background. I needed to get to her. I needed to help her.

Another hit came and I felt myself go dizzy. I heard cheerleaders laughing and at the same time I could see Jenny fighting for her life across the room as I fell to the floor. The memory was somehow blending with my reality.

I heard her continue to scream and fight, but every time I attempted to get up there was another kick to my ribs. Finally, the kicks never stopped as my attacker repeatedly put his steel-toed boot into my stomach.

With every kick, I could hear the echoed laughter of teenage girls. I could hear them calling me Large Lilly. It was a replay of when I was fifteen, except instead of a group of girls I was being kicked and punched by a grown man. I must say I preferred the girls.

Just like before, my body went numb and I could no longer feel his kicks. I knew in the back of mind that the numbness was a bad thing.

I heard Jenny scream again and I tried with everything I had to get up once more. Instead of my stomach, I saw his foot coming toward my face. I tried to reach out, but I couldn't lift my arms. I felt his large boot on the side of my head, and then the room went black.

Twenty-One
Breaking News

I heard my cell phone ringing. In my sleep I couldn't decide if it was really ringing or if I was dreaming. I kept thinking in my sleepy daze that maybe it was Lilly calling me. Then I realized my cell phone really was ringing and had been for a long time.

I jumped up quick and rummaged through the strange, dark room looking for my phone. I found it inside the couch I was sleeping on.

The number wasn't familiar. I figured it must be Renee. How she got my new cell number, I had no idea, but only she would have the guts to actually call me at this time in the morning. Knowing her, it was probably something juvenile and stupid.

"Hello!" I screamed into the phone.

"Devin! It's Dad, you awake?" He sounded like he was panicking. Dad never panicked.

"What's wrong?" I said.

I rubbed my eyes abruptly and shook my head trying to shake the sleep from my brain.

"You need to get back in town as soon as possible...something's happened."

I was already on my feet and the minute he said that I felt like I was falling.

"What's happened? Are you OK? Where's Jenny?" I blurted out as I grabbed at random pieces of clothing I had lying around the room.

I pulled on a pair of jeans and the t-shirt I wore earlier that day. I threw things into my suit-case and was ready to go before he spoke again.

"Jenny's been hurt. There were so many of them. I should've been there. She couldn't...I don't know how, but Lilly...she tried...," he stuttered.

"Slow down, Dad. Calm down and tell me exactly what happened. What about Jenny and Lilly?" I asked in a panic.

"She's...I don't know if she'll be OK. If it wasn't for Lilly she might not have...we need you home, Devin. Jenny was asking for you. Just please get to Saint Marion Hospital as soon as possible OK? I don't wanna do this over the phone and please be careful. I can't stomach the thought of losing either of you tonight. I love you, Son, and I'll see you soon."

There was silence on the other line before the screen on my phone went black. Dad had hung up and whatever was going on was bad.

Dad was sober and he was still stuttering. That alone scared the shit out of me. What the hell was going on back home?

I didn't even stop to tell Alex I was leaving. I didn't care about that. I just needed to get back home to Charleston as soon as possible. All I could do was pray that they were OK.

Questions filled my mind as I threw my suit-case in the backseat of my car. I stood beside it for a minute before I got in.

Had the world stopped turning? I suddenly felt like my brain was spinning while the world around me was still. I thought I was going to faint. I shook my head trying to clear it. Jenny needed me, and I think Lilly needed me, too. They were the only women in my world who didn't break me down or hurt me and I wasn't there for them. I needed to be there for them, no matter what.

I made it to the hospital in record time. A four-hour trip had taken me a little over two.

I jumped out of the car and ran into the hospital. When I made it to the front desk there was no one there. I was about to lose control when I noticed Dad walking toward me. He was so pale. He came up to me and wrapped his arms around me and squeezed.

I followed him to a room where my sister was laying in the bed. I stood in shock for a minute as I took in the fact that

216

she looked as if she'd been beaten pretty badly. I ran to the side of the bed and grabbed her hand.

"Jenny, what happened sweetie? Tell me what happened. I'll kill the son of a bitch who did this, I swear!"

I could feel the anger rising inside of me. I meant it! I'd kill whoever it was that had put their hands on my baby sister.

"I'm OK, just some bumps and bruises—nothing I can't handle," she said roughly. "I fought him, Dev. I even kicked him in the balls a few times. Oh, sorry...I said balls again." She attempted to smile.

She went over the events of the day. I felt a stab in the stomach when she told me about her and Lilly spending the day together and Lilly helping her get ready for a dance. She explained the after party full of drugs and older people and told me about how she called Lilly before being pulled upstairs into a bedroom by three strange men. I felt like I was about to snap with rage.

"If it wasn't for Lilly, they would've raped me, Devin. There's no telling what else." Tears spilled from her swollen eyes. "Then a bunch of people from the party came bursting into the room—they must of heard my screams—and the guys took off running. Thankfully, someone called an ambulance."

I looked around the room for the first time. I wanted Lilly there with me. I wanted to hug her and thank her for protecting one of the most important people in my life, but as I looked around she was nowhere to be found. I looked over at my dad who was in tears.

217

"Where is she, Dad? Where's Lilly?"

"Follow me," he said sadly.

He didn't say much else as I followed him to the elevator and then down the long hallway of the intensive care floor. He opened the door and walked into the room. I couldn't make myself go through the door. I just stood there in the doorway staring in. Lying in the bed across the room was Lilly, and she was covered in tubes and wires.

Her face was swollen and unrecognizable. Her hair was smothered with dry blood. There were stitches over her left eyebrow and bruises everywhere. When I got the nerve to walk to her bed, I slowly reached out and grabbed her soft hand. She didn't move. The loud machine next to her bed was beeping so loudly, but everything sounded muffled.

She was unconscious, and from the funny looking machine that blew air into her lungs, it was obvious that she wasn't even breathing on her own. My knees felt like they were going to give out on me. I held onto the wall next to me to keep myself from falling.

This can't be happening!

"Is she going to be OK?" My throat felt thick.

"I'm so sorry, Devin." Dad said to me as the tears flowed down his cheeks.

For the first time since my mother left, I cried on my dad's shoulder.

About thirty minutes after I contacted Shannon, she showed up at the hospital and cried over Lilly. She then called

Mrs. Sheffield, who was hysterical. I listened as Shannon tried to calm her. Soon she was stuffing her cell phone back into her purse and at Lilly's bedside again.

"Mrs. Sheffield is losing it. She's on vacation and can't get here for at least two days," she sniffled.

Shannon seemed upset by the fact that Lilly's mom wasn't going to be there for two days. I, on the other hand, was a little bit relieved. I knew her mother should be there, but I knew the minute she saw my face all would be revealed and I wasn't ready for that. I wanted Lilly better and I wanted to hold her at least one last time before the truth came out.

Later, the doctor came in and talked to Shannon and me. Lilly had some internal bleeding as well as some swelling around her brain.

"I think if we can get the swelling around her brain down, I'll feel a lot better about her prognosis. Right now it's hard to say. She could wake up at any time, or she could be in this comatose state for a while longer. There's no way to know until the swelling goes down a bit more. We have her on some antibiotics to fight some possible infections. I'll know more as soon as the rest of the test results come in." He seemed as confused as we were.

Needless to say, none of us felt any better after speaking to him.

I spent the rest of the night in between Lilly and Jenny's rooms.

I proceeded to internally kick my own ass. I should've been there. I shouldn't have gone to Florida. I should've been there for them. Jenny would've called me and I would've killed those spineless assholes. What kind of man could beat on a woman that way?

One that deserved to die, that's what kind.

I was in Lilly's room when the sun came up. I hadn't slept a wink all night. Dad and I had taken turns in the girls' rooms. Nurses had been in and out of both rooms all night.

We found out around seven in the morning that Jenny would be released from the hospital later that day. Lilly, on the other hand, still wasn't responding. I was slowly losing grip with reality, either from lack of sleep or from the shock of seeing the woman I loved with all of my heart on a ventilator and in a coma.

"You look like you could use this." Shannon handed me a cup of hot coffee.

"Thanks." I grabbed the cup and slowly sipped the hot liquid.

I needed anything that would keep me awake so that I was there when she woke up, or should I say *if* she woke up.

Shannon sat in the chair across from me.

"I just can't believe she's going through this again." She started to tear up.

Her words caught me off guard, and I thought maybe I was hearing things.

"Again?" I asked, confused.

"Yeah, again. You didn't stick around to find out, but when Lilly was a teenager she got teased a lot because of her size and didn't really have any friends. One day, she was approached by a bunch of the girls on the cheerleading squad and they made her think they wanted to be friends with her and asked her to meet them in the woods on the outskirts of the school property. She went, and when she got there the girls proceeded to call her names and then beat her until she was unconscious. Her mom told me more about it than Lilly did, but I know she was in the hospital for a while."

Why hadn't she ever told me about that? I thought she told me everything.

"What happened to the girls?" I asked with anger.

I could feel my grip on the coffee cup tightening.

"Nothing. Lilly refused to press charges or anything. Considering what they took from her, I would've sued the little bitches, but not our Lilly. She just switched schools and never spoke of it again. That was the last time she cried—well, until you."

Shannon quickly got up and busied herself. The conversation had just taken an awkward turn.

I, on the other hand, suddenly felt sick to my stomach. Just knowing that I was no better than the girls from her high school crushed me. I made her cry. I was paid to date her and then I made her cry.

I stepped up to the side of Lilly's bed and grabbed her soft hand again. I'd been doing that over and over again throughout the night. I'm not sure why I did it, but I think maybe it was because I needed to know that she was still warm—that she was still alive.

Suddenly, something that Shannon said ran through my mind once more.

Considering what they took from her...

"Shannon...,"

She stopped what she was doing and turned to me.

"Yeah?"

"You said those girls took something from her. What did you mean by that?" I asked, confused.

"They beat her and kicked her so bad in the stomach that she had internal bleeding along with a ton of other problems. Lilly can't have kids now."

Those last words shook me. I felt lightheaded and suddenly had to sit down. I'd taken her virginity and then said some of the cruelest things about her getting pregnant and me being stuck to her. My last words to her ran through my brain.

What if I've knocked you up? Do you think I want to be stuck to you like that?!

Thinking back, I remember her trying to tell me something before I stormed out of her room. Could she have been trying to tell me that it wasn't possible—that she could never have kids?

I felt like shit—officially. In the short time that I'd known her, I'd managed to hurt her more than any of the horrible people that had entered her life before me, and I'm in love with her.

I was going to make everything better. I was going to make it all go away. I silently promised that no matter what, I was going to make it up to her.

Shannon walked out of the room as I had my mental break down. How could have I been so cold-hearted?

I stood once more and walked over to Lilly's bed. She looked bruised and pale, but her lips were as pink as rose petals. Without a second thought, I leaned over her.

"Please wake up, baby," I whispered.

I pressed my lips against hers as I felt a single tear slide down my cheek.

"I love you, Lilly. I'm so sorry."

Twenty-Two

True Love's Kiss

Somewhere far away I could hear voices. They were followed by sharp pains behind my eyes, which I couldn't seem to open. I felt warmth in my hand and then more voices. I couldn't make them out—they were so far away.

I tried to take a deep breath, but I couldn't. I couldn't move anything. Slowly I was coming to more and the sounds around me were becoming more defined. I could hear Shannon talking and someone else—a male voice.

Was that my father? Who was that?

Then suddenly the voice was familiar.

Devin.

Instant sadness took over me, I'm not sure why. I was having a hard time focusing on anything. I tried again to open my eyes, and then a sharp, bright light broke through and I quickly shut them again. There was a loud beeping noise that was starting to aggravate me, and I wanted it to stop.

Once more, I slowly tried to open my eyes. It hurt to move them. I managed to open them and there he was—Devin. He was standing over me with his head down and it looked like he was crying.

Did I die?

I closed my eyes again because it hurt so bad to keep them open. I could hear Devin's voice again. Then there was warmth against my lips. There was softness and warmth that I never wanted to end. I tried once more to move my hand, and it moved.

"I love you, Lilly. I'm so sorry," I heard him sniffle.

Yep, I was dead. I was dead and I must've done something good in my life because regardless of the severe pain that comes along with death—I was in heaven.

I opened my eyes again. Pain shot behind them when the light came in. Devin was looking at me, and even though he still had a tear running down his face, a huge smile appeared.

"Lilly," he whispered as he wiped the single tear from his cheek.

I tried to speak. I wanted more than anything to tell him that I loved him, too, but something was stuck in my throat. Then the memories of what happened came crashing over me. I had been in a room and Jenny was being attacked. I tried to scream for Jenny—to let Devin know to go to her, but again there was something lodged in my throat. Then I realized that I

225

wasn't breathing and I started to panic. Whatever it was in my throat was keeping me from breathing.

The beeping noise in the background got faster. My arms became easy to move as terror set in. I wasn't breathing and something was choking me. Jenny was being hurt and Devin didn't know—he had to stop them. My arms were flailing about as I tried to get up and dislodge whatever it was in my throat at the same time.

"Calm down, baby. Can I get some help in here?" I heard Devin yell.

Then he was holding my arms down.

Why was he holding me down?

I heard myself make a strange choking noise and then there were nurses followed by a strange man standing right over me.

"Lilly, I need you to stay calm until I get your breathing tube out, OK? This is going to be uncomfortable."

I felt a tugging on my throat and then I gagged harder as something was pulled from my throat. Then I was able to take my first breath. It hurt my entire body to breathe, and instead of screaming from the pain like I wanted to, I heard myself make strange moaning noises.

"What's going on? Is she Ok?" I heard Devin saying in the background. "Someone, please tell me what's going on!"

"We're going to give you something for the pain, Lilly." The strange man was really close to my face.

I tried to tell him to move. I wanted to tell him to get out of my way. I needed to tell Devin to help Jenny, but as hard as I tried, nothing would come out. Finally, the pain was starting to wear off and I could feel myself becoming even drowsier. I closed my eyes for only a second and when I opened them again the stranger was gone and Devin was standing over me with worry in his eyes.

Jenny—Devin—help Jenny.

"Help—Jenny," I managed to whisper.

It felt like fire coming out of my throat. I saw the expression on Devin's face change into a mix of sadness and admiration. Then, when I couldn't take it anymore, I slept.

I'm not sure how long I slept, but when I woke up again Devin was sitting beside my bed slumped over sleeping. My vision was still blurry, but I could see well enough to see that he looked so peaceful and yet very exhausted. It looked like he hadn't shaved in a while. I was looking at a different man, physically and emotionally. I didn't move, I just sat there half awake and in horrible pain. I didn't want to take the chance of waking him up. Just sitting there watching him sleep was new.

I slowly pulled my hand out of his and ran my fingers through his dark hair. He made a soft, childlike noise and my heart ached. After everything that had happened over the last few weeks, all I could think about was how much I loved him. I loved everything about him, and his wonderful family was just the cherry on top.

He shifted again as I softly ran my fingers through his hair.

He'd said he loved me.

I was having a hard time putting the pieces together, but I specifically remember him saying it. Then another memory came and I had to wake him. I shook his shoulder a little.

"Devin, please wake up." I didn't want to yell and have nurses come in.

He jumped up like there was a fire. He blinked rapidly and took in his surroundings. Suddenly, he dropped back into his seat and grabbed my hand. He kissed my hand before laying his face into my palm.

"I'm so glad you're OK, baby. I don't know what I would've done." He continued to caress my hands with his face.

"Devin, where's Jenny? Is she OK?"

He looked up at me and softly pushed a stray piece of hair behind my ear. A slow smile developed as he ran his finger down the side of my face.

"She's OK, thanks to you. You saved her."

"But the men—they didn't?"

I couldn't bring myself to say the word rape, but he knew what I was asking.

"No, they didn't." He put his head down and took a deep breath. "I should've been there, Lilly. I should've been there for you and her, but I wasn't. This is my fault, all of it. I'm so sorry for everything I did to you. I want to make a clean start with you. There's so much I wanna tell you when you get out of here, but right now all I want you to know is that I'm in love with you and I want to be with you, no matter what."

He leaned over and kissed my forehead, then my nose, and then my lips—all very softly.

"I love you, too." I reached up and palmed his cheek.

Someone cleared their throat in the doorway and Devin jumped back like we were teenagers getting caught. I looked up and my mom stared back at me. She looked worried, which was an expression I hadn't seen on my mother much in my life. She left the doorway and came to my side.

"Are you feeling OK?" She asked as she scooped up my hand.

"I'm in some pain, but nothing I can't handle."

"I'm so sorry I wasn't here, honey. You have no idea how worried I was. I just took a mini vacation to New York to see your Aunt Barbra and I guess I should've checked the weather because, believe it or not, I got stuck in a blizzard. No flights were leaving. I'm so sorry."

She smoothed my hair back. It was strange and very motherly, and it caught me by surprise.

"It's OK, Mom. I'm a big girl," I smiled.

Then I was confused.

"How long have I been here? What's today?" I asked.

Devin stepped up.

"You've been here for a little over a week. Today's Monday. As long as you do well, you'll get to go home soon. At least that's what Doctor Ryan says."

He seemed uneasy around my mother.

"When did you get here, Mom?" I asked.

"Just now," she looked away as if she was ashamed.

No one had a chance to say anything else. There was a whistle at the door and soon I was bombarded by Dad and Jenny.

"Look who's awake!" Dad said as he hugged me.

Then there was Jenny, who I thought was never going to let me go. I laughed and pulled her hair in a picking manner.

"I love you, Lil. I'll never be able to thank you enough," she said with tears in her eyes.

She looked older, as if the experience had made her wiser in the ways of the world.

I didn't miss the strange eye contact between my mother and Devin.

I found out from Dad and Jenny later that night that Devin had only left the hospital to go to my apartment and take a shower. He wouldn't even take a chance of going all the way to his house in Walterboro. Since my place was close to the hospital, he had begged Shannon to let him shower there.

Jenny and Dad had been bringing him clothes and apparently it had been three days since he had eaten anything. I had my mother bring everyone food and practically force-fed Devin a turkey sub. Dad and Jenny laughed.

I'd never felt so much love around me in all of my life. Without it seeming weird, Dad and Jenny already felt like family. I'd already been calling Dad, Dad, for the last month or more. As far as I was concerned they *were* my family.

Two days later, I got to go home. I was blown away by how attentive Devin was to me. He helped me into my apartment, onto my couch, and then cared for me better than any nurse could. He constantly asked if I needed anything or if I wanted anything. While my mother, who usually runs the world, sat from afar and watched. It was strange.

When I got my first look in the mirror I almost cried. I looked horrible. I just sat there in my bedroom and stared at the mirror in shock. There was a soft knock at the door before Devin stuck his head in.

"I was just checking on you, babe," he said. "What are you doing?"

"Why didn't anyone tell me I looked like this, Devin? I don't want you seeing me like this—you should go home. I'll call you once I'm all better, and I look normal again." I put my head down.

No matter what, I wouldn't cry. Yeah, I looked horrible, and yeah, bad things had happened, but now I had Devin. He was all mine, I just didn't want him to see me this way.

I heard him walk up behind me, and then I felt him put his hand on my shoulder.

"Look at me," he said as he turned my face toward him. "You're the most beautiful woman I've ever seen and I'm completely in love with you." He softly traced the bruise around my eye with his fingertip. "It kills me that someone hurt you and Jenny this way. When I find out who did it I fully plan on beating them to death."

231

He leaned down, gave me a soft kiss, and I felt my heart melt.

"I do have some bad news, though. Dad's swamped at work. He didn't ask me to help, but I know I need to. I promise to come by every night to check on you, and I'll keep my cell phone in my pocket at all times. You call me if you need anything, OK?"

I giggled.

"Devin, I'm fine. Go help Dad and just come and see me when you can."

"I love you." He leaned down and gave me another kiss.

"I love you, too."

I watched him walk out of the room. I took a long, hot shower and then spent the rest of the night in bed watching TV. Shannon popped her head in occasionally to check on me. After the fifth time, she admitted to me that Devin had been calling her almost every hour to make sure I was OK. I smiled. The terrible beating and hospital stay aside, I'd never been so happy in my entire life.

Twenty-Three

Honesty's Best Policy

I stayed up most of the night in the garage trying to catch up. We were so behind on everything, not that it was anyone's fault but my own. I should've never taken off to Florida. If I had been there instead of running away like a punk, Jenny would've called me and the turn-out of this situation would've been a hell of a lot different. My sister wouldn't have been hurt and Lilly wouldn't have been practically beaten to death.

I owe her so much. She almost gave her life for my baby sister and I was determined to tell her the truth. Damn the money, damn the she-devil, damn it all! I wanted to be honest with Lilly and start over. Plain and simply put, I want Lilly completely.

I called Shannon constantly to check on Lilly, she was beginning to get aggravated with me. Being away from her when she needed me the most just felt wrong, but I had to work. Dad would never be able to do all of it on his own.

I worked all night long and ended up falling asleep on the old couch in the garage. I had a rough night's sleep and was awoken by Jenny who was digging through the paperwork on the old, ratty desk where we kept all the garage bills and stuff. I watched from afar as she figured out everything on her own. All the letters about the bank foreclosing on our property were right on top. I heard her gasp.

"Jenny, get out of those papers," I said sleepily. "That's not your concern."

"The hell it's not! Why didn't y'all tell me about this?" She held up a bank paper. "I should know if we're about to lose everything! All I could think about was a stupid fucking dance and you and dad were stressing over bills!" She swiped at angry tears with the back of her arm.

I jumped off of the couch and went to her.

"Jenny, you're just a kid, sweetie. We didn't want you to worry about it and you shouldn't have to worry about it. I'll take care of it," I soothed her.

"But, Dev, we're gonna lose everything! This is our home, we can't lose our home!" She was freaking out and I'd never seen Jenny lose her cool that way.

The payment was due in a week and I'd already made up my mind that I wasn't taking the money from Mrs. Sheffield. Regardless we were going to lose everything. Why was I lying to Jenny? Why not be honest and prepare her for the worst?

Then Jenny said something that shook my world, something that made me decide that maybe telling Lilly after the debt was paid would be a more realistic idea. She was going to be hurt by the truth regardless of whether or not I took the money. I might as well secure my family and *then* be honest with Lilly.

"I'm quitting school and getting a job," Jenny said with pure determination.

There was no way in Hell I'd let that happen.

"Over my dead body!" I said angrily. "Don't worry about it, Jenny. I already have the money to pay the bank. Just go inside and get ready for school."

I continued to work on cars alongside Dad for the rest of the day. By the time I was done and in the shower, I was exhausted. All I could think about was getting cleaned up and getting to Lilly. It had only been a day, but I missed her like crazy. She had spent most of the day in bed, and I had spent most of the day working, so we had barely talked.

On the car ride to her apartment, I tossed around the decision to take the money or not. I'd never been more confused about what to do in my life. By the time I got to Lilly's place, I was positive I was going to take the money. What was one more week when I had lied to her for almost three months?

Mrs. Sheffield was waiting outside of Lilly's apartment building for me and she had different plans.

Lucky me!

"To what do I owe the honor?" I asked sarcastically.

She didn't waste any time getting to the point.

"I've never seen Lilly this happy. I want you to continue to see her for another three months. Then you'll get your money."

"Wait a damn minute! A deal's a deal! I only have until the end of this week to make that payment, you can't do this!"

"I've spoken with the bank and it's taken care of, so what do you say? Do you want your payment made or not?"

"I can't keep doing this to her. We're in love. It's cruel. I want out now and I want to tell her the truth."

She burst into laughter.

"First of all, men know *nothing* about love—so don't even give me that bullshit," she said viciously. "Secondly, my daughter could *never* be in love with a guy like you. She's confused and blinded by her first boyfriend. Don't mistake that for love. Devin, should I remind you that I'm friends with the owners of the bank? You tell my daughter *anything* and I'll make sure you and your father lose everything as well as never work in this town again. Don't mess with me."

I couldn't say anything. She had me by the balls and I was so shocked by her viciousness that all I could do was stare at her.

"Also, you'll get out when I say you can, is that understood? Mr. Michaels, I always get what I want, never forget that. Three more months it is then?"

What could I do? What could I say? Maybe she was right about Lilly. Maybe Lilly really didn't love me. She *was* better than me for sure. There was nothing I could say to stop it, it was already started and I had to finish it or I'd lose everything, including Lilly.

"I won't say a word, but I'm not going anywhere in three months. I'm here to stay, Mom," I said sarcastically. I smiled with my teeth, but it never reached my eyes.

"We'll see about that."

Once the bitch walked away and before I went inside to see Lilly, I called the bank and asked about my dad's loan. The man told me that all was taken care of and I knew that I had to continue. As much as I hated it, I had to do it for at least three more months. I would just have to pretend that the money was never coming and I had to remember that the relationship was now real for me. Lilly was mine.

That night, even though we were both tired, Lilly and I snuggled in bed and talked. It had been over a week since we had sex and just as long since we had a decent conversation. I ran my fingers through her soft hair as we got it all out in the open.

"Shannon told me about what happened to you when you were younger." I traced the bruise on her cheek softly. I was glad to see it was beginning to fade. "Why didn't you tell me about it, baby?" I asked.

She suddenly looked uncomfortable.

"It was embarrassing—I don't like telling people about it. It makes me look weak." She shifted in bed so that she wasn't looking me in the face anymore.

"I'm sorry for what I said...that night. I had no idea you couldn't...you know," I couldn't bring myself to say it.

It hurt my heart that such a sweet and caring woman like Lilly would never experience motherhood. There were moms, like mine, who could walk away from their children like they were shit. Lilly would never do that. She would've been an extraordinary mother.

"I should've told you about the no kids thing. I tried that night. I'm not sure where you see this going with us." She swallowed hard and I could tell there were tears she was trying not to shed. "But if kids are something you want in your future, then you shouldn't count on me to be a part of that." Her voice sounded thick.

"I want you in my future. We'll worry about the rest later."

I leaned over and kissed her softly. She kissed me back harder and in fear of hurting, her I pulled back a little.

"I'm sorry," she said.

"Don't apologize, sweetie. I just don't want to hurt you. I'll give you nothing but soft kisses until you're all better," I whispered as I softly kissed the side of her neck.

She sucked in her breath.

"I'm feeling much better now," she sighed.

I laughed. She was so adorable.

"No, ma'am, not until you're *completely* healed," I playfully scolded.

"Seriously, I've never felt better." She grabbed my face and started to kiss me.

Vanilla and cherries—Lilly.

I could feel myself getting hard. Images of her face in ecstasy the first time we had sex flashed through my mind and then I went from just being hard to throbbing.

"Are you sure?" I asked in between kisses.

She didn't answer. Instead, she reached down and palmed my hardness through my pants. I hissed as she nibbled on my bottom lip. I kissed her back hard as she stuck her hand down my pants and wrapped her soft fingers around me.

"It's so hard and hot," she whispered in awe.

"That's what you do to me," I groaned into her neck.

There was nothing keeping us from having sex anymore and since I knew that no matter what we were going to stay together, I didn't stop myself.

I rolled her over onto her back and kissed her like I never had before. I stopped just long enough to pull her shirt over her head. Then everything stopped.

I stared down at her and was completely shaken. She was bruised all over. There was one large bruise on her side that actually looked like a shoe imprint. Blind rage rolled through me. I wanted to yell and scream. I wanted to find the son of a bitches that did this to her and I wanted to choke the life out of them.

"What's wrong?" She asked as she started to cover herself.

I reached up and pulled the blanket from her hands.

"Don't." The word felt like sand in my mouth. "Oh God, Lilly."

I ran my fingers softly over the large bruises all over her body. The small ones on her face didn't compare.

"They don't hurt much." She attempted to smile.

She pulled me down and kissed me again, but all I wanted to do was cry.

"I can't, baby. It's too soon. I'd hate myself if I hurt you."

I started to move away, but she grabbed my arm and pulled me back to her.

"Don't pull away, Devin, please. I need you to love me. Just make it all go away." She started to slowly kiss me again.

There was no way I could say no to her.

"We'll go slow and easy," I said in between kisses.

We did nothing but kiss and softly rub each other. I slowly removed her bra and threw it on the floor. Not once did she cover herself and her new confidence turned me on. I went straight for her nipple as I sucked it into my mouth and flicked it with my tongue.

Her breathing was erratic and her hands were in my hair, pressing my mouth to her. I sat up on my knees and pulled my shirt off. She followed me up and started kissing and touching my chest and neck.

"That feels so good," I rasped.

Somehow I lost control of the situation completely and she had pushed me over onto my back. She kissed and licked me all the way down my chest until she was at the top of my pants.

Then she roughly started to pull them down. I didn't stop her. I was hers completely. She could do with me whatever she wanted.

I had no problem letting her have her way with me. Not to mention, with her just getting out of the hospital yesterday, I didn't want to do anything that was too much for her. I let her take the reins.

Once she won the fight with my pants, she started to go down on me. Before she touched me with her mouth I saw her flinch and make a small noise. I stopped her.

"Are you OK?" I leaned up on my elbows and asked.

"I'm fine, just lay back." She pushed me back.

When she attempted to bend down I saw that she was in pain.

"Baby, stop, this is hurting you."

I sat up and slowly made her lay back. She tried to argue with me, but I covered her mouth with mine and kissed her softly and slowly. After kissing her until she was quiet, I gradually made my way down her body. I kissed every piece of skin I came to and sucked the sensitive parts. Every bruise I passed on my way down I kissed softly and made a silent promise to her with my mouth and hands to make it all better.

She grabbed handfuls of blanket and tiny, soft sighs came from her lips. The innocent noises I heard made my spine tingle and my groin ache. Lilly was natural. Everything she said and did while I worshipped her body was real and unrehearsed.

Everything I did to her was so new to her and it showed in her actions.

Making her feel good made me feel wonderful. When I made it to her pretty pink and black panties I peeled them off slowly. She panicked a little and tried to stop me, but I calmed her and began kissing her inner thigh. Her legs began to shake a little and I smiled to myself.

Her scent invaded my senses. The desire to taste her was extreme. I didn't want to scare her, so I moved extra slow. I softly blew on her sensitive spot to prepare her for what was coming next. She moaned and the sound was rough and husky.

I wrapped one arm around the outside of her hip in hopes of holding her still and then I very deliberately ran my available fingers up and down the inside of her moist lips. Her breath stopped. I used two fingers to hold her open and then slowly ran my tongue over her.

Her hips came off the bed. I wrapped my other arm around her hip and then buried my face between her legs. My mouth filled with her sweetness and my salivary glands began to pour.

I sucked and licked until I felt her body become tense. She was whining and panting. I kept going, flicking my tongue over her soft, pink hot spot faster and faster.

"Devin, if you don't stop, I'm gonna cum in your mouth," she said in between deep breaths.

Oh yes, please. I couldn't talk, but I heard myself growl with pleasure.

I kept going until finally she lifted her hips and had a very loud orgasm. She screamed my name over and over again as I licked at her new, tangy juices. She tasted so sweet. I held her hips as still as possible and didn't stop licking until I felt her entire body shaking.

I couldn't take it anymore. Now that I had tasted her, I had to feel her wrapped around me. I wasted no time as I easily climbed on top of her. Her eyes were glazed over and her face and body were glistening with a thin sheen of sweat. She looked me in the eye as I lifted her leg and slowly entered her.

This time I fit perfectly. I started to slowly thrust my hips. She felt so amazing and warm. I kept it slow and easy. No matter how bad I wanted to slam myself into her over and over again as fast as possible, I knew I had to remain calm so that I didn't hurt her.

Apparently, she had other ideas.

"Harder," she panted.

I lifted her leg higher and began to thrust my hips harder. Harder felt so fucking good. I still kept it at a slow pace. The build-up was incredible.

She was starting to squirm and whimper. She was getting close again.

"Faster, Devin, please, I can't take it." She lifted her other leg and wrapped both around my waist.

It wasn't long until I was pumping myself in and out— hard and fast. I could feel the sweat trickle down my face and back. She leaned up and started to kiss me, making my entire body ache while she moaned into my mouth. I kept going, but I just couldn't get deep enough. I wrapped my arms under her arms and around her shoulders and then started to move faster. My face was buried in her neck and I could feel her rapid pulse against my mouth.

"Yes! Don't stop. Please, baby, don't stop!" she was getting louder.

The room was filled with Lilly's cries of delight, my hard breathing, and the wonderful smacking sound of our bodies coming together.

I felt her body tighten around me and soon she was calling out my name in ecstasy. I could feel the moisture building up between the two of us as she trembled and that's all it took. I buried my face deeper in the side of her neck when I felt my orgasm take me.

I've never been a noise maker during sex, usually just hard breathing and an occasional growl when I cum. The noises and words that came from my mouth when I spilled myself inside of her were against my will.

It was the best orgasm of my entire life. I stayed inside of her until I could feel myself going limp. I could barely hold myself up I was so weak, so I rolled over to keep my weight off of her. Like a cat she snuggled up next to me and I wrapped my arm around her. I heard her breathing even out. As sleep took me away, I could think only one thing... I want this forever.

Twenty-Four
Blast from the Past

When I woke up Devin wasn't in my bed. I reached out for him and felt nothing but his pillow. Then I heard the shower water running and smiled to myself as I rolled onto my back and snuggled deeper into my bed.

I was feeling much better, it wouldn't be long until I could get back to work and things could return to normal. I climbed out of bed slowly, threw on some clothes, and went out to the kitchen. I put together a little bit of breakfast and then sat down and waited for Devin to finish his shower.

He looked so sexy when he came into the kitchen. His hair was slicked back and wet, and he smelled like fresh soap and shampoo.

"You shouldn't be out of bed, babe." He leaned in and gave me a sweet little pop kiss. "I was gonna cook you breakfast after

I took a shower. I was hoping to keep you stuck in that bed for the next few days," he said with a wink.

"I'm fine. I'll take a shower. After that you can keep me in bed for as long as you'd like," I smirked at him from across the small kitchen table.

"Do I *really* have to listen to all this mush?" Shannon said as she came into the kitchen.

Her red hair was piled on top of her head. She rubbed her eyes and yawned loudly.

I spent the entire day in bed. Devin stayed with me and we watched old movies and snuggled. Later that night he went and got some take-out for dinner. We ate in bed and shared our food. I fell asleep in his arms two hours later.

It was so nice just to be with him. While the sex was spectacular, it wasn't needed. We loved being together, just laughing and talking.

The next morning I woke up before Devin, and like a psycho girlfriend I laid there and watched him sleep. It was still so surreal that I was in love with such a gorgeous man and he loved me in return.

I can remember just a few months ago sitting at Mirabelle's with mom and wishing for this kind of relationship, and here I was, lying next to the man of my dreams.

I ran my fingers over the dips and curves of his muscled chest. I traced the outline of every tattoo my eyes could see. There were two matching stars on either side of his pelvis that peeked out of the drawstring waist on his sleep pants. The stars were designed to look as if they were crumbling and were perfectly nestled in the ripple of his lower abdominal muscles.

I left the star tats and made my way through the dark hair that surrounded his adorable navel. I watched as my fingers went up and down when I worked them across his abs muscles. The words *"All wounds become wisdom"* were inked diagonally down the side of his ribs in cursive.

I placed a soft kiss across the Japanese symbol on the right side of his chest and paid extra attention to the jagged knife that was tatted over his heart. It was magnificently detailed to look as if he'd been stabbed in the heart. Little drips of blood escaped the sides of the blade in red ink. It was the only color on his body and it stuck out.

I covered it with my hand. I didn't want to think of Devin being stabbed in the heart. I didn't want him to ever hurt. Only a man who was hurt deeply could be so shut off. Strangely, I understood his reasons even though I didn't know them and I felt honored that he had allowed me a tiny glimpse into his world.

I laid my head against his shoulder and took in the detail of the tattoo that covered the entire top of his arm. At a glance it looked like tangled, jagged vines, but looking at it closer, I could see there were words twisted into the vines. Fear...pain...sorrow...regret....hate. Each knotted word stabbed at my heart.

I reached up and ran my fingers through his hair and kissed his cheek.

"Stay," he whispered in his sleep. "Please, Lilly. Stay."

His peaceful sleep had turned into a nightmare. I could see the sweat beginning to collect on his forehead. His entire body seemed to tense up before my eyes. I snuggled closer to him and ran my fingers through his hair.

"You're having a nightmare, sweetie. I'm not going anywhere. I'm right here," I said to try and calm him.

"Mom, please don't leave me—Lilly, no!" He jumped up in a panic, his eyes wide in fear.

I sat back and let him have a moment. His panic-stricken eyes took me in until finally he reached out and pulled me back to him.

"Are you OK?" I asked.

"Yeah, I'm fine. What time is it?" He looked away and searched for a place to put his eyes so that they weren't on me.

"It's early still. Did you have a nightmare?"

"Yeah, it's no big deal." He shrugged and started to fidget.

"About your mom...and me?" I tentatively asked.

His eyes shot to mine and there was a brief flash of panic in his glazed over green eyes. Just as quickly, his smiling laid back persona slipped into place.

"So, what are we doing today, gorgeous?" He asked with a smirk.

He had completely ignored my question. We had never talked about his mother. I'd always sensed that it was a sore subject, but I gathered from my conversations with Jenny that his mom had left them when they were young.

"Devin," I reached out and laid my hand over his arm. "Do you wanna talk about it?"

"Yes, I wouldn't have asked if I didn't want to talk about it. Wanna have another movie in bed day?" He nuzzled my check.

"That's not what I was talking about, sweetie." He tensed up next to me. "I meant do you want to talk about the nightmare and your mom?"

His sweet and smiling face went dark.

"Just drop it, please."

He climbed out of bed and went into the bathroom. I heard the shower water turn on and I knew I had pushed the wrong button. I felt awful.

I followed him into the bathroom and stood in the door way. He stuck a hand into the shower water to check the temperature then he noticed me standing there.

"Come for the show?" He asked as he slowly started to untie his drawstring pants.

"Are you gonna give me a show?" I flirted back.

"Come here." His voice was stern and demanding.

I walked to him then leaned up to kiss his soft lips. The kiss started out soft and sweet, but soon Devin took over and our tongues were fighting for ground.

He backed me up until I felt the bathroom counter meet the back of my thighs. He stopped kissing me and quickly turned me to face the bathroom mirror. I watched our reflection as he very slowly kissed the side of my neck then bit down on my earlobe. His eyes never left mine in the mirror. It was so sexy.

He worked his hands around the bottom of my t-shirt, then lifted it and took it off of me. I was standing there in my panties in front of him and I couldn't bring myself to look at my naked reflection. I knew once I saw myself my mood would turn sour.

I turned my eyes away. I could only imagine how my pale, chunky body looked next to his firm, tan one.

"Don't look away," he said roughly in my ear.

I flicked my eyes back to his and held them there. As long as I looked into his eyes, I was fine. I just didn't want to see myself.

He ran his hands up my sides and brought them around to my stomach.

"Watch my hands," he rasped.

"No," I whispered.

I felt my expression drop. Looking at his hands meant looking at my stomach.

"Do you have a problem looking at yourself?" His breath blew into my ear as he nibbled softly on the lobe.

It felt so good and I let my eyes flutter closed.

"Open your eyes and look at yourself." His voice was rough.

My eyes popped back open and took us in. Like I had expected, his body looked darker and firmer compared to mine.

"I love looking at your body. It's so sexy and succulent." He ran his nose down my hairline and breathed me in. "I love kissing and tasting you here." He brought both his hands up and cupped my breasts. Then he slowly worked his hands back down my body until he was at my panty line. He dipped a finger inside my panties and ran it across my pleasure point. "And I especially love kissing and tasting you here."

My legs wobbled and a tiny noise escaped my lips.

"Did I mention that you taste amazing?" His tongue peeked out and licked quickly at the side of my neck.

He moved his finger again, barely grazing me on my most sensitive spot. My body begged for him to put pressure there and to move his fingers lower and deeper.

"I bet you want to be touched here," he pressed. "I bet you wanna cum. Don't you?"

"Yes." My voice sounded deep and seductive. It surprised me when I heard it.

He slowly started to push my panties down. Once they were at my ankles I stepped out of them. He ran his hands down my arms until they were cupping my hands. He intertwined our fingers as his kisses moved to the back of my neck. Then, very unexpectedly, he brought my hands up and placed them against my chest. Using his hands, he gently massaged my breasts with my own hands.

My skin rippled as he pressed my hands against my body and slowly worked them down over my stomach. They went further down, until he was pressing my finger into my moisture. My body was tense as I leaned my back against him.

Then there was a rhythm as he used my finger to massage my clit in a circular motion. It felt amazing, and before long I was starting to pant and moan softly. His hands left mine and the motion stopped.

"Don't stop," he whispered in my ear as he moved his hands up to caress the rest of me.

Hesitantly, I continued his rhythm on myself. His eyes beat into mine. At first there was a tiny bit of embarrassment, but once I felt his hardness press into my back and heard his breathing increase, I knew I was turning him on.

I nibbled on my bottom lip as the ache increased in my lower stomach.

"Next time you're alone and you touch yourself, I want you to fantasize about this moment."

The mirror was beginning to fog up and soon I couldn't see our reflections anymore. He spun me around and lifted me onto the bathroom counter like I weighed nothing. He pulled me to the edge of the counter then lifted me again as he pushed himself inside of me. I wrapped my legs around his waist and my arms around his neck.

Within seconds, I was coming apart and he moaned his approval as he gripped my ass. It was fast and hard. The bathroom was full of steam and heavy breathing. I heard him groan my name in my ear as he slammed himself inside me one final time.

252

It wasn't until I was done with my shower that I realized what he had done. He had effectively taken my mind away from all the questions I had about his mother by seducing me. I hated that he was so slick to use sex against me, but at the same time I wanted to applaud him.

*****

After that day I never mentioned his mother again. I knew in the back of my mind that Devin was more broken than he let on, but who wasn't? I just wished that he would talk about it.

A week later we went shopping with Shannon.

"I hate shopping malls," Devin said as he sucked on his cherry slushy. "It's full of teenage boys in skinny jeans and twelve year old girls with too much make-up on." He pointed to a boy with a green mohawk. "That boy's pants are tighter than the chick's that's with him."

"Skinny jeans are kind of the thing now," Shannon laughed.

We were on the hunt for the perfect birthday present for our friend Erin, and Devin had tagged along. He looked funny, all tall and tattooed among the girly shops. Every now and again I'd catch him shaking his head and rolling his eyes. He was such a guy.

"Lil, you know you want a pair of skinny jeans," Shannon joked.

"Um, hell no. You'll never catch me wearing skinny jeans or anything camouflaged," I said as I browsed.

"I don't care what you wear. I prefer you naked anyway."
Devin snaked his hand behind me and grabbed my ass.

I smacked his hand away and felt my face heat up. Being affectionate in public was new for me and I think he got a kick out of making me blush.

Shannon rolled her eyes. "Why no camouflage?" she asked. "I think some of the pink camo stuff is cute."

"The whole point of camouflage is to blend in. A girl my size ain't blending into anything."

Shannon and I laughed while Devin shook his head.

He hated when I made fat girl jokes, but it was kind of my thing. Growing up I learned quickly to make the jokes before anyone else could. It slowed the teasing if I made people laugh with me instead of at me.

"I gotta pee. I'll meet up with you guys in a bit, OK?" Shannon said, as she left the store.

Devin and I walked out behind her and made our way to the next store, passing Victoria's Secret on the way.

"OK, now that's more like it. Come on," he grabbed my hand and pulled me toward the store.

I'd always made it a point to *never* go into Victoria's Secret. I knew what that bitch's secret was and it had everything to do with stringy panties with not enough fabric to cover my ass.

Shannon had once tried to talk me into buying a pair of thongs, but the thought of that string going in and never coming out always scared me. Losing the thin line of fabric was a very real possibility for a girl my size. Not to mention, looking like a sumo wrestler was never my thing.

"I am *not* going in there." I pulled my arm back.

"Why not? You'd look hot in that black thing over there," he whispered in my ear as he nodded at a sheer piece of scrap fabric hanging in the showcase window.

"I think not," I blushed. "I'd never wear something like that."

"Not even if I said pretty please with a cherry on top?" He leaned in and wrapped his arms around my waist.

"Nope, not even then." I latched my arms around his neck.

We stood that way as people walked around us and paid us no attention.

"What if I promised to suck the cherry on top?" he whispered against the side of my neck before planting a soft kiss behind my ear.

There was no winning when he talked to me like that.

"OK, fine." I peeked up at him through my dark lashes and saw a soft smile spread across his face.

"I can't wait to get you home and see you in that thing," he smirked.

Home. The way he said it made my heart skip a beat.

He intertwined his fingers with mine and turned back toward Victoria's Secret again.

I followed behind him and face-planted into his back when he came to an abrupt stop.

"Well, hello, Devin. How are *things*?" Renee asked with a sneer.

I didn't need to see her face to know it was her. I'd never forget her voice. I guess I'd hoped that I'd never see her again, especially not while I was with Devin. Ever since the day I found out that the Renee that ruined my life was the same Renee that used to be his side piece, I'd had a tiny fear that we'd run into her while we were together. My biggest fear had happened.

"I'm good," he said with a clipped tone.

Then it happened. Her eyes left his face and met mine. Her expression changed from amused anger to one filled with total rage.

"Don't tell me you're with *her!*" she pointed at me with disgust on her face.

"That's none of your business," he evenly replied.

"Oh my God, Lilly? Large Lilly?" she threw her head back in laughter and I felt Devin's body tense. "Didn't we deal with you that day in the woods?" She laughed to herself. "Oh my God, I still remember your face that day. It was fucking priceless. I thought I'd never see you again. I see you still have that weight issue thing going on." She motioned with her hand at my body.

I felt like I was dying a thousand tiny deaths. The embarrassment I felt could never be put into words. Why'd she have to do this now? Why in front of Devin?

"I can't believe you actually switched schools because of that. We were just fucking around with you. A girl your size could take some roughing up," she continued. "And then your

256

bitch of a mom called the school on us. You got me kicked off the cheerleading squad, you fat cow!"

Devin looked down at me with questions in his eyes. I could almost hear him asking me why I didn't tell him. Then I saw something else written in his eyes...anger. His face was turning bright red and I thought for a minute that he was going to yell at me and join in with Renee and call me mean names like we were in high school again.

Instead, he turned his attention to Renee and took a menacing step toward her, causing her to back up a little.

"If you ever talk her like that again, you'll regret it for the rest of your life. If you ever come near her again I'll personally make your life a living Hell. I've never put my hands on a woman in my life, but if I even think for a minute that you're causing this girl," he pointed at me. "A single minute of stress or heartache I'll personally come to your house and choke the living shit out of you. Do you understand?"

His voice was a sinister whisper and I watched as Renee's face turned from red to white. She gawked back at him like he was a mad man before shaking her head and backing away.

His body relaxed and his facial expression softened as he turned to me.

"Are you OK, baby?" His voice had softened, too. I loved it.

"I'm fine, a little embarrassed, but I'm OK." I reached down and picked up the bag I didn't even realize I'd dropped.

"You have nothing to be embarrassed about." He leaned in and kissed the tip of my nose. "If anyone should be embarrassed, it should be her for acting like a massive bitch. You, on the other hand, are perfect."

He kissed me and everything and everyone around us disappeared.

That night he stayed at my place. He was an insatiable beast and I loved it. He didn't take his hands off me all night. I blame the tiny piece of scrap fabric he bought me from Victoria's Secret. We made love until we were both exhausted and passed out.

Twenty-Five
Mommy Issues

When I left for work, Lilly was still sleeping. There's nothing more beautiful than a sexually satisfied Lilly sleeping like an angel. I never thought there'd be a day when I had to force myself to leave a woman to go to work, but she was a magnetic force. Being around her made me feel like I was balanced, like I wasn't breaking apart and splitting into different directions all the time.

Since meeting her there had only been a handful of moments when I felt my usual madness and all of those moments had something to do with either her or Jenny being in some form of pain. Other than that, I felt whole again. I hadn't felt that way since before my mother left.

I sang along with the radio while I worked on a blown head gasket in an old Chevy. For the first time since I was a boy, I didn't feel like there was a fifty pound weight on my shoulders.

"You sing like shit," Jenny said as she threw a piece of candy at me.

I was glad to see she wasn't affected by the big, traumatic scene from a few weeks before. I had to give it to her, she was tough as nails. I couldn't be more proud of her.

"More candy? What did Josh do now?"

"He beat the shit out of Justin and embarrassed me at school."

"Justin?"

"My date *that* night," she shrugged. "It wasn't his fault. He was just being a normal teenager and getting drunk."

"He shouldn't have left you alone like that. I'm glad Josh got a piece of him. Anymore news on the guys? I'd love to get my hands on them."

Jenny could never lie to me. She had a tell sign and for years she'd been trying to get it out of me so that she could make sure she didn't do it. There was no way in Hell I'd tell her so she could lie in my face. It was the silliest thing, but every time she lied her nostrils flared a bit.

I watched as she shuffled her feet and then turned away.

"Nope, nothing," she said as she dug into her little bag of candy for another piece.

"Now look me in my face and say that," I said.

She turned my way and her nostrils flared before she even started to speak

"Cut the shit, Jenny. I'll just go ask dad. Did they find out who they were or anything?"

"They did, but I don't want you getting your ass arrested for murder. Just let it go and let the cops deal with it. I'll tell you if you promise not to touch them. We don't got the money to bail your crazy ass out of jail."

"I promise." I held my hands up.

"You promise what?" She asked.

"I promise I won't touch them."

A baseball bat to their knees wasn't technically me touching them.

She told me and the worst part was I knew the bastards from high school. They were out on bail, so soon, very soon, I'd see them again. Eric Fitch, Ryan Lang, and Chuck Mitchell—I had a bat with their names on it.

"Don't tell Lilly I told you, OK? She didn't want to tell you for the same reasons I didn't want to tell you."

"I won't say anything."

And I wouldn't.

I felt a tiny sting at knowing that Lilly had withheld information from me, but I guess I can understand why she did.

I stayed home that night, but only because I had a guy bringing over a car super early. Lilly was going back to work tomorrow anyway, so instead, we stayed on the phone until we were both falling asleep.

The next morning I got an early start and spent most of the day working. Life was good and I couldn't wait to get back over to Lilly's and be near her.

I heard a car door outside the garage so I walked out and was met with a tall, gangly man standing beside a Mercedes. He was older and balding a little, but still dressed pretty nice. I could tell by looking at him that he wasn't from Walterboro.

"Can I help you?" I asked.

"I'm looking for a Harold Michaels. Is he here?"

"No sir, but I'm here. What can I do for you?"

"Are you Devin?"

"That's me." I suddenly felt uncomfortable with him being here.

He reached out his hand for me to shake it.

"My name's Dan Archer. It's nice to meet you."

I shook his clammy hand, but I couldn't say the same. It wasn't nice to meet him. If anything, he was slowing me down and keeping me from my girl.

"Can I ask what this is about?"

"I'm here about your mom, Laura Michaels."

I hadn't heard her name said out loud in so long and it was like a slap in the face. He needed to leave.

"She doesn't live here anymore," I said dryly.

I turned and rudely walked away. I didn't know who he was or what the hell he wanted, but anything that had to do with *her* I wanted no part of.

"Devin, you need to hear this!" He called after me.

"Don't talk to me like you know me, and I don't need to hear anything except my shower water. Get lost."

I turned again.

"Your mom and I were together for the last seven years," he said loudly.

"Good for you. Although, I wouldn't be too proud of that if I were you." I was halfway across the yard when I realized he was following me. "Dude, if you don't get the hell off of my property I'm gonna kick your ass!" I started back toward him.

I would, too! I didn't need this shit. My dad and Jenny didn't need it, either. We were moving on with our lives. My life was just starting to make sense and the last thing I needed was anything that had to do with the woman who birthed me.

He didn't move as I got in his face.

"Devin, just listen."

"One," I started to count.

I was already passed being pissed off. I was giving him a chance to turn and leave.

"There are things you need to know." He started to panic.

"Two." I swear if he was still standing there when I got to three I was going to punch him square in the face.

"If we could just wait until your dad's here, I really have something I think you all should know."

Oh, hell no! He was not rubbing this crap in my dad's face. My dad didn't need to see the man my "mother" was fucking. He didn't need to know that this man even existed.

"Time's up, Fuck face...three." I snatched him up around the collar and hauled his scrawny frame upward.

He pulled back as if he was going to run, but I was much stronger. I pulled back my arm ready to feel his nose against my fist.

"Devin, your mom passed away last week!" He shouted in a panic and I could see the sadness in his eyes.

Everything stopped. My fist sat suspended in the air and all the oxygen left my body. Black spots danced in my vision and I felt my other hand loosen around his collar.

"Are you OK, buddy?" I heard him ask.

"I'm not your fucking buddy." I shoved him away. "How'd she die?" I croaked.

"Lung cancer. I only came because I thought you and Jenny should know. I would've liked to talk to your father about this. I bare no ill will with him. Your mother and I met a year after she moved to Maryland."

Maryland. That's where she ran off to. That's where she's been all these years, living her life as if Jenny and I never existed and now, she was dead.

I never got a chance to tell her how badly she scarred me. I never got to tell her how I felt, how I hated her for turning me into a heartless bastard. I hated her for leaving me and Jenny. I hated her, and now she was gone. She's been gone for many years, but I think there was always a part in the back of my brain that thought I'd see her again one day.

I was disgusted by the fact that as much I as hated to admit it, I'd hoped to see her again. She was gone. My mother was dead.

"Leave."

"Devin, I think I should talk to your father."

"I'll deal with my father, you leave."

I'm not sure what it was in my face that made this guy turn and leave, but he didn't hesitate.

I watched as he walked back to his luxury car and pulled away. I felt as though my feet had grown roots. I couldn't move, I couldn't breathe, and the worst part was it hurt so bad knowing she was dead. She didn't care about me a bit, yet here I was deep inside mourning her.

No way could I tell dad and Jenny. No way.

Suddenly, all I felt was anger. How dare she die without saying goodbye to us? She died from lung cancer, not a sudden death. She didn't die in a car accident or have a fucking massive heart attack. She had found out that she was dying and she still didn't come to say goodbye.

I lost all control of myself as I rampaged through the garage. I pulled over tool-boxes and busted out car windows with a tire iron. Poor Lucy got the brunt of it.

After I destroyed the garage, I was inside tearing through the refrigerator. I sucked down one of Dad's beers, but it wasn't enough. I could still feel. I ripped open the liquor cabinet and grabbed dad's large bottle of Crown Royal. I didn't even bother with a shot glass as I downed the burning liquid. The fire in my throat seemed to relieve the pain in my chest.

I needed to not feel. I didn't want to feel anything.

I wished to Hell that Dan Archer had stayed so I could pound my fist into his face. I was full of anger and now I was also full of liquor and I needed a release of some sort before I fucking exploded.

That's how Jenny found me, drunk out of my mind, sitting at the kitchen table.

"Devin!" She came busting in the back door. "Are you OK? Someone destroyed the garage and busted a window in your car. What the fuck happened?" She was panicked.

Her wide green eyes beat into me...so innocent. She was just a baby when that bitch left us and now she had the nerve to leave again.

I'd kill anyone who ever tried to hurt her...anyone. Actually, I had a date with a baseball bat and an attempted rapist's face. If he was man enough to beat a female senseless, then he was man enough to take the beating that was coming his way.

My chair skidded across the floor as I jumped up. Eric Fitch. I knew where he lived. He thought he was going to hurt my Jenny and my Lilly and get away with it. Well, he had another thing coming.

"Are you drunk? Devin, what the hell's wrong? What's going on?" The worry in her eyes fueled my rage.

I turned away and headed for the back door. The screened door was ripped off of its hinges as I tore through it. Then I was at my car. I was drunk, I could feel myself dragging, but it didn't matter.

I couldn't find a baseball bat, so instead I picked up the tire iron I had used before and hopped into my car, broken glass and all.

"Devin!" I heard Jenny scream after me as I squealed tires down the road.

The ride to his house was a blur. I had drunk too much and I could still feel. I was so angry I was seeing red.

I ran into the back of a car when I finally made it to Eric's driveway. I beat the hell out of the door for what felt like hours and then finally he answered. It pissed me off more when I saw the look in his eyes. He remembered me and he knew why I was there. He knew it was my baby sister.

I didn't even say two words to him.

"Look, man, I'm sorry." He held up his hands like a little bitch.

I yanked him down the front porch steps to the middle of his yard and then I began to unmercifully beat the living shit out of him. I'd left my tire iron in the car, but I think using my fists felt better. It hurt so good to beat him in the face. My knuckles cracked with each hit.

He called for help and at one point I was almost positive someone else was screaming for me to stop, but I couldn't and I didn't want to. I wanted him to hurt the way Lilly and Jenny had hurt. I wanted to break him the way that I was broken.

Once he stayed down and I didn't see him moving anymore, I dropped to the ground next to his limp body. There was blood everywhere, but I didn't care. That bastard needed to bleed.

When I stood I could feel myself leaning. I hoped that I could make it to the car, but the liquor was in my veins and no matter how badly I wanted it to numb me, I still could feel.

I felt like I was coming apart, like there were pieces of me trying to run away from each other in opposite directions, and it was ten times worse than before.

How was I ever going to feel centered again? How was I ever going to feel anything other than pain and anger again? I needed to feel centered. I needed to be alive and I needed to be balanced again.

I turned back to my car and hopped in. I needed Lilly.

Twenty-Six

Comfort

I hadn't heard from Devin pretty much all day. My first day back at work sucked and I'd spent the day excited to see him. He was supposed to come over, but he never did. I called him and texted, but I heard nothing.

At one point, Jenny called and asked if I had heard from him. I could tell by her voice that something was wrong, but when I asked she said nothing. That of course made me worry more.

As much as I hated it, the idea of him and another woman popped into my head. He was gorgeous and I knew women found him attractive. It would hurt to find out he was seeing someone else.

I sat up in bed watching TV with my phone in hand. I kept almost dozing off and jumping, and then finally, at some point, I fell asleep.

A loud pounding on the door woke me. I waited for a bit hoping that Shannon would get it, but then I remembered she wasn't home. I peeled the comforter back and climbed out of bed. Then I remembered I was worried about Devin and ran to the door.

Once I got to the door, I checked the peep hole and saw his face. Relief filled me and I suddenly felt a rush of happiness. I opened the door with a smile on my face that soon melted when I saw his messy appearance.

The doorframe held him up as he leaned all of his weight against it. Expressionless, bloodshot eyes stared back at me as he lifted his hand and ran it roughly down his unshaved face. His hair was disheveled and there was blood on the front of his shirt. Panic rose up as I took him in. I rushed to him and ran my fingers down his body, as I checked for injuries.

"You're bleeding! Oh my God, Devin! What happened? Are you OK?" I went on and on as I checked him over.

"It's not my blood," he slurred.

I took a better look at his gorgeous face. His unfocused eyes attempted to meet mine and it was then that the smell of liquor reached my nose.

"You're drunk?"

"Abso-fucking-lutely." He attempted to move toward me and almost fell over.

I wrapped my arms around him and helped him into my apartment. Once we made it to the couch I let him collapse onto the cushion before I went straight to work on his clothes. I removed his blood-stained shirt first and threw it to the side. Quickly, I checked him over again just to be sure that he wasn't injured somewhere. His skin felt cold and clammy against my fingertips.

His knuckles were busted open, so I went to the bathroom and got a wet towel and the first aid kit. I cleaned his fingers then wrapped them up.

I felt fingers in my hair and looked up to see a very drunk Devin starting back at me.

"You're so fucking beautiful," he whispered as his heavy head fell against the back of my couch again.

Shaking my head, I dropped onto my knees on the floor and removed his boots.

Once I was done getting Devin out of his shoes, I went to the hallway closet and pulled out a blanket for him. When I got back to the couch, he was standing there looking back at me in all his tattooed, muscled glory. He was still leaning a bit to the side when his eyes locked on mine.

"Come here," he rasped.

He looked as if he was about to crumble and I couldn't tell if it was the alcohol or if something was really breaking him down.

"Are you OK, baby?" I asked.

He closed his eyes and sighed. "I love it when you call me baby."

I went to him and he groaned as I softly ran my hands up his chest and put my arms around his neck. On my tiptoes, I softly kissed the line of his neck and his chin.

"Tell me what happened, Devin."

When he finally opened his eyes, he looked at me differently. The calm and collected Devin was gone and an anxiety-ridden shell of a man stood before me. His shoulders felt tense beneath my fingers and his eyes held a crazed demeanor.

"I need you, Lilly." He captured my face softly in his hands as he slurred the words.

"Please tell me what happened?"

"Make it go away, baby," he whispered as he leaned in and started to kiss me.

I let him as I melted against his body. He collapsed against the couch once more, but this time he took me with him. Not once did he break our kiss, and soon, I felt his velvet tongue against mine. I kissed him back and let my fingers play in the hair at the back of his neck.

He broke the kiss and started down the side of my neck.

"I need you, Lilly," he repeated against my skin.

"I'm here." I bit at my bottom lip to stop myself from moaning.

"Please, just make it all go away," he drunkenly begged.

"I don't know what's going on, but tell me what to do to make it better. I want to make it better, Devin." I stopped him and stared into his eyes as I waited for his response.

"Don't leave me," he said desperately.

272

"I'm not going anywhere. I'm here. I'll do whatever it takes to make it better." I wanted to cry.

He looked so hurt and afraid. It was strange to see such a strong, confident man so lost and unsure.

He flipped me onto my back on the couch and crawled on top of me. His movements were less calculated—slower than usual.

"I want you. I need to be inside you," he said aggressively.

His hands were clumsy as he leaned back and started to remove my flannel pants. He growled in appreciation when he saw that I wasn't wearing any panties. I said nothing as he angrily pulled at my shirt to get it off of me.

"I want to see your skin. I need you," he kept repeating.

Leaning up, I quickly pulled my camisole over my head. Instead of his usual slow sexual way, he fell on top of me again and quickly entered me. It caught me so off guard that I gasped. My body easily accepted him, so there was no pain, but it was so unlike Devin that for a brief minute I felt fear.

Once I looked up into his face my fear melted away and all I wanted to do was make whatever was hurting him go away. He looked down at me and although there were no tears on his cheeks, he looked like he was about to cry. He buried his face in my neck so that I couldn't see his face anymore.

Something was definitely wrong. I held on to him and my heart broke as he rocked against me over and over again. The couch creaked with his every thrust and the sound of our bodies smacking echoed throughout the room.

273

"I only want to feel you, baby, nothing else, just you," he whispered into my hair.

His movement became jerky as he sped up. He thrust into me over and over again, harder each time. His hot breath pounded against the side of my neck. I said nothing as he found comfort in my body. I just held him close to me and every now and again, I kissed the side of his neck.

I felt his body tense up as he growled out his release and slammed into me one final time. His full body weight pressed against me when his arms went weak and he dropped onto me completely.

When he finally removed his face from my neck and looked down at me I could see the realization in his eyes of what had just occurred. I never said no, but he never really asked. Quickly, I cupped his cheeks with my hands and kissed him softly.

"Did I hurt you? I never want to hurt you," he said with a thick slur.

"It's OK, I'm OK," I whispered.

He said nothing. He just stared back at me like he was afraid I'd push him away and run for my life. Then his expression changed, and tears filled his eyes. I'd never seen a grown man cry in my life and my heart crushed inside my chest as he buried his face in my neck once more and wept loudly.

"I'm going to lose you. I am. You're the best thing that's ever happened to me and I'm going to lose you." He drunkenly cried.

Twenty-Seven

Damage Control

I woke up the following morning with swollen, busted knuckles, a splitting headache, and only one memory from the day before.

My mother was dead and I, as much as I hated to do it, had to break the news to dad and Jenny. I tried to get up, but I was pinned beneath an arm. It was Lilly's. She was holding me close to her chest sleeping in the sitting position on the couch.

Her poor neck was going to have one hell of a kink in it. Then I remembered everything. I'd destroyed the garage and then beaten Eric Fitch within an inch of his life. I was sure that once I got home there would be cops there waiting to take me to a jail.

The final memory slammed against me and I felt even sicker to my stomach. I'd shown up at Lilly's house and pretty much attacked her. Yet, here she was holding me close and taking care of me.

I slid from underneath her arm and softly laid her down on the couch. I pulled a throw blanket over her then went and took a shower. Thankfully, I kept an extra set of clothes at her place, so I had something to change into.

When I walked back into the living room all showered and fresh, Lilly was sitting up on the couch with big sad eyes.

"Are you OK?" She asked in a scratchy voice.

She looked exhausted and had barely gotten any sleep last night I'm sure.

"I'm fine. Are you OK?" I asked.

I needed to know that she was OK, and that I didn't hurt her or do anything that would push her away.

"You scared me last night." She tugged on the end of her hair then twirled it around her finger.

That was all it took. I went to her and dropped to my knees in front of her.

"Lilly, I'm so sorry. Please forgive me. I'd never do anything to hurt you. I don't know what came over me. I got some bad news yesterday and I just needed you. You always make me feel better."

"What was the bad news?" she asked.

I told her everything. I started at thirteen when my mother left and ended with yesterday when I had found out about her death. When I was done, there were tears on my cheeks and I was in Lilly's arms again.

"Do you want me to go with you to tell Dad and Jenny?" She was so selfless.

There would be a time when I would have to tell her the truth about how we started, too, but it could wait a little longer. Too much had already happened. We needed a drama break.

"Please. I need you to be there."

Dad cried like I expected him to. I think deep down he had always thought she'd come back. I also think he was upset by the fact that he wasn't there for her in the end. Dad was just like that. Even though she had run out on him, he still felt like it was his duty to take care of her.

Jenny didn't really respond. If she did, she waited until she was out of our sight to do so. More than likely that's what she did. Jenny wasn't one for tears, especially in front of people.

Lilly stayed to help me clean up my mess in the garage and then we took my car to get the windows fixed. I never heard anything from the police so I assumed Eric Fitch had lived and wasn't planning on pressing any charges. The bastard got what he deserved. Lilly wasn't too happy about it when I told her that I had beat him so badly, but she had to know I'd find out. As a man who loved her and my sister so deeply, there was no way I wouldn't have defended their honor.

By the time I was taking her home, it was getting late and we both had to work the next day. I was grateful to Lilly for skipping out on work for me, but I couldn't ask her to do it again.

The plan was to drop her off at home and go home to be with Dad and Jenny, but once I got to Lilly's door something inside me needed to stay. Thankfully, she asked to me stay and so we got ready for bed and crashed early.

When I woke up it was still dark out. A sliver of light from the cracked bathroom door lit a small corner of the room. Thinking that Lilly was probably just using the bathroom, I rolled over and tried to go back to sleep.

I was almost out when I heard her gagging in the bathroom. I climbed out of bed and went to her.

"Baby, are you okay?"

"Yes! I'm fine." She gagged again. "Please don't come in here."

I didn't listen. Instead, I got a cold washcloth and handed it to her. She was dry heaving, and her skin looked pale.

"Did you eat something bad, sweetie?"

"I think so. I'll be out in a minute."

I left her alone and went and waited in bed. I heard her gagging more, and then I heard the water running as she brushed her teeth.

When she climbed into bed it was late and we were both so tired that we fell back to sleep instantly.

I had another dream about my mother leaving me, except in this nightmare, we said goodbye to each other. I didn't feel any fear or sadness. Instead, I felt the warmth of Lilly's hand as she held it. I looked over to see her standing next to me smiling.

"Are you leaving me, too? "I asked.

"I'm not going anywhere." She squeezed my hand.

I woke up with a happy smile the next morning.

278

Twenty-Eight
Impossible Possibilities

"I'm not sure what I'm doing wrong. I hardly eat and when I do eat I can't keep it down. This stomach bug is kicking my ass, yet I'm still freaking gaining weight!" I said in aggravation. "My damn pants won't even button anymore."

No way would I go out and buy a bigger size. I swear I'd be one of those sloppy women who wore sweatpants every day before I went up a size.

"That's what happens when you get comfortable in a relationship. You and Devin have been seeing each other for close to five months. That's kind of early to be getting comfortable, but hey, to each his own," Shannon said as she flipped through a magazine.

"Yeah, I guess so. I don't know. Wow, it *has* been almost five months. That's crazy." I flashed a big, happy smile.

I was thinking about everything that had happened in the last few months—so many things, bad and good. Devin was worth the bad things, he was everything I could've asked for.

I suppose at some point I should tell him about the money. He wasn't with me for the money; Devin wasn't that kind of guy. Things couldn't have been more perfect, and like Shannon, he was clueless about it. It wasn't like I lived the life of a person with millions, so how could he have known?

"Oh my God, I'm cramping so freaking bad. This period is kicking my ass big time. I wish Aunt Flo would go straight to Hell." She sat back and rubbed her lower stomach. "You wouldn't happen to have a tampon on you would you? I really don't feel like walking over to the store. That crazy-eyed boy is working today. You know, the one who stares at you the entire time you're in there?"

"Yeah, he's creepy." I reached into my purse and dug around and then it hit me.

I couldn't even remember the last time I had a period. I wasn't regular all the time, as in I didn't get it on the same exact date every month, but I'd never missed an entire month before. As I sat and thought about it, I hadn't had a period in *at least* three months.

"What's that face about? Do you have one or not?" Shannon asked.

"Shannon, I haven't had a period in over three months," I said, confused.

A list of all the reasons for a missed period ran through my mind.

Cervical cancer, cysts, an awful female disease that would make my boobs fall off. Everything I ran through my mind was bad. It would be my luck that I'd die from some gruesome disease right after finding love and happiness.

"I know this is kind of a touchy subject, but do you think you should get a pregnancy test?" Her eyes got large. "What if you're prego?"

"Trust me, that's impossible."

"Hey, you never know. Crazier shit has happened, Lil."

"Babies are not in my future, but I guess I should set an appointment and have myself checked. I hope it's nothing serious." I frowned.

"Yeah, it can't hurt. I hope it's nothing, too. But could you imagine Devin's face if you *were* prego though? He'd totally shit himself." We laughed.

A week later we weren't laughing anymore. A week later we stood over a piss stick in the hallway bathroom with a big bright pink positive sign.

I shook it like an old thermometer then looked at it again. It was definitely positive.

"Well, if I'm reading this right," Shannon held up the box for the pregnancy test. "You're pregnant."

After years of being told I'd never have children, I should've felt happy. I should've been elated with the possibility of holding a little baby in my arms and being called mommy, but I wasn't. All I felt was fear.

It wasn't supposed to be happening for me. All the specialists I had gone to when I was younger swore it would never happen. In my mind something was wrong and if something wasn't wrong, something would be. I couldn't have been that lucky.

I tried not to think about it until after my appointment. There was no need to get my hopes up or make Devin crazy for no reason. He'd hate me. I'd promised him that it was impossible. We'd had unprotected sex because conceiving wasn't something that would ever happen for me and yet, there was a little pink line on a stick that said it had.

Later that night Devin came over and we lounged in bed and watched TV. He attempted conversation with me so many times, but I didn't feel like talking.

"Are you feeling OK, baby? You've been quiet all night and you barely touched your dinner. Are you *still* having stomach problems?"

"Something like that," I responded.

"You can talk to me about anything, you know?" He smiled down at me.

"I know. I'm really OK."

I wanted to tell him so badly. I wanted him to hold me and tell me that everything would be alright, but a tiny voice in the back of my head kept repeating that I could never have a baby. My body couldn't and if I was really pregnant, I'd lose it.

Devin had entirely too much going on in his life, I didn't want to add that to the list.

On appointment day I lied about having to work. It was something I wanted to do alone. I sat in the waiting room and did something I never did, I bit my nails. When the nurse called me back I got a bad case of anxiety. Something deep down was telling me that the doctor would have bad news.

When Dr. Dandridge came into the small examination room I was sitting on the exam table in a paper gown. My fingers were starting to hurt from squeezing them together so hard and even though the room was warm, I felt like I was freezing all over.

"Long time no see, kiddo," Dr. D said with a big white smile.

I had started seeing him when I was younger, right after the big traumatic teenage mob attack. He was the only doctor that I went to that didn't make me feel like I'd die within the hour if I didn't suddenly lose fifty pounds. I always felt very comfortable with him.

He was a younger doctor and very friendly—tall and skinny with big, blue eyes and salt and pepper hair. Shannon came with me on my last appointment and she'd had a crush on him ever since.

"So, what's new?" he said as he tapped his pen against his clipboard.

"Um, I haven't had a period in three months. I took a pregnancy test and it was positive. I'm kind of thinking there might be something wrong." I nervously cracked my knuckles.

"Hmmm, well, let's have a look and see what's going on, shall we?" He continued to smile, but I could see a small hint of worry in his eyes.

He knew my situation. He knew that a baby wasn't a possibility.

He did a vaginal exam first. I kept peeking down at him and every now and again I'd catch the perplexed look on his face.

Something was definitely wrong.

"Well, Lilly, your cervix is definitely different."

What the hell did that mean? Was that bad? Was my cervix covered in cancer and I'd be dead in ten hours? The Facts man! I needed facts! I had stuff to take care of. I had to make sure Devin and his family were a part of my will and I needed to say my goodbyes.

I was in the throes of a very massive panic attack and he was leaning back like he was on a Caribbean cruise. All he needed was a fruity drink with a freaking umbrella sticking out of it and a pair of sunglasses.

He pulled down my paper gown to cover me and then he rolled back on his stool and removed his plastic gloves.

"Let's do an ultrasound," he said as he rolled over a large piece of machinery with a tiny TV screen on the front.

He covered the bottom of me with another sheet before pulling my paper gown over to reveal my chubby stomach.

The clear jelly he squirted on my stomach felt warm and then he was gliding a little white wand over the surface.

The black and white screen lit up with a fuzzy picture. It looked like the screen that popped up when you forgot to pay your cable bill. There was nothing there, just a mass of black reminding me that my stomach would never house a child and then, there it was.

The profile of a baby—it's overly large head and tiny nose. Two arms and two legs sprung from its tiny center. It was hard to make it out on the screen, but it was definitely a baby.

I looked away from the screen and down to my stomach as if I needed to make sure that these pictures were definitely coming from me and that he didn't sneak and stick the little wand on another patient who had accidently walked into the wrong room.

He was still pressing it against me, moving it around to show me different views of the small person that was tucked away inside my stomach.

I was in shock and from the look on his face, he was shocked as well.

"Congratulations, Lilly. It looks like you're about fourteen weeks." Dr. D's big, blue eyes crinkled at the corners with his big smile.

As if I didn't understand, and technically I didn't, I asked, "Fourteen weeks?"

"Yes ma'am. The baby measures a little over three months."

"But I was just in the hospital, they didn't say anything. Is *it* OK?" The words sounded as if they'd been crushed.

"Well, somehow they missed it, and yes, *the baby* seems to be OK. I'll have to have some tests done, of course," he beamed.

The baby—there was a baby in there. I looked down at my stomach again before turning back to the screen. I was in shock. Maybe I was dreaming. It couldn't be real.

Then he pressed a button and a noise sounded. It was a heartbeat, strong and steady, soothing me and letting me know that it was real. I was pregnant and my baby's heart was beating.

"Want to know what you're having?" he asked.

"Can you tell that now?" I was still in a state of disbelief.

"Sometimes we can, if the baby's willing to show us. Do you want to know or do you want it to be a secret?"

"What am I having?" My voice sounded off, like a really cool female robot from the future.

"It's a girl."

In that moment, my life was changed forever. A perfect little piece of me and Devin was coming—a little princess.

After setting four different appointments to four different specialists, I left the doctor's office.

Dr. Dandridge had assured me after double checking everything over and over again, that I was indeed pregnant and the baby and I were both healthy. The follow-up appointments were just a precaution because of my past health issues, but it was definitely happening.

I cried once I was alone in my car. Happy tears streamed down my face and euphoria filled every crevice of my body.

On the drive home, all I could think about was Devin and what his reaction might be. His words from the first time we'd had sex rang through my mind.

Do you think I wanna get stuck with you like that?

Would he hate me, or would he be happy? A lot had changed since that very first time. We were together and we were in love.

How would I go about telling him? It's such a sensitive time for him and his family with the second loss of his mom. Maybe a baby would be a welcomed thing for his family *because* of the loss of his mom.

I think Dad and Jenny would be ecstatic. It was Devin that I was worried about. If a baby wasn't something he wanted, I'd have to let him go. I could do it alone and I could financially take care of a baby.

I decided that no matter what happened between Devin and me, the baby was a blessing, and I was going to treat it as such.

When I pulled up at my apartment, I sat in my car and laid my hand over my belly. Now that I knew why I was gaining, the extra weight around the middle didn't seem like such a curse.

When I walked into my apartment I was met by my mother. She scared the crap out of me and I screamed a little.

"What the hell, Mom?" I clutched my chest. "I'm so having my locks changed. You're trying to give me a freaking heart attack!" I reached down and picked up my dropped purse.

"Where have you been? I went by Franklin's and you weren't there. I called your phone and you didn't answer. What's going on with you, Lilly? It's like you never have time for me anymore."

For the second time in my life I saw my mother frazzled. The first time was when my father left.

"Everything's fine, Mom, I've just been busy is all." I went into the kitchen and grabbed a bottle of water.

"Where were you?" she asked again.

"I had an OB appointment."

I wasn't going to go any further than that. I'd tell my mom when the time was right, but somehow it felt wrong to tell her before I told Devin.

"Everything's OK I'm assuming?"

"Yes, everything's good."

She eyed me for a few before finally sighing loudly.

"What aren't you telling me?" She started tapping her freshly manicured nails on the kitchen counter. "Ever since you met Devin you've been different. At first I liked seeing you happy, but now I feel like your pulling away from me."

"I'm not pulling away. I just have someone to spend time with now. We're in love." I flashed a big happy smile.

"Don't be ridiculous, Lilly. You don't know what love is." She ran her fingers nervously through her hair.

I'd never seen my mother look so unsure and with the way she was acting, I was almost convinced that the doctor had called her and told her the big news already.

"I think it's time you stopped spending so much time with Devin," she said flatly, like I was some fourteen-year-old girl that had to listen to her.

It wasn't going to happen.

"Did you just hear me, Mom? I love him. I'm with him every night."

Her eyes got large as she looked me in disgust.

"Are you having sex with him?" She looked so irate that I stepped back a little.

"That's personal," I blushed.

"Oh my God, you are! What have I done?"

What had she done? She had nothing to do with it.

"You didn't do anything. It just happened, but he's a great guy and I adore his family. I'm not saying we're going to get married or anything like that, at least not any time soon, but you need to get used to Devin being in our life now."

I wanted so badly to tell her that he was the father of her granddaughter, but I wouldn't take that away from Devin. If I was the first to know for sure, then he should be the second.

"Over my dead body!" She screamed.

I'd never heard my mother raise her voice like that and it really freaked me out. Maybe I should've been more worried about her response to the baby and not so much about Devin's.

She didn't even give me a chance to respond before grabbing her purse and running out the door.

She just needed some time to cool off. Once she had some time to relax, maybe a spa visit, things would be better. Soon I'd invite her to lunch somewhere and fill her in on the big news. She just needed some time.

I knew Devin was busy at work so I didn't call, but I did send him a text.

Me: *I miss you. Is it cool if I come by and see you a little later?*

Devin: *I miss you more. Absolutely! I can't wait to see your sweet face. I'll be done with work around five.*

Me: *OK. See you then.*

Devin: *OK. I love you, beautiful.*

Me: *I love you, too.*

I'd tell him that afternoon. I'd lay all my cards on the table and pray that my hand was good enough to win.

Twenty-Nine

Rule Changes

I stared down at her last text.

I love you, too.

I never thought there'd be a time when those words would warm me. I loved Lilly and I was happy. For the first time in my life, I was really content. I'd kept the fact that her mom was paying our loan in the back of my mind because it didn't matter anymore. Her mom would never tell and I'd decided I wouldn't either. It didn't matter why we met. The fact was we did meet and she was the best thing that could've ever happened to me.

I couldn't wait to see her later. I hadn't been able to stop thinking about her all day and I fully planned on taking my time and kissing every square inch of her body later.

It kind of threw off me that she wanted to come to my house, instead of me going to her apartment as usual, but I'd do whatever she wanted. It had been a while since we had sex in my bed. It sucked having to be quiet because of Dad and Jenny, but it was good just the same.

I loosened the lug nuts and removed a flat tire from a Caravan that was brought in. The tire needed to be replaced since the wires were starting to come out. The woman hadn't said anything about replacing the tire, but she had four kids and there was no way in Hell I'd let her leave here with her tire in such bad shape.

I'd take it out of my pocket, no big deal.

I was humming along with the radio and not paying attention to anything around me when I heard a car door slam.

The she-devil rounded the corner and my entire day went to shit.

"You!" She pointed at me. "You stay the hell away from my daughter, got it?"

Her face was flushed in anger. It was a big change from her usual reserved, bitchy nature.

Then her words sank in. She was telling me to stay away from Lilly. My heart skipped a beat and I suddenly couldn't swallow.

"What?" I forced the single question out.

"If you want your money, stay away from my daughter! Break it off. I didn't mean for it to go this far. I didn't think you'd actually start to care for her or that she would honestly fall for you. I want better for her. I specifically said not to touch her and you did it anyway!"

I felt as if I'd been slapped in the face. Why would Lilly put our personal business out there for the world to know, especially her bitch of a mother? It felt wrong for her to know such delicate things about our relationship.

"I love her. I won't leave her alone. We belong together." I tried to stay calm and be as respectful as possible.

She was a total pain in the ass, but she was still Lilly's mom and if I planned on spending the rest of my life with Lilly I needed to start being nicer to her mother.

"Don't you want better than this for her?" She motioned to the dirty garage around us.

I wanted Lilly to be happy and I knew I could make her happy. I wasn't the richest man in the world, but the one thing I knew about Lilly was she didn't care about material things. She loved me and she wanted to be with me. We could make it work together.

"I can make her happy," I said coolly.

"If you care about her at all, you'll stay away from her, and if you want this house, this land, or this shack you call a business, you'll break up with her and never find yourself in her presence again."

This wasn't happening! It couldn't be happening.

Calm, cool, and respectful went straight out the fucking window.

"You bitch! Do you get off on this? Do you go around and ruin people's lives for enjoyment? You can't play with people like this! I won't do it—I can't do it." I threw my lug wrench across the room and it crashed into a wall before pinging to the floor.

"You'll do it or you'll lose everything. I'll make sure Lilly can't stand the sight of you. Once she finds out about you cheating on her that's all it'll take. Don't think for a minute that I can't pay of some piece of trash to lie for me." She was beginning to calm down which meant she felt like she had the upper hand again. "I'll do whatever I have to do to secure my daughter's future. I've already got a nice young man picked out for her— he's a lawyer. Can you compete with that?" Again she motioned to the area around the garage. "Do right by her Devin, let her go. If not, you get nothing and I'll ruin your life."

With those final words she turned and walked away. She wasn't willing to even listen to my argument, and honestly, I was tired of arguing. Lilly was more important to me than the house or the business.

It was time I came clean. I was sick of having that bitch pull me around like a puppet.

I'd tell Dad and Jenny, too, since this meant we were more than likely going to lose everything. They loved Lilly as much I did, they'd understand, and as a family we'd make it work. The only difference was now I included Lilly into that situation.

She was my future, my everything, and I'd do right by her. I'd start over fresh somewhere and be the best Devin I could be for her. Even if it meant losing her, I was going to come clean. Hopefully, she'd understand. Hopefully she'd forgive me and we could move past it and start over fresh.

I finished up all the work in the garage, and when Dad came in we quietly cleaned up some old oil and swept the place.

Once I was done, there I went inside and took the hottest shower my skin could handle. Lilly would be there soon and the possibility of my life being flipped upside down was hanging in the balance.

I knew Lilly. What I was going to tell her was going to hurt her and thinking about hurting her was making me nauseated. The last thing in the world I wanted to do was hurt her, but if I wanted to feel secure in our relationship, it needed to be done. I had to tell the truth.

"You look like you just saw a ghost. What's on your mind?" Jenny asked as she flopped onto the couch next to me.

"Just thinking. What's up with you?" I asked, hoping to change the subject.

"Josh kissed me," she blurted.

I swung my attention to her.

"Did you punch the shit out of him? Do I need to punch the shit out of him?"

I would, too. No questions asked.

"I think I like him, Dev." She blushed prettily.

My baby sister, the tomboy, the girl who could kick the asses of every boy in her school, blushed. The room suddenly felt smaller.

"Well, I should hope so. Y'all been friends for a long time." I played it off.

"No, I mean, like, I really *like him* like him. Is that OK? I mean, do you like Josh?"

Alarms went off everywhere in my mind. She was talking about dating. I knew the day would come at some point. My sister's a pretty girl, but I was hoping it would be after college once she got out of her awkward wannabe-boy stage.

"As long as it's what you want, I guess I'm OK with it. If he hurts you, I'll break his legs."

She squished herself closer to me and threw her arms around my neck.

"Don't worry, if he hurts me, *I'll* break his legs." She smiled and gave me a kiss on the cheek.

She was going to be the death of me.

"Listen, Jenny, I need to sit down and talk to you and Dad tonight about something serious. OK?"

"You're going to ask Lilly to marry you?" she asked hopefully.

"That would be kind of fast, don't you think?" I laughed. "No, I'm not asking her to marry me, but it's something important, so don't be at Josh's house all night, OK? And no making out and shit, video games only or I'll kill him, got it?"

She shook her head. "Yeah, yeah, yeah... I'll be here and if he lays a finger on me, I'll break it for you."

I laughed as she walked out the front door and left me alone with my thoughts and fears. Today was a game changer all around and I was starting to worry about whether or not I'd win the game.

Thirty

Big News

I drove the thirty minutes to Devin's house with a huge smile on my face. I still couldn't believe how much my life had changed in the last couple of months. I used to be so lonely and now I had a wonderful guy in my life that I loved with all my heart and a baby on the way.

I'd had the entire day to think on it, and I'd decided that I was ecstatic about the baby. I'd already started thinking about the baby names I liked and all the fun stuff I was going to buy. I thought about houses and buying a new "mom" car.

Even with all the good stuff running through my head, I was still worried about whether or not Devin would want to be a part of all of it. I hoped more than anything that he would.

Jenny would be the perfect aunt and Dad would love our little girl like there was no tomorrow, but what about Devin? What would he say when I told him the wonderful news?

The subject of kids had never been brought up, mainly because our relationship was just getting started, but also because the subject of kids hurt so badly. It had never been a possibility for me and it killed me to think about how lonely my future looked without little ones running around.

I sat under a red light praying for it to turn green and pulled out the ultrasound picture that the doctor had printed out for me. I couldn't wait to show it to him and get his reaction.

It felt like the trip to Devin's house had gotten longer. By the time I arrived in his driveway, I was almost jumping out of my car and running to his front door. When I knocked, a swirl of anxiety hit me. What if he didn't want the baby? What if he wanted a family, just not with me?

What was I thinking? He was Devin Michaels, the sweetest, most unselfish, loving man I knew. He was the man that I had fallen madly in love with, and the man that I wanted to spend the rest of my life with. I shook all the bad thoughts out of my head and knocked once more.

He pulled the door open, smiled, and then held open the screened door, inviting me in without saying so. The ultrasound picture was burning a hole in my hand. It took everything in me to not open it and throw it in his face with a big smile.

"Hey, baby." I leaned up and gave him a pop kiss.

He kissed me back then wrapped his arms around me and hugged me close for a long time. He was acting awfully strange and for a brief second I panicked and thought that maybe he somehow knew about the baby already. That was impossible, of course, since other than the doctor, I was the only one who knew.

He let go, stepped back, and just stared at me while sitting on the couch. I sat beside him and held his hands in mine. He didn't even notice the picture in my hand. He looked as nervous as I felt and again I wondered why.

"I thought about you so much today." I brought his hand to my mouth and kissed his palm softly.

"I thought about you, too. I love you, Lilly," he said, flatly.

"I love you too, Devin. More than you could ever know."

This time it was his turn to kiss my hand. He pressed my cool palm against his check and looked back at me. He didn't even notice the folded picture in my hand. Something was definitely wrong.

"I need to tell you something."

Alarms went off in my head.

"I need to tell you something, too. That's why I came to you, but you go first. What I have to say can wait a few more minutes. Are you OK? What's wrong, baby?" I slid closer to him and wrapped my arms around him.

"I don't know where to start," he said. "I guess I should start with how wonderful I think you are. You're the sweetest woman I've ever met and I thank God every day that I met you."

He was starting to sweat. Even his hands were starting to sweat in mine. He cleared his throat and pulled at his collar.

Then suddenly I knew what he was doing. He was breaking up with me. Right before I was about to tell him that we were having a baby, he was telling me he wanted nothing more to do with me. I could feel it. His next words were going to kill me and I was going to have to drive home with a part of Devin tucked safely inside me.

Years from now, when I would look into my daughter's eyes, I'd see him, and it would kill me, but I wouldn't let it break me. I had more than just myself to think about now, and if it was the last thing I did, I'd protect my baby, even if it meant staying strong and not breaking down over our break-up until after she was born.

I sat quietly and tried to cover the worry that I hoped wasn't showing on my face.

"God, this is so much harder than I thought it'd be." He started to breathe heavier. He knew his words were going to crush me.

I knew it, too.

"Devin, you can tell me anything. No matter what it is, I'll understand. Just tell me what's wrong and I'll fix it. I love you, Devin, and I..."

He cut me off by holding his hand up for me to stop before I could finish.

"You're going to hate me when I say this. Promise you won't hate me, I just want to be honest with you."

He wanted to be honest.., that meant there was another woman involved. I had to remember to be strong once he broke it off. I could take it.

"I could never hate you, Devin," I whispered.

This was it, the end of us. He was about to break up with me.

"Do you remember the first day we met?" he asked.

"Of course, I remember."

I definitely did, I counted it as one of the best days of my life.

"Well, it wasn't by coincidence that I came in your store that day. Your mom told me to go in your store. She told me where you worked and where you hung out. She made it easy for me to get you to go out with me."

"I don't understand," I said, confusion written all over my face "What does my mother have to do with this? You've only met her a handful of times."

"I met your mom before I met you. I met her at the bank one day. I was making a complete fool out of myself begging the bank to give Dad more time to make a payment on the house. We were fixing to lose everything, Lilly, everything that we worked so hard for. We owed the bank eight thousand dollars and we were fixin' to lose it all. We didn't have that kind of money," he pleaded.

"I still don't understand what any of this has to do with my mother," I said.

Inside I already knew. Instead, I sat there quietly praying that he wasn't about to say the words that would shatter me completely.

"The bank turned me down. They told me there was nothing I could do except pay the balance owed. I went crazy and punched the bank manager. I was arrested, but I wasn't there long before your mom bailed me out. I had no idea who the hell she was. I'd seen her at the bank before I showed my ass, but I was still shocked when I stepped outside the jailhouse to see her standing there waiting for me and well..." He stopped.

"Well?" I asked.

I needed to hear him say it. I needed to hear him tell me that my mother bought him for me. I had to hear it!

"She made me a proposition that I couldn't refuse."

OK so maybe I didn't need to hear it. Maybe hearing it would rip my heart out, slam it to the floor, and spit all over it.

"How much?" I asked.

I didn't want him to finish after all. I could feel the bile rising in my throat. The room suddenly started to spin. I leaned my head against the back of the couch and closed my eyes, hoping it would slow the spinning.

"How much did she pay you to sleep with me?" I asked calmly.

"It wasn't like that, Lilly. I fell..."

"I said how much?" I yelled loudly. "What was the going price for my virginity?"

"I wasn't supposed to touch you. It was strictly forbidden, but I couldn't stop myself with you. You make me so weak." He grabbed the tops of my arms as if willing me to understand.

"Oh, but let me guess, I'm just so *beautiful* and *sexy!*" I threw his words back at him. I felt disgusted that I'd let him see me naked.

Just knowing that the entire time he was probably turned off by me made me sick to my stomach. My mom didn't have to tie a porkchop around my neck to get the dog to play with me; she just had to pay the son of a bitch!

"You are, baby. You're so beautiful and I..."

"Don't you dare call me baby! I'm not your fucking baby, and I'm sick of your lies already! Just tell me how much!" My voice cracked and that pissed me off even more.

I didn't want explanations. I didn't want to hear another word except for the amount of money I'd paid to have Devin in my life for the brief time he was in it. I needed to know how much it cost me to conceive my child.

My heart was officially broken and it hurt worse than being kicked by a mob of spiteful cheerleaders, worse than a grown man beating the shit out of me. It hurt like nothing I'd ever known in my life.

"Twenty-three thousand all together. She gave me three thousand in the beginning and I was supposed to get another twenty when I....." He stopped.

"When you what?" I asked.

303

The fact that I couldn't cry was starting to scare me. For the first time in my life, I was OK with bursting into tears. I welcomed the damn tears, anything that would relieve the amount of pressure on my chest, but no tears came. Instead, I just stared at him like a crazy person.

"You get another twenty grand when you what, Devin?" I growled.

"When I break it off with you," he whispered. "But now that I'm being honest with you, I probably won't get the money and I don't care anymore. I don't want the money. I'm prepared to lose everything...everything but you."

When he said those words, instead of hearing I love you and I don't want to lose you, I heard, *Why bargain with your mom, when I could just be with you and have more than twenty grand? Why fuck with the mother when I could have the daughter who's loaded with millions?*

He kept his head down the whole time. Of course he couldn't look me in my face. For months he stared me in my eyes and told me things I'd never dreamt of hearing a man say to me. Months!

I took a deep breath, trying to calm myself.

The room was closing in on me. I needed to get out of there. I needed to run far away and never see his face again, but just the thought of being without him already started to burn my stomach.

I felt like someone had just knocked the air out of me. How could my mother do this to me? How could she dangle something so perfect in my face and then snatch it away? I'd never be able to forgive her for this.

I wasn't breathing and the lack of oxygen was making my head swim.

I stood quickly and the room spun harder as I turned toward the door. I felt his arm on me to help me from falling, but I ripped my arm away from him as if his touched burned me. It did. The memories of his touch burned me all over.

"I am so sorry, Lilly," he said.

I could hear what sounded like sadness in his voice, another act, I supposed.

Then he was in front of me on his knees holding my hand. "Please, forgive me. I'm so sorry. Please, forgive me."

It was unnatural to see Devin on his knees begging. Such a beautifully broken man, but I'd seen people do worse for money. Money! It's what made the world go 'round and I'm so lucky that it was kind enough to snatch me up and sling me around with it.

"Don't be sorry because I'm not. I can't be sorry. If anything I should thank you."

I looked down into his face. Even on his knees he was almost to my shoulders. I wanted to scream at him. How could he do this to us? We were going to have a baby!

"Thank me? For what?" he asked, confused. "I'm a horrible person and I hurt you, regardless of what you're gonna say, I know I hurt you. I just..." I cut him off.

"You just did what you had to do to take care of your family. I'm glad that I could help y'all out. I'll make sure your balance to the bank is paid."

His head snapped up with anger on his face. He looked so heated, that for a second I feared he would attack me.

"I don't want her damn money!"

Her money? Did he not know all of it was mine?

A tiny bit of hope bloomed inside of me before I squashed it good and hard. A lie....he was *still* lying! Oh he knew, he knew it was mine and that's why he was down on his knees in front of me begging.

"As far as you hurting me goes, that's just stupid. You gave me more than I gave you, trust me." I could feel the tears tearing through my eyes.

The lump in my throat suddenly felt too large to swallow. I tried to clear it before continuing.

"The time we spent together was a lie, at least for you it was," I choked.

"No! Not everything I..."

I cut him off again. "Let me finish. Even though the time I spent with you was just an act, I didn't know that, and I'd rather have a moment of wonderfully altered reality no matter how much of it was false. I'd rather have had it fake, than never at all. At least now I can say that I know what it feels like to be in love."

I somehow managed to smile through my pain. The liquid in my eyes felt like it was going to spill over at any minute and it wasn't long before I could feel the tears streaming down my face. It was over. He was going to be gone out of my life for good as soon as I walked out the door and got into my car.

"Thank you, Devin. You'll never know why I'm thanking you, but just know that once I walk out that door, I'll be just fine.

I would be, I had no other choice.

I swore to myself I'd never let him find out about the baby. It would be just another reason for him to suddenly want to be with me. I thought he was just as deep in this as I was. He'd said he loved me for money; I didn't want to hear him lie again for our baby.

"Please, Lilly, don't leave me. I love you so much."

His words echoed like they were screamed across a deep canyon. That's how it would forever be—me on one side and him on the other. I couldn't hear his lies anymore. It hurt every time he said he loved me because I knew it had nothing to do with me and everything to do with my money.

There were so many things I wanted to say, but nothing would come out except, "I'll never know if you're with me for me. I'm sorry, Devin. I can't."

I finally took a good look at him and saw the tears on his cheeks. He reached out and grabbed my hand, but his touch made me nauseated. I shook his fingers away from mine, turned, and walked away.

I could hear him calling from behind me, begging me to please just give him another chance, but Hell would freeze over before that happened.

The tears kept coming as I made my way to my car. Once I was inside, they poured heavily.

I knew it would be a long while before the tears stopped. I had never in my life felt that kind of pain. It cut me so deep emotionally that it physically hurt. My stomach hurt, my chest hurt, everything inside me hurt.

Was I dying inside?

This is what it's all about. This is why people are afraid to fall in love, because losing the person you love hurts like Hell.

I cried the entire drive home.

Thirty-One
Payday

I'd rather get my ass kicked five times a day every day for the rest of my life than feel the pain I felt in that moment. When Lilly walked out of my door and I knew I'd never see her face again, the small part of me that had started to flourish because of her suddenly died.

Just when I was starting to feel alive again, Lilly pulled out a metaphorical gun and shot me at close range in the heart. It was like she didn't even hear me begging her. She just stared off into nothing like I'd broken her and deep down I knew I had. It wasn't enough that I was shattered into a million pieces my entire life, I had to drag a perfectly put-together person into my world and shatter her as well.

My legs suddenly gave out on me and I collapsed onto the front porch. The fact that I was never going to see her again ate at my heart. Parts of me screamed to go after her, but I knew she didn't deserve that, nor did she want that. She deserved better.

She was too good for a piece of shit like me and I'd give her a chance at a better life without me. It was the least I could do.

I was about to lose what little bit I did have. I had nothing but broken parts of a man to offer her.

Her tail lights disappeared down the road and felt my insides take their final breath. She was gone. It was over and the best thing for me to do was let her leave.

I went back inside and collapsed on the couch again. Part of me wanted to go drown myself in Dad's liquor cabinet, but I didn't deserve to be numb. I deserved to hurt, deserved to feel my heart crumble inside of me.

I don't know how long I sat there staring off into space. Time ceased to exist, but at some point, I heard Jenny talking to me. She was snapping her fingers in my face trying to get me to flinch.

"Dev, you're scaring me, damn it! What's going on? I swear to Christ you're gonna drive me to drink!"

Then she reached back and smacked me across the face. The sting of her tiny palm shook me as it snapped my head to the side. I wanted to beg her to hit me again. I deserved to have my ass whipped.

"She's gone," I croaked.

"What do you mean she's gone?" She didn't even ask who I was talking about, she just knew. "What did you do, Devin?" She sounded panicked.

Not only did I hurt Lilly, I dragged her into my world and let my dad and Jenny fall in love with her, too. They were going to hurt, too. They were losing her, too. How could I not have seen this coming? Lilly had become a part of our family and I had single-handedly ripped away Jenny's sister and my dad's daughter. That's how they looked at her. That's what she had become to them.

I couldn't even bring myself to tell Jenny what I had done. I didn't want her to see what her brother really was; I didn't want to see what I really was anymore. I was beneath any descriptive word I could think of, worse than a piece of shit, worse than selfish.

I didn't even respond. I just got up, grabbed my car keys, and left. I don't know where I planned on going, but I ended up parked outside of Lilly's apartment. I didn't get out of the car and bang on her door. I didn't go beg her like I wanted to, I Just sat there. Somehow, knowing she was within reach soothed me.

At some point, I fell asleep sitting up in the driver's seat of my car. When I woke up there was a bird on the hood staring at me, judging me. I worked the kink out of my neck and cranked the engine. There was no need to prolong the inevitable. I had to go home and tell my family it was time to start packing. We had living arrangements to make and I had to start job hunting as soon as possible. There was no way in Hell I'd take that bitch's money even if she *did* offer it to me.

When I got home Dad was sitting at the kitchen table eating breakfast. I fell into the chair across from him and it slid across the linoleum floor.

"Well, you look like Hell," he said as he scooped up a fork full of eggs.

"Maybe that's because I spent the night there." I sounded as hollow as I felt.

"You need to eat somethin' and get a shower. You can't win a woman back smelling like a dog. Then I want you to take the rest of the day off and go on over there and get our girl." He got up and rinsed his plate in the sink.

"Dad, she'll never forgive me for what I've done. You don't know the half. I wouldn't blame her if she never talked to me again. I love Lilly, so I'm going to let her go." I rested my elbow on the table.

"I wasn't talking about Lilly, although I sure wish y'all would patch things up. I meant our other girl."

"You been drinking already this morning?"

"Nah, I'm sober. I found this on the floor." He pulled a black and white picture from his pocket and slid it across the table to me. "I'm talkin' 'bout this girl."

I looked down at the ultrasound picture. Printed in white digital font was the word *Girl* with a dotted line pointing to a gray blob in the in middle of the fuzzy picture. The name *Lilly Sheffield* was printed vertically down the side of the picture.

At first I was confused. Lilly has specifically said she couldn't get pregnant. Yet, there was her name printed very obviously on the picture.

312

It looked like a blurry mess, but I could make out a little leg and a tiny foot, and in that moment, my world fell around me like tiny fragments of bright, white light. It made my skin tingle as it rained down on me. The oxygen I was about to exhale was held hostage in my lungs by my heart that had suddenly quit beating.

Lilly came yesterday to tell me something. She wanted to tell me we were going to have a baby. She was probably ecstatic, she was probably the happiest she had ever been in her entire life when she showed up at my door, and I had gut punched her with the truth. I had squashed that happiness in an instant.

I had made her cry. I put her in a state of shock. I'd seen the shock on her face. I'd hurt her more than she'd probably ever been hurt in her life. My now ex-girlfriend, the love of my life, the woman who walking around with my heart nestled snuggly inside of her, and I had made her cry.

I felt myself snap. I stood quickly, and my chair left a skid mark on the linoleum. Dad was saying something to me, but I had tunnel hearing and nothing made it through to my brain. My joints felt stiff as I moved across the house to the front door.

I ended up at Lilly's apartment, but she wasn't home. I'd go to every place I could think of until I found her. I needed her to breathe my existence back into me and to gather all the tiny fragments of life that were floating around me and put them back together.

I found myself at her mother's front door. An older man in a suit answered.

"I need to speak to Lilly Sheffield."

"Follow me."

He turned to walk away, and like a pup, I followed behind him. He was taking me to see Lilly and when I got to her I'd refuse any other option but for us to be together.

The last time I was in this house I was kicked out, and I'd probably get kicked out again, but I had to try anything and everything to get her back. Yes, for the baby, but also because since the moment she walked out my door I hadn't felt alive. I wanted to live.

When we got to a set of brown paneled doors, the older man stepped aside and motioned for me to enter. The door was heavy and silent as it opened. The pit of my stomach was telling me that it felt wrong, and when my eyes connected with Lilly's mom instead of Lilly, I knew why.

Like daggers, her eyes pierced me. Had this been a cartoon, fire would be flying from them and burning me to death. I'm sure my eyes mirrored hers as I stared her down, unwilling to blink.

"I hope you're proud of yourself," she hissed.

"Are you proud of yourself?"

She was sitting behind a desk, stacks of unopened invitations laid out in front of her. As I took her in, I noticed her tense shoulders, the purple circles around her eyes, and a few misplaced pieces of hair. She was upset, and that let me know that she had seen Lilly.

I moved closer to her desk and stood there.

"Where is she?" I asked.

She didn't respond. Instead, she reached into the desk draw and pulled out a piece of paper. She held it out to me and I snatched it from her.

"I believe this is what you came here for. Take it and get out of our lives." She turned away as if dismissing me.

I stared down at the check in my hand. It was written for fifty thousand dollars. The bitch was paying me off. That little, thin piece of paper would take care of most of my problems. I could cash it and pay off the loan and everything would just be fucking great, except it wouldn't be. As long as Lilly was gone, nothing would ever be good again.

All the pain I felt was because of this stupid check. A sudden streak of anger rang through my body, and before I knew it, I was ripping the check up in Mrs. Sheffield's face. I'd live on the streets before I cashed that check and I knew that both Dad and Jenny would agree. They'd want nothing to do with that money just like I wanted nothing to do with it. I wanted Lilly.

"What are you doing? Are you insane?" she asked me.

"I don't want your damn money." I continued ripping the check into tiny pieces.

"But you'll lose everything!" The look on her face was almost comical, and had I been in a laughing mood, I would've laughed.

I was in no laughing mood, I was on a mission.

"I've already lost everything. Now, tell me where she is."

She didn't respond. She just sat there staring back at me like I was from another planet.

"Fine, I'll keep searching until I find her."

I turned to walk away. I was done with that bitch and all the heartache she had caused Lilly and me.

"Wait," she called after me.

"What?" I growled, as I turned back to face her.

She shook her head for a minute like she was in shock.

"You really love her, don't you?" she asked softly.

"What do you think?" I yelled as I started toward the door again.

"Wait, I have something for you." She came around her desk and stood before me.

Her eyes were warmer and her small smile looked real. For a second, I was taken aback by her sudden change in facial expressions.

She held out a piece of paper and as much as I wanted to snatch it from her and rip it to sheds, too, I stopped and read it. It was the deed to the house and shop. The loan had been paid in full and the property was now in my dad's name.

Fury ripped through me again and I almost did rip the paper up.

Who the hell did this bitch think she was?

"I told you! I don't want your charity! You own it now!" I said as I balled up the paper and stuffed it into her hand.

"Devin, I didn't do this. Lilly told me to make sure you got this."

"I don't understand? If you didn't..." she cut me off.

"I live here, I drive fancy cars, and I shop until I'm blue in the face, but the fact of the matter is, none of this is mine. Lilly owns everything, all the homes, all the cars, and all the money, it's hers."

I couldn't believe what I was hearing. My face was stuck in shock. Tears were stinging my eyes. How could she not have told me?

"Lilly doesn't like people to know," she answered, like she had read my mind. "When my parents died we weren't on very good terms. They weren't happy with the way I was raising Lilly. Truth be told, they had a right to disagree. I was a horrible mother, still am." A rare flash of weakness struck her eyes. "They left everything to her. She still likes to live like she's not rich, but the truth is, Lilly has more money than she could spend in a lifetime."

All that time she was a rich heiress and I was just a dirty garage boy. There I was thinking I could do right by her and make her happy, when the truth was she needed *nothing* from me.

"I can't believe this..."

"Devin, she loves you. She's hurting and I'm going to do something, for once in my life, that'll make *her* happy. I'm going to do exactly what she asked me not to and I'm going tell you where she is." She stopped and took a breath. "She was making a stop at Franklin's to quit her job, and then she'll be staying at our beach house for few weeks until things blow over. That's where you'll find her."

She leaned over and scribbled something on a piece of paper then handed it to me.

"Here's the address. Go make her happy." She smiled sadly.

In no time, I was in my car. I had to make one stop and then I was headed to the beach to get the love of my life back.

Thirty-Two

Priceless

I'd never spoken to my mother the way I did when I got to her house. After leaving Devin's, I went straight to her. I'm pretty sure I broke a few antique vases and I'm almost positive I told my mother I never wanted to see her face again.

She asked for forgiveness. Everyone wanted forgiveness. Everyone thought it was OK to play with my life; they thought I'd just get over it and move on. News flash! I didn't need any of them! I had my own daughter on the way and I'd make sure to always make her feel like she was good enough. No matter what she'd know she was a miracle.

"Did you think I was incapable of finding someone on my own? What made you think you needed to pay someone to be with me?" My screams echoed off the marble floors of my mother's foyer.

"I wasn't thinking! I only wanted to make you happy, Lilly. I saw the way you looked at that couple that day in the café and I knew that no matter what I had to do, I'd make that happen for you because you deserve it!"

"But you *paid* him, as in prostitution! It wasn't real, Mom! It doesn't count if it's not real! He was pretending that he cared about me and now I'm in love with him! How do you think that makes me feel?" Tears rushed down my cheeks. "Am I that disgusting to you? Have I ever been anything that you could be proud of?" The dam had broken.

Years of not feeling good enough and being picked on came crashing over me. I cried so hard my chest burned. My words were coming out in sobbed screams. I cried because no matter what, I was never able to make my mother proud. I cried because I'd given all of me to a man who was pretending, and I cried because in less than six months I'd have to see his face every time I looked at my daughter.

"Disgusting?" she asked breathlessly. "Lilly, you're so much more than my daughter to me. You're all I have. You're the only person in the world who cares about me. You're my best and *only* friend. I'm sorry if I don't know how to show you these things. I'm sorry if I seem like a cold, heartless bitch, but it's all I know. You're the best thing I've ever done in my life and I couldn't be more proud of you. I have a safe in my room with every craft you ever made me and every award you ever won. No mother has ever been more proud of her daughter."

For the first time in my life, my mother's bitch exterior cracked and she cried. We reached a new level in our mother, daughter relationship and even though I didn't forgive her, I understood better. While I would never go about it the same way she did, I know I'd want the same thing for my daughter, complete and total happiness.

I'd tell her about the baby at some point. Too much had happened and I wanted to take some time to gather my thoughts first. We had a long road ahead of us, but she was still my mother. She was trying to do right by me in her own little way, even though it was the wrong way.

"I'm going to quit my job, and then I'm going to go stay at the beach house for a while. I need time, Mom, but I need you to do something for me." I dug into my purse and pulled out the paper I had drawn up earlier that morning.

It was the deed to Devin's house and garage. It was paid in full and in Dad's name. It was sad that a single piece of paper was the reason behind all of my pain, but I couldn't hate it. Some good had come out of the situation and as much as I wanted to hate my mother and Devin both for what they'd done to me, they still did something *for* me as well. I'd have that something wrapped in a pretty pink blanket in the near future.

"Make sure Devin gets this." I handed her the paper. "And don't tell anyone where I am. I'll be back to get my life in order soon."

Mrs. Franklin cried when I told her I was putting in my two weeks. I had too much going on in my life and I was missing entirely too much work anyways. I'd still be sure to purchase something once a month to keep her afloat, but I didn't have the time to work there. Mrs. Franklin had become like a mother to me and it hurt to do it, but she understood.

Shannon on the other hand was in complete shock. I told her everything and she was pissed that I never told her about the money, but once she checked her checking account she got over it pretty quick. It didn't matter anyway, once I confirmed that I was definitely pregnant she forgot all about everything and went straight into baby shower planning mode.

Not to mention, she had been holding out on me on some stuff, as well. Come to find out, her and Devin's friend, Matt, had been seeing each other for the last month.

"Yeah, good luck with that one." I laughed.

"No luck needed. He's not getting into these panties until he proves himself. I think he's on a mission and I'm enjoying his attempts. It's kind of hot."

Good ole Shannon and asshole Matt. That was going to be interesting.

I was collecting all of my things from the back and putting items in boxes when Mrs. Franklin came in.

"Oh, your necklace came back in. I meant to call you and let you know, but things got crazy around here."

She pulled out a little box.

"My necklace?"

I had no idea what the hell she was talking about.

322

"Yes. Is says here you put in the order for it to be engraved a little over a month ago," she said as she looked over an order form.

She laid it on the table and walked out front when the doorbell rang.

I pulled open the little box and inside was the locket Devin had purchased the first day I met him. *Lilly* was engraved on the outside of the sterling silver cover. I cleared my throat and swallowed hard. I was afraid to read what was on the inside—afraid of more lies.

I pushed on the side of the locket and it popped open. The engraved script jumped out at me and my eyes pooled with tears.

You will forever be priceless to me.
I love you

I felt myself fall into an old desk chair as the tears fell harder. I held the necklace in my hands and replayed the first day I had seen his face. I considered it one of the best days of my life.

I read the inside of the locket again and it hurt. It was a lie, too. I wasn't priceless to him.

"You are." I heard Devin whisper as if he'd heard my thoughts.

I looked up to find him standing in front of me with a look of sheer worry etched into his face. He looked as though he hadn't slept and his eyes were puffy and red. It was weird to see him that way since he was usually so calm and collected.

He dropped down to his knees in front of me and cupped my hands. I wanted push him away. I wanted to run out, but I was so weak. The parts of me that were drawn to him, the parts in love with him, were so much stronger than my will to leave.

"I was just coming to get this," he ran his ringer over the chain of the locket. "So I could bring it to you. I don't think I've ever been happier to see your car parked out front." He took a deep breath and his face crumbled before my eyes. "I know about the baby."

I knew he'd find out once I realized I'd accidently dropped my ultrasound picture at his house. After thinking it over all night, I'd decided that I'd tell him anyway. Dad and Jenny wouldn't want to miss out on the baby's life and I wanted them to be a part of it.

"I came to tell you about her yesterday. I didn't lie to you, Devin. I was told I couldn't have kids. I'd never try to trap you that way, and I won't ask you for anything, I promise."

"Her." He dropped his head at the word before looking up with tears in his eyes. "I want to be there. Please, let me be there for her... and you."

"I'd like for the baby to be a part of your family," I said.

I watched as his shoulders visibly relaxed a bit.

"And you?" he whispered. "Will you be a part of my family, too?"

"I don't know. Did you even care about me at all, Devin, or was it all because of the money?" I stared into his eyes and prayed that I would see honesty.

His eyes fluttered closed for a brief minute before he matched my stare. "Before I met you, I only barely existed. After my mom left, I spent every day of my life feeling like I'd never see the light again and like every part of me was going in a million different directions at once. Then I met you, and everything inside of me balanced out. You're the light in every dark part of my soul and I'm drawn to your warmth. I was so broken before you and somehow you put me back together. Maybe I should, but I don't regret taking your mom's offer. You're the best thing that's ever happened to me and I can't bring myself to regret it." He dropped his head into my lap and cried. "I just know I'm sorry I hurt you and if I have to spend the rest of my life making up for it I will. Anything I have to do just to be close to you, I'll do it. Because honestly, when I'm not near you I feel like I'm going to fall apart again."

"And the money?" I croaked.

"What about the money? I don't give a damn about your money. Not even thirty minutes ago I was ripping up a check for fifty thousand dollars and ready to live on the streets. I only care about you and the baby. I've worked since I was thirteen and I'll work for the rest of my life. I just wanna take care of you and our baby." He softly laid his hand over my stomach. "Please give me another chance, baby. I love you so much."

His love filled me, and for some crazy reason that I didn't understand, I believed every word. Maybe I was an idiot, maybe I'd kick myself in the ass in the years to come, but I loved Devin and I wanted to feel the way he made me feel for the rest of my life.

"I love you, too, Devin."

I reached out and wiped the single tear that fell down his cheek and he wrapped his arms around me and stuck his face into my neck.

"I almost lost you," he whispered.

"Almost, but now you're stuck with me. I'll be all pregnant and cranky and you'll love it."

He tearfully smiled back at me.

"Sounds perfect," he leaned in and kissed my stomach before coming up and kissing me softly on the lips.

Epilogue

I worked late at the garage with Dad. We were swamped at the shop and since Jenny was coming home from school for a few days, we needed to get everything done. By the time I got home, all the lights in the house were out and I knew everyone inside was asleep.

I pulled into the driveway of our three bedroom house and felt pure happiness for being home with my family. I made sure to quietly shut the front door since the last thing I wanted to do was wake up Emma.

I crept into our bedroom, and, without turning the lights on, I made my way through the dark bedroom and into the shower.

After my shower, I slipped through the bedroom to my side of the bed and turned on the lamp. The dim light illuminated a small portion of the bed, but it was enough to see my beautiful wife sleeping. Her dark hair spilled over her pillow and a light flush made her soft cheeks pink.

Instead of being in her toddler bed in her room, Emma was balled up next to her mother's pregnant stomach, her tiny three-year-old fist balled up under her chin.

It was such a beautiful sight that I didn't want to move them over to make room for myself. Lilly's eyes popped open when she felt me adjusting Emma's small frame.

"Hey, baby." She flashed me a sleepy smile. "Sorry, she had a bad dream." She ran her fingers through Emma's hair.

"It's OK, sweetie." I leaned in and gave her a tiny kiss. "Go back to sleep. You need all the rest you can get, baby."

She turned on her side facing me and tucked her arm under her pillow.

"Mom stopped by today." She rested her other hand across her stomach and smirked. "She took Emma to the park for few hours. When they came back, Mom had mud all over her pants. It was so funny."

"Your poor mom doesn't stand a chance with Emma. She's so much like Jenny." I reached out and ran my fingers over Emma's soft cheek before settling my hand on Lilly's stomach.

I felt a small bump against my palm and smirked.

Lilly hissed a little then shook her head. "He's been doing that all day. I think he's ready to come out." She softly rubbed her stomach.

"He's gonna be a hard ass like his daddy." I smiled proudly.

"Yeah, like I can handle a mini you running around," she laughed.

I loved her laugh. I loved everything about her. I tucked a strand of dark hair behind her ear.

"You're the only person in the world who knows how to handle me." I leaned in and gave her a kiss.

"Imagine what the world would be like if I weren't here to keep you tame. That makes me a valuable commodity to the community," she giggled.

"No, baby, that makes you priceless."

Acknowledgements

For me, this is the hardest part of writing a book. Telling a story is the easy part, but sitting down and trying to thank the people who have supported you is very difficult, especially when you have lived a full life filled with wonderful people. That being said, I'll give it a shot.

This may sound weird, but I'd first like to thank any person who ever said a rude thing to me about my weight. There's never been a point in my life that I wasn't overweight, so this happened a lot in my world. At the time, the things you said were very hurtful, but looking back now, I'm glad you said them. You single-handedly fueled this story. You planted the idea in my brain and watered it every time you said a hurtful thing to me. So, thank you.

Secondly, I'd like to thank my Beta readers, Mary Smith, Melissa Andrea, Ruthi Kight, and Katy Austin. You ladies are amazing, and I appreciate the late night messages and your honest opinions. I'm very blessed to have met such wonderful people throughout the entire publishing process. I'm amazed by the amount of support I receive from people I've never met in person. Again, I thank you guys.

To every blogger who jumped on The Fat Bitches Blog Tour and to every single person near and far who have helped to promote or supported my work. I love you all more than you could ever know.

Last by not least, to my wonderful husband Matthew. You took the insecure girl I used to be and turned her into the confident woman that I am today. Thank you for telling me I'm beautiful every day for the last eleven years of my life and thank you even more for meaning it. The love that you have shown me over the years has nourished me and helped me blossom. I love you, baby.

Made in the USA
Lexington, KY
15 July 2014